'We must tear down Ussian! We must curse every brick, every stone, every inch of land. We must curse the Cyclones, and those who are red-haired, and those who wait at the delta. We must curse the fantasy of the Zuni Bird. We must burn Ussian in sacrifice to the one-eyed lord, the Divine Mutant inside us all, the Master who has changed us in this new time. We must reject and destroy ourselves in order to be saved, we must take our places in the Mutant dream ...'

Two-Eyes is the second volume in a new and outstanding science fiction series in the great tradition of *The Lord of the Rings*.

Also by Stuart Gordon

One-Eye
Time Story
Suaine and the Crow-God

Stuart Gordon

Two-Eyes

Panther

Granada Publishing Limited
Published in 1977 by Panther Books Ltd
Frogmore, St Albans, Herts AL2 2NF

First published in Great Britain by
Sidgwick & Jackson Ltd 1975
Copyright © Stuart Gordon 1974
Made and printed in Great Britain by
Richard Clay (The Chaucer Press), Ltd
Bungay, Suffolk
Set in Linotype Pilgrim

Table of Contents

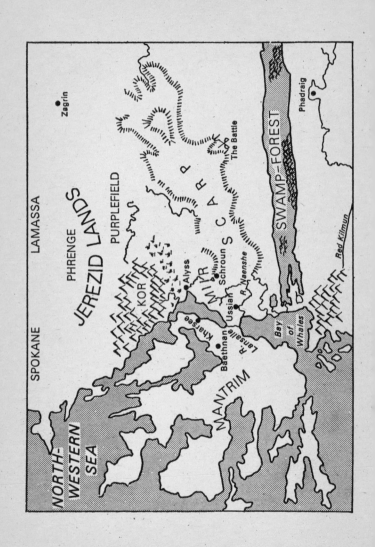

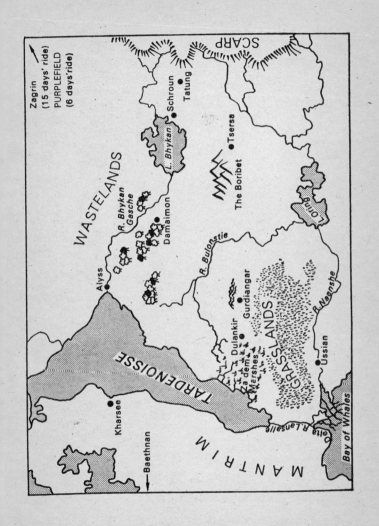

Introduction: The Plume of the Zuni Bird

The delta was dangerous, mysterious – and always growing.

The river Naenshe surged out from tree-lined eastern bluffs, hit shelves of black rock, and divided into three leaping brown torrents. Its many foaming brows struck at the lagoon-chain of the placid Lansalle, overwhelmed the dreaming river from the north. The Naenshe muddied, chivied, and flurried the Lansalle through the miasmic, labyrinthine delta; drove it out into the landlocked Bay of Whales. Married, the choppy brown currents brooded deep into the discolored sea, taking away from Miir as much as they'd given.

This place of clashing waters terminated the two great systems of lakes, rivers, and canals which defined and fertilized the sweet southern land of Miir. It was a wilderness of sucking currents, of sudden bores washing through the reedy alluvial islands which teemed with squalling birds. Even when the sky was clear and the mists dispersed, there was no sure telling where the gleaming mudflats ended and the sea began. It was a giant elemental arena; the currents jousted most violently when the swollen rivers met spring tides pushed higher by southwest gales. It was only after the Equinox that the birds returned. They chose to settle on the western side of the delta, where conditions were relatively less violent, where the islands and mudbanks sometimes remained permanent until the autumn. Innumerable, overcrowded, and precarious, they made the delta raucous with their squabblings. It was no ideal sanctuary, but it was the only place in this part of the world where they were relatively safe from man. Relatively.

On summer nights the wildfowlers came into the labyrinth with the Naenshe chewing all around them. They were local men and women, small and quick-footed, armed with net and bag. They wore cork life jackets and carried a consecrated amulet to protect them from the wrath of the Zuni Bird. Trusting in their speed, stealth, and knowledge of the delta, they prayed nevertheless for luck and a clear night. The mudbank configurations changed too often for maps to be anything but dangerously misleading. The fires kept burning on low hills to the east and west of the Lansalle – the eastern in Miir, the other in peninsular Mantrim – were the only reliable references, and then only on clear nights. The delta gave no guarantees, vouchsafed no secrets. Boats failed to find a way in, or, if succeeding, subsequently they usually grounded or got lost in the endless and restless maze. It demanded homage on foot; in return for its riches it demanded an acceptance of frequent death. One instant you could with care be treading a ghostly moonlit mudbank link to one of the islands where the birds were thick, and the black lagoons about would be nearly still, just chuckling against the mud they were sculpting, merely rippling the lunar reflections. And perhaps the very calm would warn you, so you'd stop, and turn your head, and when you heard it, you'd think at first it was your imagination. But then you'd see it – a dim phosphorescent turbulence in the night – a tumbling wave, your height or higher, a monstrous froth roaring over the mudbanks and lagoons. Then, rooted to your final spot, you'd see the shades of beating wings eclipse the moon in that instant before the waters took you.

And as you drowned the Zuni Bird would come to claim your soul.

All the local people who wildfowled for a living had such visions at one time or another. They came to terms with their fear, or they starved. The small delta communities were poor, and there was little other work in the area, particularly since the last Jerezid invasion of Miir. The Cyclone brotherhood of Mantrim had been active in the area since the invasion. Though their Colleges were mostly located deep in Mantrim, it appeared that they had a special interest in the delta.

Once, the Cyclones had been respected wanderers, a brotherhood of healers and wise men working for the common good. Now they were remote and secretive in their dour Colleges; they had grown wealthy. Now they stayed apart from the people, they were disliked, they did nothing for the common advantage and were feared because of their esoteric powers. And though, supposedly, they had no interest in political power, the financial exactions which they laid upon the people living on the Mantrim side of the delta had increased since the Jerezid Warlord's invasion. For two hundred years the brotherhood had held the Rights of Gift and Exemption in the Delta Province; now many thought their tyranny as bad as that of any warlord or bureaucrat. All the talk of their tax-gathering representatives about needing more Gifts to assist the growth of the Project impressed the victims not at all. What was the Project? It was something to do with the delta, for Cyclones were frequently seen in the area, engaged in inexplicable activities. To the people of the area, the Cyclones were simply another irritation which made life more difficult.

They considered the Cyclones to be black magicians, but they were not afraid of the brotherhood. They reserved their fear for the Zuni Bird.

The Zuni Bird, they knew, existed in the delta's violent outer margins. Singularly lonely, immortally brooding, the Zuni Bird was pure spirit which could assume whatever form it wished. If a tidal bore or sudden wave took a life, then the Zuni Bird was in that wave, and had created it expressly to destroy the hunter. More than Spirit of the Two Rivers, the Zuni Bird was the vengeful protector of the many species which used the delta as sanctuary. The wildfowlers thought of their bane as a spirit of the drifting mists, as an eerie song too pure and high for gross human ears to register. When the moon was full, they said, it selected a distant outer islet and assumed the form of a great and beautiful bird – slender-necked and wingless, with plumage of snow-white electric, and ruby eyes which shone as it preened amid the torrents. To see it was to have your senses destroyed. For generations they'd told curious strangers the tale of how the myth-hero A'Yaya was 'overwhelmed by divine ecstasy' when he looked upon the Zuni Bird, of how he emerged from the delta mad – but holding in his right hand a gorgeous white plume which radiated light and healing power. This was the time after the Middle Kingdom when many people were being born sterile and the future seemed bleaker than the past – but, said the story, those whose bodies were brushed by the miraculous plume became fertile, and Miir lived. Veneration of the Zuni Bird became widespread, the aims and philosophy of Miir's most famous institution were decisively influenced by A'Yaya's discovery: eugenic necessity became an art of life. When the women of the original Tarasse College in Ussian came to choose a name for their emergent order, they called themselves the Feather Guild, and the greatest maker among them they called the White Feather. The plume itself, vitality spent, eventually became part of the White Feather's ceremonial regalia. Of A'Yaya it was said simply that he was in a state 'beyond need of human praise.'

The tale ended with a warning which no longer made strangers laugh:

'You will die a futile death if you seek the Zuni Bird. For it is not to be seen again until the Flowering of the Fifth Element approaches. First the Herald will see and bear witness in a dark time. Then many will see and bear witness.'

For a century or more this had been thought no more than apocalyptic extravagance, the language of myth, a primitive belief which need not be taken too seriously by sophisticated people.

Now it was thirty-five years since mad Analee had borne incoherent witness in a dark time, staggering ecstatic from the delta with a white plume in his hand even as the refugees were streaming past the delta into Mantrim.

The plume had been beautiful – many wildfowlers still alive remembered stroking it, touching it with reverent fear to their faces and bodies. But it had none of the curative powers spoken of by the myth. It was just a feather. This had been a disappointment, a doubt. But Analee's ecstasy had been undoubtedly genuine, he'd been transfigured, nobody had understood him, he'd had to be restrained. Obviously, he'd met *something* out in the violent margins – what else could it have been but the Zuni Bird? Then Analee had disappeared. Some said that the Cyclones had taken him. The tale of his ecstasy flashed through beleaguered Miir; from the delta to the city of Ussian – from Ussian to Alyss, Danaimon, Schroun, Gurdiangar, and every smaller place. The Zuni Bird became a symbol of resistance. On Ussian's walls it was depicted as a radiant snow-white spirit. Analee's strange exploit raised Miir's hope as Kalnakill and his Jerezid army ignored the age-old conventions – the Zuni Bird lived, barbarity could not prevail. And when Kalnakill made it clear that he expected Miir's people to abandon their beliefs and tongue in favor of the Jerezid Dogmas and the General Synthetic, the people began speaking of the prophecy in A'Yaya's Tale. Was Analee the Herald? Was this the time of the Fifth Element? If so, then the Jerezid invasion was a trivial physical irritation. It was time to bear witness to the glory of the Zuni Bird. Thousands set out for the delta.

Kalnakill denounced the Zuni Bird as a mass delusion. For a time he ordered his soldiers – conscripts from the northern lands which he'd conquered already – to prevent people setting foot on the delta.

He soon desisted.

For one thing, he learned what other conquerors of Miir had learned. Miir was different, Miir was soft and seductive, the continued use of fire and sword in this gentle land would surely stimulate revolts elsewhere. Miir was too well-loved by other peoples: they thought of it as a restful paradise. Worse, he realized that he too was growing to love the land; in his relaxation he was beginning to question why he strove to extend his Jerezid domains. Soon, he was planning to withdraw.

The other reason for desisting was that nobody who went into the delta came out. Nobody repeated Analee's success. The flood of believers soon became a trickle. And the wild-fowlers, who'd grown sick of watching the delta swallow its bright-eyed victims, advised the seekers to go away. They said that the Zuni Bird was already too fat with dead souls, and that perhaps there had been a miscalculation, for the Fifth Element showed no signs of Flowering. They said that Analee had been all very well, but that the subsequent hordes of blundering suicides had only succeeded in ruining the hunting. Life was not easy.

Mantrim was not invaded. And the Cyclones said nothing, though they continued to observe the delta, presumably engaged on their incomprehensible Project. Of Analee, nothing more was heard.

Kalnakill withdrew with his armies, leaving behind a consul and a token force. Over twenty years later, Kalnakill died while attempting to capture the distant southern hillcity of Phadraig. His son Khassam succeeded him. Khassam, as rapacious, did not trouble Miir.

The years passed, and many in Miir came to agree with the rising Formalists of Ussian that Analee had been a hoaxer, that the Zuni Bird did not exist. And again, only romantics and wildfowlers openly expressed belief in the Zuni Bird. But the Cyclones were still at the delta.

After thirty-five years, Khassam marched on Phadraig again.

A bizarre and critical time was inaugurated, affecting every land.

And an invisible war which had been thirty-five years in the fighting began to grow visible in the light of a changing reality.

A war to do with whether or not the Zuni Bird should fly through Miir.

Part I: The Long Night

1 : Namahon and the Cyclone

'Wait, just a minute. I must look back – just once.'

Namahon was twelve years old, a curly-haired boy with an open face burned nut-brown by Miir's hot summer. His yellow-flecked gray eyes were brooding, his voice was wary. It was the first time he'd spoken to the Cyclone who was taking him to sanctuary in Mantrim since they'd stolen out of festive Ussian on horseback a half hour previously. The Cyclone was a dark, shaved, forbidding man in his early thirties. Namahon wasn't yet sure of him; the Cyclones had a bad reputation and were particularly unloved in Ussian. But when they had climbed out of the valley in which Ussian lay and the sunlit north grasslands rippled before them, Namahon found he had to call out. Reining in beneath the great fir tree which marked this point, he turned to look back without waiting for a response, he lost his eyes in the bowl of Ussian.

The Cyclone's name was Lonawi. He had expected this : it was natural.

Spare inside the loose white shift which he'd hitched up around bare legs for easier riding, he checked his dun stallion with a sharp thought and looked back at the boy. His mouth puckered briefly with wry sympathy. Namahon was seated utterly still and gazing down the slope, a diminutive figure, his green traveling robe spread on the panniered flanks of a chestnut mare too big and broad for his knees to grip. There had been no time to find an ideally sized mount. However, the mare was strong and sweet-tempered, and Namahon was managing well.

Lonawi reined in beside Namahon, who didn't acknowledge him. It was cool in the shade of the tree, the afternoon was humid, and the climb – they'd avoided the paved road – had been steep. And Lonawi could not deny that Ussian was very beautiful, though its tastes were not his. Understanding something of Namahon's feelings, he let the boy stare mutely and stiffly for a short time. Then he bent over, spoke reasonably :

'Every minute spent looking back increases the risk of re-capture.'

The boy looked up sharply. His face was intense.

'I look back because I will never see Ussian again.'

'The climate will change. When it is safe for you to . . .'

Namahon shook his head; his jaw was set.

'I will never come back.'

'Do you mistrust our offer of sanctuary? Your mother re-quested it.' Lonawi's gesture was amused but impatient. 'We're not ogres.'

'It's not that. You carried my mother's letter, she trusts you, her judgment is usually very good,' said Namahon in a rush. 'And part of me at least is glad to go.' He lowered his eyes to the sandy soil. 'But I go knowing I will never come back – even if I want to.'

'How do you know that?' Lonawi was curious.

'I feel it!' Namahon met the Cyclone's eyes and found them fathomless. 'I feel it! And whatever the Formalists say, or you for that matter, I *know* my feeling is true!' Then, misinterpreting Lonawi's ambiguous expression, he hastened on to add : 'I don't mean to insult you by comparing you with the Formalists, but I'm not looking back for a small reason. It's because I won't see Ussian again, I want a picture to hold in my mind.' He laughed with a disturbing, too-adult bitterness. 'Maybe when I'm old I'll write boring poetry remembering only how beautiful it looked when I left on the day of the Harvest Festival! They say you forget all the ugliness. Curse me if I do!' He gestured forcefully at the elegant city spread in the bowl of the valley below. Lona-wi watched and said nothing. The boy was high-strung, with years of pressure pent up inside him : best for him to get it out before it festered further. Despite the risk, Nama-hon's arm fell to his side; he was sad. 'Look,' he said, 'the sun's coming down the valley. The whole city dances around the river. It knows it looks beautiful. Look at the round windows in the Kuwa Quarter behind the Market; they're like a huge green emerald. They're part of why

Ussian's called the Green Emerald. I have friends in the Kuwa Quarter – there they take you for who you really are, they don't get angry if your behavior isn't Formalist.' He looked up helplessly. 'I hate it ... but I think I must love it too ... I *had* to look back....'

The chestnut mare moved to reach some tempting grass. Namahon broke off, stared away.

'Looking back is addictive,' said Lonawi, his expression unchanged.

'Yes, but ... why today?' Namahon demanded intensely. 'Or why couldn't today have been gray and miserable? Why must it be a Festival day, with flags, and bells, and colors, and people in the streets? Even the dredgers on the river are decked with flags. *And* the Jerezid Consulate. Not even it looks ugly today. And the Tarasse looks cheerful, but it's a lie! It's full of dull and spiteful people who hate my mother. And I'm deserting her.'

'You're not deserting anyone but yourself by thinking like this,' Lonawi said in a very quiet voice.

'Yes, I am!' Fighting emotion, Namahon nodded violently. 'I could easily have given you the slip, but I didn't want to. Or I did want to, but I couldn't!' His troubled eyes sought out the spiky red-brown buildings which had been his home. The various heights of the Tarasse College dominated the city from their sprawling, sloping site on the north side of the river Naenshe. 'It was horrible there,' he said, low-voiced. 'Hate behind the smiles. All the time they watched me, hoping to catch me out so they could discredit Tschea. Now I'm free ... but she's still there, and my half-brother and half-sisters. They're too young to know why the Forma-lists hate them. Why does she send me away and not them? Why do I endanger them by letting myself go? What's hap-pening?'

His shoulders slumped.

Lonawi looked at a lonely, uncertain boy. The Cyclone wiped his brow; even up here the air was close and breath-less. He looked about.

'We must go. Once across the Lansalle we'll be safe.'

His voice was definite. Nodding silently, Namahon twitched the reins away from Ussian and followed the

Cyclone, his yellow-flecked eyes flicking from side to side but not back again.

Lonawi intended to ford the Lansalle at its shallowest point, midway between the delta and the long lake from which the river flowed – Tardenoisse. This meant passing northwest through the grasslands. The tough-stemmed grass grew thick and above head-height, it hemmed and overhung the paved and narrow road, its lancelike tips stirring restlessly as a thickening sky warned travelers that the thunder rolling farther west was coming their way. With Lonawi leading, the pair passed an irregular stream of people on foot, horse, or wagon : people hurrying to Ussian in time for the celebrations. Brightly dressed in their best clothes, the passersby scowled at the forbidding Cyclone, but gazed curiously at the boy behind. Namahon's face was shadowed by a hood, he met no eyes, he gazed at the blackening sky or at Lonawi's back. He was regretting his behavior at the fir tree. He should have controlled himself better. He resolved not to make such a display of himself again.

He looked forward to riding through the thunderstorm.

But the storm veered north and missed them; when at last the grass began to thin out, the twilight air was heavier and more oppressive than at any time before. Lonawi had hoped to reach the Lansalle by nightfall, but the river was still some way distant through the woods and arable fields which began where the grasslands ended. And he knew Namahon must be very tired; his instructions were to make haste, but not to exhaust the boy completely. So he turned off the now-unpaved road as it descended through the first extensive woods, signaling for Namahon to follow. When the two horses had picked their way deep into the trees Lonawi dismounted; unpacked, tethered, and fed his horse while Namahon slithered painfully from the mare and stood uncertainly, feeling sick.

The Cyclone took the mare.

'I'll look after her. Get firewood before the light goes.'

Namahon went peering for wood, wondering what was the point of a fire on a night like this. Sweat was running down his aching body, and the haze in the sky was such that the newly risen full moon was apparent only as a silvery smear. He stopped between two huge trees which between them blotted out half the sky. He listened. The world outside Ussian was strange. He felt very unreal, as if he might wake up and find himself back in the Tarasse at any minute. But the night-woods whispered, and the Tarasse was already distant. He shook his head sharply. The dreaminess persisted, though he no longer felt quite so sick. Everything was so still, as if waiting ... and the waiting was connected in his mind with the feeling that he would never see Ussian again. It was frightening; he resisted the urge to turn and flee aimlessly. Was the air making him feel like this? Or his exhaustion? He started. That bush! It moved! And what was that sound? It was growing too dark! Heart hammering, he turned and limped back past looming trees with his few sticks, too stiff and confused to relax.

The Cyclone was bent down to the ground, coaxing a fire into existence with tinder he'd collected on his own account. His eyes were gleaming and his prominent cheek-bones reflected the still-small flame. He paid no attention as Namahon put down the sticks. Namahon remained standing. He realized that, in addition to taking care of the horses and building the fire, the Cyclone had put up a lean-to – an angled canvas sheet roped around two trunks.

'Hungry?' asked the Cyclone, without looking up from the fire.

'I – I'm not sure. . . .'

'Sore?'

'Yes,' said Namahon with more conviction. 'But not very.'

The flame caught firmly. The Cyclone fed it carefully; he sat back.

'Now we have a fire,' he said with evident satisfaction. 'Do you like fires?'

'Yes,' said Namahon again, sitting down stiffly on the other side of the fire. An insect buzzed him; he tossed his head with irritation.

'Please relax,' said the Cyclone. 'Your face is so distant I can't help feeling nobody's at home. Let us at least be companions. You may call me Lonawi, and I will call you Namahon – if you permit it.'

'Yes,' said Namahon, unsmiling, 'Lonawi.'

'Good.' Lonawi selected objects from his pack. 'Here. Catch.'

Namahon brought up his hands just in time to catch the lumpy bag and the clasp-knife which followed it across the fire. Opening the bag, he found a mixture of vegetables. 'Peel them,' said Lonawi as he unpacked a pan, 'and soon we'll have a meal. Then perhaps you'll join me in a small service recognizing this sanctified day.' He added more wood to the fire, shadows leaped up the trees, the horses snickered nervously. 'The harvest's a complete failure. But that's no reason why we shouldn't raise our spirits as best we can. Do you know the Foundation Tales? Or are they too old-fashioned for a modern lad like yourself?' Lonawi gave his voice a provocative twist.

Stung, Namahon plunged the knife fiercely into the ground.

'The Stick-People call the Tales lies and rubbish, unfit for the minds of growing ... Uniques. . . .' Namahon was reluctant to use the term. 'But Tschea taught me to love the Tales; they hate her for that as well. And in the city there are people like Tah Ti the Boaster. He tells many strange stories.' The boy laughed sharply. 'He'd better watch out, Cuinneale will get him, Cuinneale doesn't like stories!'

'Cuinneale?' murmured Lonawi. 'I've heard of him.'

'Tschea would have become White Feather when Inila retired three years ago,' Namahon continued passionately, 'but Cuinneale influenced the other Red Feathers and Clarai was voted instead. Clarai listens to him, and the Jerezid Consul listens to her. The people have to agree with him because he's friendly with the Guard Commander. He's horrible, he changes people into dull Formalists like himself, it can't make him happy, because he's always attacking someone. Tschea says it's because he hates himself and can't admit it. He's got the Guild and the Patterning orders under his thumb – he was Chief Shaper. The Preconceptuals are scared of him; only the Leapers still support Tschea and won't go Formalist, they can see through him. But they're not very strong.'

He took a potato, hacked savagely at it with the knife.

Lonawi was slicing herbs. 'So she has no friends in the Guild?' he asked. 'Nobody to help? Is that why she came to us?'

Namahon stiffened suspiciously.

'Why do you ask?'

Lonawi shrugged. His bald pate gleamed ruddy in the firelight.

'Doesn't matter. Careful with that knife.'

The boy fell silent. Lonawi was agreeable. Now it was completely dark save for the fire and the moon's hoary smear through still foliage; it grew darker when Lonawi set the pan on a griddle over the glowing fire. Namahon brooded silently, distant, wrapped up in his cloak. And the Cyclone wondered how much Tschea's son guessed or knew. Probably nothing concrete. He could hardly know of the activities of the Inner Vortex, nor of the Project, but ...

'Do you know?' Namahon asked suddenly, looking up.

'Know what?'

'Why Tschea approached you. Why this happened so fast.'

Lonawi sensed the cutting edge of Namahon's intelligence.

'I'm only in the Second Degree of the Outer Vortex,' he said equably, stirring the stew. 'Just an agent used for the odd jobs. The Master gave me my orders, that was that. I'm simply taking you to Baethnan....'

'I don't believe you.'

'What do you mean?' Lonawi sounded slightly severe.

Namahon fingered the rough stone amulet which hung around his neck.

'I can feel it's part of your orders to say things like that,' he replied emphatically, 'so that I don't get worried. But isn't it part of the Cyclone creed that people shouldn't be kept ignorant of what they're fit to know?'

'True.' Lonawi nodded, lips slightly parted in interest.

'Would your Master deny that creed? Aren't you fit to know the nature of your mission?'

Lonawi burst out laughing.

'I know what's fit for the Second Degree to know!'

'Well then, how much is that?' Namahon demanded,

pressing forward eagerly, quite forgetting his fear. 'Why am I going to Baethnan? They say that Analee was taken to Baethnan, that Baethnan knows all about the time before the Great Forgetting ... so why Baethnan?'

'Didn't your mother tell you?'

'I don't think she knows why herself!' There was a note of bitterness in Namahon's voice. The woods stirred, very briefly; the breath of breeze was quickly suffocated. 'She pretended it was all just to get me out of the Tarasse, but I think she wonders if you Cyclones influenced her mind. Is that possible? It's said you can do that. Don't we have the right to know? Doesn't your creed extend to others?'

'I repeat: we're not ogres.' Lonawi was quiet, perhaps reproving.

The boy sighed. 'The air's so strange,' he muttered. 'Has been ever since those creatures were discovered and brought back to life by Khassam....'

'The mumen?' Lonawi's face was blank, almost invisible.

'Yes, that's right, the thirty mumen!' Namahon nodded vehemently. 'I know the Middle Kingdom Lays. The mumen were the limbs and principal agents of the Divine Mutant, they were his interpreters, they spelled the world with their dancing of his strangeness.... The air's so strange,' he repeated. For a moment he was silent. Then – 'Khassam's taken them to Phadraig with his invading army. Perhaps they should have been left beneath the Spirit-Mountains where they were found. I heard it said that they were only found because a Jerezid patrol was chasing Nikosner through the mountains.... Just think ... if Nikosner hadn't been exiled from Miir to Kor, the mumen would never have been discovered in those vaults.... I wish they'd been left undisturbed....' And he shuddered, wrapped his arms around himself, and breath rattled out between his teeth. 'Everything's so *creepy* tonight....'

'Here,' said Lonawi, handing over a bowl full of stew. 'Eat.'

Namahon was hungry. The food quickly vanished. Then for a time they stared at the fire's glowing bed. Occasionally, the horses snickered nervously. And Namahon knew that the night pressed them as heavily as it lay on him. The atmosphere was filled with many strange currents.

'Why do you Cyclones stay locked up and secret in your Colleges?' he asked, needing to talk. 'I thought that once you were wanderers, depending on people's charity and goodwill. It's said you're all very rich, but then people would say that anyway, since they don't like you....'

'We still wander.' Lonawi felt the boy's need to talk aggressively. He smiled, and tapped his head. 'There are immense distances to be wandered without moving a step. And it's only to the outside we seem locked up and secret – though truly, there is no outside. Our doors are open.'

'Yes – then why are you so unpopular? You've only been allowed to build one College in Miir – and many people think Dulankir's more like a fortress than a College!'

'It lies between the north wind and the delta.'

Namahon shivered. 'What does that mean?'

But Lonawi was imperturbable across the glow of the fire.

'It means that Dulankir is well sited where it is,' he said.

And Namahon felt the night creeping through him, pulling at him.

'Is it true that adepts of the Inner Vortex can make themselves invisible?' he demanded, a hint of desperation in his voice.

'Anyone can be invisible when they learn how not to be noticed.'

'Do you believe in the Zuni Bird?'

'Of course!' Lonawi was mock-serious. 'Do you take me for a Formalist?'

'I don't know what I take you for. Tschea told me never to take people at face value; she said to meet them in the eyes and see them there.' Namahon grimaced, fidgeted, abruptly answered a much earlier question. 'No. She has few friends in the Tarasse. Few risk being associated with her. They might find their preconceptions being turned down as' – and he adopted a pompous adult tone – 'artistically nonfunctional!' His laugh was jagged. 'My mind's jumping about like a grasshopper tonight. I feel ... it's horrible! The night crawls, it's trembling with what's about to happen, it's building up with currents of conflict in every direction!' He jerked his head to the south, spontaneously, toward the delta. 'Images press on me! I see so many people, all waiting, the eastern horizon glows ... Ussian's on fire! Oh, there's a horrible tumult in my head' – and he stood up, gripping his skull in both hands, features twisted in distress. But as Lonawi half-rose the boy's hands fell away, and his voice grew trancelike. Lonawi waited where he was.

'Oh ... I'm in such a strange place ... in a mirrored house where ghosts dance, all differently. I hear a child laughing, a very young child.... What am I doing? I'm painting – painting on a wall....'

'What are you painting?' asked Lonawi gently.

'... Painting eyes,' said Namahon in a faraway voice, 'red, yellow, purple, orange eyes, they're all running and dripping down the wall ... and the ghosts ...' He started. 'They're the ghosts of people who are solid and real in the world tonight, but something awful's happened, something to do with the mirrors, and the laughing – they stopped believing they were real. The laughing ... it's ... oh ... I see a man ... he's real, I can't see through him, he carries a strange machine, it's ancient, filled with power, it reminds me of the delta.... He's looking in a mirror, he thinks it's a door, he's going to go through.... No! No! Don't go through there!' And Namahon shuddered, his head fell, and he shook it, took a deep breath. 'Now I'm at a door,' he said in a bewildered voice, 'another door ... my mother ... she's trying to kill him, her eyes are ... it's the mirrors! Help them ... they want to reach the delta, I don't know what ... Lonawi! Lonawi! I'm going mad!'

'Be calm,' breathed Lonawi. 'It's the night. I also sense many strange images.' And he thought of the general order:

Do not speak of the Project outside the Colleges.

The night was getting through to him, it was true, and it was very disturbing, despite his trance-preparation for the approaching crises.

'. . It was so *real*,' Namahon whispered. He sat slowly, ashen in the darkness. 'I've had such scenes in my head before, but never so vivid ... the red-haired man, and Tschea, both drowned in this ... conflict.' He shivered. 'And the mirrors ... and the laughing, which I can't ... but *through the mirrors* ...' He looked up sharply. And Lonawi knew that he was clearly seen by the boy in the dark. '... What of the Unmen of Lamassa? Isn't it true that they came through their mirrors from another dimension, that they can influence people at great distances through ordinary mirrors?' Ignoring what Lonawi said, he hurried on, somehow driven to speak what lay on his mind. 'Tah Ti says the Unmen can only materialize outside their land if invited ... or if land's vacated, cursed by its own people. And with so many mirrors in the world ...'

Lonawi interrupted, in a tone which brooked no denial:

'This isn't the time to speak in reflections. It is time we celebrated the Harvest Festival with a short observance.'

And in fact Namahon was glad to agree; the ceremonial chants of praise seemed to establish a small center of calm in the pit of the unfriendly night. Later, though, he stared at the remains of the fire and could not sleep as Lonawi squatted motionlessly, staring at the sky.

He thought about his father, Algon.

He knew he'd recognize his father immediately – if ever they should meet.

Apparently a wild and unlettered barbarian, Algon had spent a total of three days in Ussian when Tschea was a controversial Green Feather newly from Schroun. In those three days they'd met, Contracted, and turned the Tarasse upside down. The Preconceptuals had tried to drag Algon away for the usual biotests, but he'd cracked their heads together. When the stiff-faced Darsan Guard had drawn bows on him, he'd joked his way out of the situation. Algon had gone, and not come back.

'Very sensible of him too,' Tschea had told Namahon many times, always with the same wistful humor, 'seeing as he took the Jerezid Consul's brand new landsailer with him – without asking. It was a very popular gesture, at the time....'

Over the years, Algon reached the status of a Tarasse-myth. Tschea had risen on the myth – before Cuinneale used it against her.

He'd vanished. But he'd left more than a son. Namahon felt the comforting weight of the rough amulet in the hollow of his neck. Tschea had passed it on to him the first time he'd asked about his father. Now it was a connection in a time growing very disconnected. He wouldn't see Ussian again. *Or perhaps only as a glowing reflection*, he thought, gazing at the harvest moon. It was like a milky, blinded eye, in the south ... over the delta. He shut his eyes. *Now is all....*

Now. A leaden night in a breathless wood beneath a fatal moon, with threads in his head drawn from a much-extended *now*.

2 : Celebration of the Harvest

In Ussian, too, the evening was close, unrelieved by any of the winds which had been scattering the ripening harvest far and wide. There was little to celebrate in the high price of grain – it was a day made for idleness – but the city swarmed with determined celebrants and seekers of Contract. The Green Emerald's polyglot population depended on the season: tonight, the more-or-less permanent core of about fifty thousand was swelled almost double. The local population was no less various in appearance than the spendthrift tourists who thronged the arcades and public places. Miir had grown from a great diversity of peoples attracted to the Tarasse since the sterile times: the Tarasse conferred pleasure, prestige, and profit on those accepted.

Tonight, the city's pleasures were in great demand. Bars, bordellos, gaming houses, redweed dives – they were doing a roaring trade. The Market betwixt Kuwa Quarter and squat brown Jerezid Consulate was crammed with visitors from the northern lands, from Phrénge, Kór, Spokáne, Aquínte, and savage Purpléfield, from Zagrín, the distant Jerezid capital. They spoke freely in General Synthetic, believing that nobody here understood the official Jerezid tongue. The people encouraged this illusion.

At sunset, bells began ringing from both sides of the river. There was a general motion toward the Chuunlan Oval, the great white stadium recently built down by the river, adjacent to the labyrinthine maze of the Tarasse. All day long ox-carts had been ferrying materials here from the wharves and the south side warehouses, sweating red-tattoo work-gangs had been erecting temporary booths outside the Oval. And the sloping groves in the reddening Maple Park high above the Oval had filled with people who had no chance of getting in. Many of them thought it the best place to be in any case. There was no crush, and from this height they had a bird's-eye view of the Celebration. The position had the added attraction of being on a level with or higher than the terraced gardens and promenades of the Yeki House, the nearest spur of the Tarasse. Maple Park was a popular place from which to watch the beautiful, bizarre women, men, and Uniques. For their part, the inhabitants of the College came to the Yeki House gardens in order to be seen in their new styles, relationships, and personalities. It was one of their many games, one whereby current status and situation was telegraphed to the watchers in the Park – to admiring relatives, glamor addicts, political observers, and the simply curious. The game was among the oldest in the Tarasse, dating from the time when the College had been a closed institution; it had come to be a 'done thing,' a near-dance of exaggerated movement, gesture, greeting, and re-buff. Of late, the dance-element had grown increasingly Formalized; spontaneity had all but died from the terraces of the Yeki House. Still, the movements themselves were an accurate pointer to the current mood of the Tarasse, and the custom remained popular.

So many people, visitors and citizens, had come early to Maple Park to spend their holiday viewing the lives of the famous. Shouting at bored children and wiping their brows, they had watched all day with knowledgeable intensity and identification.

'There's Sos'to with her new Contractual!'

'A Jerezid flunky – she'll never make the Red with him!'

'But what's she got growing from her shoulders? – that purple thing?'

'A membranous ruff. Haven't you heard? The Patterners can grow them from you now. It's remarkable what they can do.'

'I don't know. I think it's hideous.'

'Oh, it suits her. It goes with her tattoos. . . .'

And late in the afternoon Tschea the Red Feather appeared briefly by herself. She scanned the Park with what looked
like an amused grimace before going back inside. When
evening fell and the Yeki House terraces emptied, those in
the Park argued about her while eating, drinking, and scanning the bright crowds which converged on the Oval as the
bells continued to toll. The white-walled stadium filled
rapidly with the eight thousand who'd obtained their seats
from the Lottery or through connection. The high-crested
boxes and the mosaic-stepped enclosure on the eastern side,
the Dragon side, were still empty. The procession from the
Tarasse was due any minute: city Guards and mounted
Darsans in blue-gold uniforms were clearing the marbled
Inila Way, pushing back the thousands who couldn't get
into the Oval but wanted a sight of Clarai as she passed.
Thousands more had already enveloped the bare ground
about the Oval. Carrying lanterns, posturing in masks and
ridiculous costumes, wearing summer flowers and ears of
corn in their hair, they surged among the temporary shanty-
town of booths, bars, sideshows, and places to eat. The ramshackle streets stretched down to the railed bank of the rapid
brown Naenshe; the rivermen were alert and ready to fish
out drunks who fell in, but nobody doubted that the Naenshe would claim its share tonight. For the night was thicker
than the day had been; the air was hot and difficult to
breathe; the bars of wine-merchants and brewers were sell-
ing out already. Sending emergency messages back to their
cellars in the city for fresh barrels, they agreed they'd never
known anything like it. Such humidity! So many people –
and so few of them with smiles or songs: so few happy
faces.

Then eyes turned up to the southern side of the valley to
the signal-fire atop it. The blaze indicated that the moon was
risen over the peak of Shain Tree Hill. It was time for the
procession to begin. Those in Maple Park propped themselves up on their elbows. In enervated groups beneath
spreading maple crowns they talked, their conversation
terse.

'What a night! The air's so heavy. What's going on?'

'What's going on? My head's going *around*, I'll tell you that!'

'The Grand Master's not coming. He's fallen out with Clarai. . . .'

'He's fallen out with everyone. Who loves a Cyclone?'

'You remind me. Tah Ti has a strange tale to tell at the moment.'

'You don't take that idiot seriously? What does he say?'

'Cuinneale will clip Tah's wings, mark my word!'

'Cuinneale will clip everyone's wings. He—'

The speaker's words were drowned out by the swell of cheers from below.

'Look! Clarai's carriage. The White Feather!'

And some of those in the Park stood and cheered as the White Feather's open ox-drawn carriage appeared around a bend of the Inila Way three hundred feet below. Escorted by mounted Darsans, her carriage was followed by others as ornate; they looked like colorful beetles from high Maple Park as they wound through the close-packed sea of the crowds below.

Others in the Park showed no interest; they remained where they sat or lay on discarded clothes – loving, bored, disdainful, or simply unable to move. Some of those standing resented such disrespect to the White Feather, and several drunken fights were breaking out among the maples as Clarai's carriage passed through the Dragon Door and into the Oval.

There were over a thousand people in the procession. It took several minutes for all of them to pass into the Oval. When all of them were inside, the great bronze-relief gates of the Dragon Door were shut and the tens of thousands outside turned to their own entertainments, feeling that they'd cheered and applauded enough for one night.

The lucky ones inside the Oval stood for the entry of the procession from the Tarasse. They craned for a good view of the White Feather as she showed herself from her gold-lit box above the inner buttresses of the Dragon Door. To most of them she was a distant figure, not so much a human

being as a symbol of Miir, her body embellished all over by
the traditional White Feather tattoos. Ussian's freethinkers
thought the White Feather Display the most dehumanizing
prerogative of Her Eminence. Her face alone was free of the
ritual designs.

Framed in black hair, her face was strong and beautiful, and it belied her forty-five years. Her face was a prac-
ticed mask on occasions such as this. Who knew what
she thought with nearly ten thousand gazing at her, with
nearly ten thousand bowing to sound the sonorous hum
of respect? Cuinneale? Perhaps. The gray ghost was behind
her in the box, standing where he could see without being
seen, so lacking in presence it seemed possible that he had
no real substance. The illusion was betrayed by his eyes –
restless black beads, finely meshed about with crow's-feet,
always on the move. They watched Clarai take the applause. Clarai from the streets. Now she was Miir. It was
his doing. So subtle, so patient he'd been. Sowing the
ground for his vision of the perfect art. Now the reaping
was threatened by the Leaper warning that some dire new
influence was abroad – an influence connected with Khassam's revival of the mumen. Cuinneale didn't believe it.
The Leapers remained arrogant, quite capable of crying
wolf in an attempt to diminish his authority. Tschea was
probably behind it. Tschea! Through a side embrasure he
scanned about the enclosure. It was filling with ranks of
Red, Green, and Purple Feathers, with languid Contractuals,
excited Uniques, brow-mopping guests, off-duty Patterners,
and hopeful men currently vying for prestigious Contracts.
Cuinneale narrowed his eyes at some of these in the last
group. They were dressed and conducting themselves with
complete indifference to Formalist values. The rules of
admission to the Tarasse would have to be tightened up,
or bad art would creep in despite his vigilance.

His pale forehead was beaded with sweat. He made no
attempt to wipe it off. His hands remained invisibly clasped
beneath wide sleeves.

Clarai withdrew before the applause faltered too obviously.

Her wide eyes met Cuinneale's with a question as lights were dimmed all around the Oval. She indicated the third chair. Down below, only the sandy central arena remained lit. All about, an expectant hush.

'Where is he?' Her voice was lazy. 'Where's our Consul, our Clumsy Peacock? Is his lateness deliberate? Does he mean to slight me? Or' – she paused to let green-coiffed and -clad attendants clothe her tattooed, naked body in a loose white robe, let them place the white plume in her raven hair – 'has he heard the Leaper warning of strange influences?'

Cuinneale showed no surprise. He met her sharp-eyed gaze as the attendants slipped the heavy-stoned Matriarchal Necklaces around her neck. Outside, they awaited her sign.

'Chimalus is primitive, but not credulous to the point of stupidity.' Cuinneale's eyes fell to the jewels where they gleamed dimly against the illustrated swell of her breasts. 'Besides, the rumor has been checked. I don't believe he's heard it. His spies tell us everything.'

'I think I know him better than you.' Clarai seemed amused as she turned back to the balcony in new guise. 'I think perhaps tonight has given him a headache – a species of diplomatic seizure. Like the Grand Master he ducks the celebration of a ... completed harvest!'

She turned to the Oval. Framed in sudden light from beneath the wooden balcony, she gave the silent signal.

Inside and outside the Oval, heads turned up to the trumpeters stationed at twenty torchlit points about the topmost perimeter.

Trumpets came gleaming to twenty mouths. They waited there for Clarai to give the sounding signal. They waited as motionless in the torchlight as the flags and pennants above the stadium. All breathing seemed to fade from the city. Clarai raised her arms up above her head.

Everything was poised for the moment of their descent.

She's disturbed, Cuinneale decided; *tonight needs careful shapes*.

Her arms swept down to her side. The gleaming trumpets sounded.

Distant by his fire atop the valley the signalman heard the fanfare, and shivered in the heat of his fire. The moon was a

pallid glimmer above the dim bare flanks of Shain Tree Hill
behind him. It was all so eerie. And he so far from the Celebration....

Duty-bound, he stared hungrily down as the fanfare was
drowned out by thousands greeting the commencement
with deep-throated relief.

Fire, flowers, gleaming flanks.

Fourteen tumbling horseback clowns came sweeping into
the arena from the western Door of Hundred Heads, star-
bursting from the gargoyled colonnades, posturing, whoop-
ing, somersaulting on their mounts.

Three Communal Hearth teams came running from the
Dragon Door, young dancers of both sexes, garlanded and
streaming silken corn-yellow as they curved toward the galloping horses, seemingly bent on collision.

While, springing right out of the theatrically startled
crowd, the Fire-Dancers from Danaimon came leaping in
swirls of flame-colored cloaks, carrot-haired and naturally
ecstatic. Jumping the barrier, each took the Fire-Hoop from
a novice; from different points the ten of them bounded
into the dangerous center with the flaming hoops whirling
above their burning heads. The crowd drew breath. Disaster
seemed inevitable. Frail flowers, flaming hoops, horses
careering with cavorting madness on their backs – how
could the disparate groups survive each other long enough
to merge in a single dance? Forty-two dancers, fourteen
horses, a limited space, colliding....

Some strained to get a better view.

Others averted their eyes.

Then, somehow, each group was safely through the
others, and turning back to merge in common purpose,
tentatively mingling. The opening shock of danger was over.
Now the dancers flirted with their danger and grew patterns
from it, tight and intense. Now they dissolved these explor-
atory patterns as the yellow dancers flowed out like dreamers, the fiery ones darted, and the horses whirled about the
whole, their flanks almost brushing the barriers at the side.
From this wide expansion the first climax built. The rich-
trapped horses began to close the circle on the yellow and

the red, their drumming hooves a menacing cannonade. While the yellow weaved hopeless flight around and through the beleaguered center, the Fire-Dancers joined issue with the threatening clowns. These madcap geniuses – several of them Uniques – howled with mock hate and triumph as they somersaulted through the Fire-Hoops thrust in their path by those who danced in Vaira's Way. The ten Fire-Dancers fought valiantly to protect the reaping of the yellow, but they were pressed farther and farther back by the snorting horses and their elemental riders. The circle grew tighter, tighter – now red and yellow waved back to back as the horses stormed about them. Red was blown into yellow; the corn would burn before storm blew it down—

No. For the fearsome clowns leaned in, plucked up red dancers and tossed them to the outside of the whirling circle. The red spun back past lashing hooves as the clowns flung streaming yellow up and over. Red leaped up with flaming hoops on high as yellow burst out; ten clowns slipped off and left the fiery ones on horseback. The clowns tumbled between tails and nostrils into the center, yellow returned, and red slipped off; now all were inside the circling horses save four clowns left to guide the animals off in four directions. The inner circle of human dancers was left at the center of the arena, a torchlit whirling of red and yellow and patchwork colors, too intricate for individual motions to be followed; a spellbinding fusion, flame-petaled mandala – it was Celebration. Enacted as it always had been enacted.

One of the Fire-Dancers was called Marck. He was twenty, he was high in Vaira's Way, dancing in the flame. Tonight was the first time he'd ever been in Ussian. He'd never seen so many people. Nor sensed such a heavily electric atmosphere before. The city wasn't joyful. Perhaps cities never were. None of that bothered him now. He was beyond himself. He was a dancing jet of flame. He was unaware that not all the spectators were fully absorbed in contemplation, that some were distracted and looking about, that others were talking as he danced so joyfully.

He wasn't aware of Tschea's eyes.

3 : The Red Feather Tschea

Hazel-eyed, electrically restless in cloudy lemon, Tschea sat high at the back of the Dragon enclosure. She was close to an exit tunnel. She was ready to use it. Her mind was much too restless to let her go on sitting here. With moody, fragile concentration she stared over a descending forest of nodding plumes, intricate hair-styles, and bizarre, unquiet profiles, and she considered the hypnotic whirling of the dance.

Joy from the dancers, she thought, *and self-deception from everyone else. Nobody wants to believe the Leapers. But tonight's unnatural; just such a night as they forecast. Tonight it happens. It must be tonight. Or very soon. And who'll be pretending celebration then?*

She sensed unacknowledged worry everywhere. *I'll explode,* she thought, *if nobody else does.* She ran fingers through coils of hair like white light, touched tentatively at the blue-gold starburst tattoo on her forehead. The night was so nervous, but she had to relax. She couldn't afford to get into disputes tonight. She could recognize that energetic irritation was clouding out her sadness at Namahon's leaving. In fact, her irritation amounted to a darkly fervent wish that the alien influence of which the Leapers warned would hurry up and overwhelm this falseness about her. And let it swallow her also! She'd come to the Tarasse with ideals, with a free spirit and clear vision. Now the Tarasse was a pointless game which she played to spite those who didn't want her to play. It was no good. She'd lost her way in social distraction, in a hardening climate, found secondhand purpose in lonely opposition to the Formalist value-system.

No, she told herself, *no despair. I'm not that weak.*

But Namahon was gone. Her favorite child. Had she done right? She wasn't exempt from the doubt she sensed all around her. Down in the arena, new dancers were feeding in to replace the old, and drummers started throbbing a fast beat which hurt her head. A middle-aged man seated imme-

diately below her broke out in laughter at some joke the
plump woman in purple beside him had made. His laughter
quickly became uncontrollable, hard-edged. Tschea found
herself on her feet.

'What's wrong, Tschea? Your face frightens me.'

Tschan, Tschea's older hearth-sister from Schroun by
Lake Bhykan, was nervous. The night, the drums, the laughing which wouldn't stop – and Tschea standing over her
with a face so set, so grim, so premonitive.

Tschea looked down. Tschan was lying on cushions with
her auburn-haired head on Kryle's chest. Her present Contractual was pleasant, predictable, and unimaginative – precisely the type the Formalists approved. Tschan had been
pert, neat, mercurial. Now her face had filled out, and the
swell of her belly beneath embroidered white linen told
that she was pregnant again. Her eighth Unique? – or was it
her ninth? To Tschea there was unreality in what she saw,
unreality in the Tarasse normality of Tschan and her eighth
or ninth Contractual, in their pretense that nothing was
amiss. Struggling to make sense of it, Tschea stared without
answering, not in malice but incomprehension. Who was
Tschan? Who was Kryle? Who did *they* think they were?

'Sit down, or go away, but stop staring at us like that!'

Tschan read contempt in Tschea's gaze. To Tschan, the
Red Feather was continual humiliation, and possibly a vam-
pire thief of Tschan's own rightful energies. Tschan had
reached the Purple, and secretly she knew that the Red was
forever beyond her. Tschea was a rebuke in every respect:
in her early success and self-reliance, in her very presence.
Tschan's tattooing was extensive, imaginative, but to her it
seemed crude compared with the delicacy and imperial
style of Tschea's single starburst. The line of Tschea's neck
and bare bronze shoulders was still flawless, suggesting to
Tschan that her own fashionably sprouted membranous ruff
was an unfortunate affectation. And through cloudy lemon
Tschan could see that Tschea had kept her shape, was still
almost slim. After all, she'd only had four children, over-
rated at that. Worst of all, it was Tschea who was famous in
Schroun, not her. Tschea had rejected the honor of their
Hearth, and she'd never gone back. Tschan returned fre-

quently, was greeted warmly every time ... but never a
more substantial recognition. It was always Tschea they
wanted to know about – Tschea's scandals, Tschea's conflicts, Tschea's lovers, Tschea, Tschea, Tschea!

The laughing man was choking on his sudden emotion,
and the alarmed woman in purple was thumping him on
the back. Now other instruments had joined the drums, but
there was something lackluster about the music. Still Tschea
hadn't answered, still she stared, so that Kryle was half-
mesmerized, and Tschan could no longer take her intensity.
Tschan thrust herself up on one arm.

'What is it? Have you lost your tongue?'

Tschea gestured almost imploringly at the spectacle, looking down so her jaw and the slant of her cheeks were caught
in light from the arena. 'This music has lost its fire!' she insisted. And, palms cupped in mime, she scooped up the
music of pipes, flutes, and drums and flung it at her hearth-
sister. Tschan flinched. 'Listen! The spirit's gone out of it.
Just the form is left. The times demand a different music
altogether; this is hypocrisy!'

'It sounds all right to me!' Kryle's baritone was hollow
with false heartiness. Tschan laid a hand on his velvet knee,
and she stared up blankly, aware that neighboring heads
had turned at Tschea's voice. Tschea knew it too. She
shrugged, already regretting the uncharacteristic stridency
of her insistence. Why bother? But Tschan's hostility hurt,
even now. They had been close. If only she could get
through to Tschan without exposing herself to fresh
charges of arrogance and egotism. If only.

'I know you don't believe what the Leapers say,' Tschea
said quietly, 'but at least consider it – for your own goods.'

'You're like a child,' Tschan rebuked her, 'always dreaming.'

'The air is strange. I know you feel it.'

'And where's friend Hilgo tonight? What's wrong with
you?'

'There's an extra element in the air tonight – you must
feel it!'

'Three years since you Contracted with him for a musical
prodigy. . . .'

'Tschan, please listen!' Tschea bent closer, under stern control.

'...Nobody can understand your objection to him,' Tschan continued, firmly deaf. 'His pedigree's immaculate – Master Songmakers on both sides of his family....'

'Hilgo's an excellent fellow,' added Kryle.

'Keep out of this,' said Tschan swiftly, uncomfortably.

'... Tschan, please ... our art's as stale as ...'

Tschan was all too conscious of people listening. She refused to let Tschea provoke her into uncomfortable thoughts, into what Cuinneale called 'morbid irrationalism.' 'Tschea, dear,' she interrupted quickly, loudly. 'Let me give you some advice. I understand how high-strung you are. But you're almost thirty-four. It's time you faced reality. If you don't consummate with Hilgo soon you'll be asked to resign. The Four-Year Rule applies to you too, you know. Have you considered Hilgo's feelings?' She shook her head and hurried on: the sadness on Tschea's face was discomfiting. 'Self-pity won't help. You weren't voted White Feather – neither was I. And because Hilgo's not a ravishing barbarian like Namahon's father is no reason for you to reject him. Nor for you to talk like a Leaper and project your morbid depressions on everyone else. People are always asking me if you were the same as a child and I have to tell them, yes: just the same – self-willed, moody....'

'You know very well that Hilgo was not my choice.' Tschea's sharp tone undercut Tschan's loudness. 'I'll see you later,' she added, turning. And she left them for the exit tunnel, sweeping platinum coils from her face, urgently swift. Several people turned to watch her go, and scanned Tschan and Kryle before looking back to each other, or to the arena.

'She is an unbalanced person,' Kryle commented.

'Oh, *she*'s not unbalanced, it's the world that is!' Then Tschan looked quickly into Kryle's brown eyes. 'A joke,' she said anxiously. 'An ... an irony ... no more.'

'Yes,' said Kryle, attempting to smile. 'An irony.'

For of course both of them and many others were not-thinking about the Leaper predictions. Despite their oppo-

sition to Formalism, no one thought of the psychics as
enemies of the Guild. The Leapers read the influences of
Above and Below; they appointed the most favorable times
for Unique births. Not even Cuinneale could persuade
people to ignore their vague warning, not even he could con-
fine it completely.

Now the dance was over, the music was fitful, tentative,
as if unsure of its right to be heard. There was an interval.
The crowd buzzed as heavily muscled red-tattoos raked the
floor of the arena smooth. The interval stretched, the musicians stopped playing, then started again. The Opa Theater
of actors and mimes should have immediately followed the
dancers, to enact the popular ritual play: *Tattoos of the
Ghost*. There was no sign of them. Perhaps they'd been held
up on the road from Alyss in the north. Then why wasn't
an alternative on? Such disorganization was unprecedented.
Sweating stadium officials gathered at the Door of Hundred
Heads, shouted contradictory orders at each other, at the
dancers and other acts. Nobody seemed to know what they
were doing, as if their minds were scrambled.

'Send the dancers on again.'

'No. Get them out of the way! Everyone, get out of the
way!'

'You told me the Theater was here. You clearly—'

'Idiot! I *asked* you *if* they were here. You nodded, I
thought....'

Then Cheli, the Keeper of the Oval, furiously bustled
down from her box above the colonnades. Cheli was a retired Red Feather of great, shaking bulk. She waded into the
shameful misunderstanding with wine on her breath.
'What's going on?' she demanded. 'Have you taken leave of
your senses? Get the Orators on!'

The twenty black-and-silver-robed Orators did their best
to hold the crowd's attention, but from the start their
massed declamation was competing with a restless background buzz. In the box above the Dragon Door Clarai
stroked her chin and watched stonily, Cuinneale had gone
to find out what was happening, and the third chair remained empty. The Clumsy Peacock hadn't turned up from the
Jerezid Consulate.

Beneath the colonnades, Cheli was still haranguing her officials with a great wealth of invective when a breathless boy brought word that the Opa Theater had arrived outside.

'They were attacked by Nikosner's brigands!' he blurted.

'Impossible! Nikosner's been ...' Her voice faded away.

Her red-robed bulk covered the flagstones with remarkable speed.

Outside the Oval, the painted wagons of the Opa Theater were surrounded by a silent crowd. The members of the Theater were slumped on the stony ground. Some talked warily, angrily, others were silent, but all looked exhausted, disheveled. A frail white girl was gazing at the bloody bandages on her arms: she seemed to be in shock. Attempting to comfort her was a tall, spindling man with protuberant eyes and a bulbous, turbaned head. Cheli recognized him from previous visits of the Theater as its leader, Ahnem. Using her weight to advantage, she pushed past gawking people and came up to him.

There was blood on his face, a tic beneath the right eye.

'I am Cheli. What happened?'

Ahnem's words came low, rapid, resentful.

'Nikosner. Without warning. Out of the grass. We have ... two dead.' His voice rose. 'He abducted three of my actresses – my Bree among them. We have several badly injured – we need doctors, not spectators!' He jerked his head around the people waiting in shadow all about. 'Can't you do anything but stare? Do you think we attacked ourselves?'

Cheli took him by his quilted arm.

'You're certain it was Nikosner?' she pressed.

'Yes! His laughter – like an animal screaming. Like a ...' He wrenched his arm away, and his voice was bitter. 'We were assured that Ussian's Guards had driven him from the grasslands, that it was safe to come. Is that not so?'

'Yes,' agreed Cheli ponderously, unable to think straight, 'you were assured. But Nikosner has not been seen for many ...'

Ahnem spat, just missing her painted toenails.

'So much for Ussian's assurances!'

Angry faces about him expressed agreement. Members of

the Theater had closed in around her, their faces hostile, as
if it were her fault personally that Nikosner had attacked
them.

'You'll be fully recompensed,' she promised, still calm.

Ahnem looked at her with angry contempt.

'Even now,' he said rapidly, 'who knows what the viper
does with my Bree, my flower – because of Ussian's assurances!' Leaving Cheli red-cheeked with mounting anger, he
started to turn away, then checked. 'One other thing,' he
tossed over his shoulder. 'The brigand left a message for your
Cuinneale. It seems they are friends. *"I remember"* – that is
what the brigand said! Now, send us doctors!'

They turned their backs on her. Cheli buried her face in
her hands and massaged her weary eyes. The night was unhinged with weight and bad fortune. What could she do?
She could hardly ask the Theater to perform.

And – Nikosner's message for Cuinneale . . .

Leaving instructions that the Theater-people were to be
given whatever they needed, Cheli returned angrily through
the gawping crowd to the outer porch of the Door of Hundred Heads. There, beneath a torch guttering from a bracket
between two grimacing white gargoyles, she ran into Cuinneale.

'What is happening?' he asked very quietly, quite without expression, his bleached hair colorless and his face dull
red in torchlight. But his eyes arrested her. She wondered
how to put it. She had no love for Cuinneale; she thought
of him as an upstart.

'The black mage Nikosner is back – with his brigands.'

Perhaps Cuinneale's mouth tightened, but she couldn't be
sure.

'Neither black, nor a mage,' he murmured. 'Why exag-
gerate? As Nikosner he is bad enough. . . .'

'He has a message for you,' Cheli added carefully.

'A message?' His eyes narrowed, and the crow's-feet grew
pronounced.

What skeleton is this that nobody knows of? she wondered.

'It is *"I remember"*,' she told him in a neutral voice.

Cuinneale stepped closer to her. His eyes seemed large.

'Does anyone else know of this ... message?'

'Not as far as I know....'

Then she realized what he was trying to do. His eyes seemed like saucers, spinning into her head. There were people all about, but none of them dared disturb what seemed like a close conference between Cheli and Cuinneale. She fought. But she was taken by surprise, and her mind was already confused by earlier drinking and present madness. Soon, only the two black eyes were spinning inside her head, and Cuinneale's voice—

'You will forget all about this message. I am going to walk away. When you see me pass out of your sight, you will forget....'

Cuinneale slipped back into the porch. In a few seconds, Cheli appeared to start, to look confused. What was she doing, standing here dreaming? Why couldn't she think straight tonight? Hadn't she just been speaking to Cuinneale? It was all so vague tonight. Angry at herself, she returned through the Door of Hundred Heads to sit out the rest of the crippled Celebration.

4 : The Book of An

What else could I have expected? At least she didn't ask where Namahon is. How long till they find out he's gone?

Avoiding the Dragon Door, Tschea had sought a less conspicuous exit farther around the perimeter of the Oval. Now she stood by the white outer wall, gazing at the crowds which eddied around the booths, at the spiky background heights of the Tarasse, and up past steep Maple Park to the starless night with its moon-smear in the south. What should she do? She couldn't bear the thought of going back to the enclosure. She had no wish to return to the Tarasse. She could duck into the crowds but, even without her red feather, she was certain to be recognized, and tonight she shied away from recognition. Moreover, movement was uncomfortable, and her lemon dress was sticking to her

body in this drenching night-heat. So for a time she rested
where she was.

Algon's son was gone. She felt a double emptiness.

Cuinneale would have scotched an open departure; he
would have found a reason to keep her boy within striking
distance. Namahon had taken too much on her behalf. Her
three younger children lacked his potential, his strangeness,
and they'd never been singled out so viciously. Now Namahon was gone. If the Leapers had read the signs truly, then
a powerful center like Baethnan would be among the safest
of sanctuaries during the coming days – one, moreover, in
which Namahon's potential could develop properly as it
never had under the Shaper teachers. If the Leapers were
wrong – then she and her other children would have a lot
for which to answer. But the weight of tonight made an
error seem unlikely; what worried her more than possible
expulsion from the Guild was whether she'd done right in
sending him to Baethnan. The College derived an ambiguous
reputation from its study of ancient lore. And many said
that the Cyclones were dark. She found such ambiguity
strangely compelling; it echoed aspects of her own life
which she'd never understood. Why had she sent Namahon
to the Cyclones, whom she didn't altogether trust? She
knew that she had a dark side, and so did Namahon. It was
the darkness of Algon, who'd gone, and not come back. Algon had come with such contrasts, with such a range of
light and shade in his being. He had drawn her like a moth
to flame, a moth who wished to burn gloriously. Now, on
sustained impulse, she'd sent his son to Baethnan. Why?
Had she been compelled by some external force of which
she was unconscious? Since her foundling childhood she'd
felt that she was being ... watched.

Had she sent Namahon to a sanctuary? – or had she sacrificed him?

She left the wall. Circling the upper perimeter of the
booths and half-empty dancing platforms, she picked her
way past lovers and little groups of redweed dreamers who
lay by the rock-gardened spur leading up to Maple Park.
She followed the ivied sandstone of the Tarasse walls to
the flagstones of Inila Way. The marble gleamed, reflecting

the light of torches, braziers, and the lit windows of elegant buildings between Inila Way and Naenshe. She hesitated. Why this slinking in the shadows? Where was she going? Tonight, Ussian's people were here, on this space about the Oval. Thousands milled. Night was on top of them. Night lay on everyone. Why pretend she was different? So, having circled it, she entered the crowd.

Soon she saw Tah Ti, not far away, seated on the counter of a booth. As usual the Boaster was the center of an argument. She watched him from a distance; she couldn't hear what he was saying, but she could see that it was exciting the people around him. There he sat with his tawny cat, Reb, upon his shoulder, with his hooded eyes flicking from one angry face to the next, his silver-streaked green plaits tossing energetically with each new, more inflammatory point. Tschea found herself pushing forward to hear what he said. Worming her way through the close crowd like an urchin, she realized that nobody was paying her the slightest attention. She wore the general expression; she found it strangely exhilarating. She pushed her way till she was within fifteen feet of the Boaster, and stood by high-hatted travelers from distant Spokane and listened. She respected Tah Ti for his inventive eloquence, for his jibes at the growth in power of the city Guards, at Cuinneale's inanimate intimate relationships, at Jerezid taxes and the Consul's losses in Clarai's games. Tah Ti was not afraid to speak out his angle of any truth.

Tonight, as she'd suspected, it wasn't the failings of Ussian's society he was railing about.

'... Moreover, in the Book of An,' the Boaster was insisting in his sharp, nasal voice, 'the book the Cyclones keep locked up at Baethnan, the one they say blights the unprotected reader – in that book it's said that the Divine Mutant wasn't human in any sense. The Mutant was the projection of a certain group of *ideas* – for when order failed with the Great Forgetting, time and space became a flux in which *idea* and *matter* were indistinguishable from one another. Thought formed and materialized itself in the clashing elements, and it found no rest. The Mutant was the conglomeration of that tormented essence which was human thought in the time after the Great Forgetting – the Middle Kingdom!'

The crowd muttered at the Boaster's energetic insistence, but Tah Ti continued through spasmodic shouts of disagreement. 'The Mutant had no stable existence save in the very instability which it epitomized; the world turned, that age ended, and the Mutant's essence was petrified in new order, its nature faded and was forgotten. . . .'

Tah Ti shrugged. The tawny cat on his shoulder shifted, its bushy tail curled around the neck of its master, and its eyes reflected torchlight and wan faces.

'But the world spins on; there are cycles which seem to repeat themselves . . and in the Book of An, it is said . . .'

Many sensed they didn't want to hear what he was about to say. Uproar broke out. He was jostled by those closest to him, and a bony finger stabbed into the pit of his stomach.

An old man interrupted. 'Tah Ti, your talent's impressive, but you are so *credulous!*'

A spate of other voices showered him with belittlement.

'Was it reading the book which blighted your brain, Tah Ti?'

'Did the Cyclones ask you in and tell you all about it?'

'No, don't you know, Tah Ti's friendly with spirits who bring secret knowledge that even the Cyclones don't know about!'

'Then why haven't the Cyclones come begging him for his knowledge?'

'Ah! They have! But Tah Ti turned them away as unworthy!'

From her cramped stance, Tschea could see Tah Ti waiting for the shouting to subside, his stark face haughtily patient. She wanted to shout out, *'Let him speak,'* but she held her peace. Then she saw a Guard, scarred and leather-strapped, breaking through the crowd to the Boaster. Tah Ti stared back calmly enough.

'Tah Ti, once you were amusing with your diversity of illusions, now you've become an obsessive nuisance. I heard you yesterday by the wharves, and there you were also troubling people with this Book of An.' The Guard's voice was contemptuous. 'Can your mind accommodate no more

than a single delusion now? Have your visionary arteries
hardened?'

The Guard's voice said he'd be glad to give Tah Ti trouble.
The crowd's laughter was edged. Then Tah Ti shouted hotly,
standing.

'Pigs! Listen, damn you!'

People stared, caught in surprise. Tah Ti talked too much,
but he'd never been abusive. Now he was shouting so
angrily that even the Guard moved back a step, his right
hand moving automatically to his side. But the sword remained undrawn, for Tah Ti's eyes had caught him. 'What I
tell you now is true!' Tah Ti bellowed. 'I have no more
diversity, just a single truth! My former diversity was no
more than the half-formed jungle of what I know now!
Of what's about to happen. Come on, you don't need me to
tell you. What a night! What's astir? Nikosner's back in the
grasslands, the Opa Theater has been attacked....'

What? thought Tschea, *Nikosner back? Namahon* ...

'... Why would Nikosner return unless he knew that
there are circumstances approaching which will benefit his
chaos? And you – look at yourselves. How is it you listen
to Tah Ti the garrulous fool when normally by now I'd be
getting your soft fruit in the face? Now let me tell you about
the book – yes, the Book of An... !'

His voice was quivering with such intensity that he'd
cleared a small semicircular space before him; even the
Guard had edged farther back. And the cat on his shoulder
shifted lazily as he told a rapid story, punctuating it with
frequent jabs of his fingers, tosses of his plaits.

'I was over in Kharsee on the other bank of Tardenoisse
when they threw the recruiting Cyclones out of the town.
And I was there when the storm fell on Kharsee that same
night – the storm which the Cyclones denied raising. I took
shelter in a cellar by the docks while buildings tumbled all
around. And there, taking shelter with me, was an old blind
giant. He was ... strange. The pupils of his eyes were rolled
up and useless, the whites alone stared. He'd lost his voice,
and he could only whisper, or croak like a crow. He told me
he'd been trained as a boy by the Hou'ons of Lamassa the
witchland. He said the Cyclones don't know half as much

about the Unman mages as they like to think they do. He gave me no name, no history, but his aura was compelling; he was like a slab of rock on fire inside. And while the storm raged over us, he began to tell me about the Book of An, which he had seen – to his cost. . . .'

The audience was growing in every direction, and he held it quiet, speaking now in a hushed voice, stroking the cat under its chin, steadily.

'. . . He told me of how the book came to be written, and what fate befell An for writing it, of how the book was lost, and found, and lost, and found again . . . of how it played its part in the wars of the Third Jerezid Dynasty a century ago. And he told me of what the book has to say about this time . . . about *our* time. . . .'

He paused to take a breath and to judge his situation. They waited for him to speak, taut faces stretching in every direction from this booth which he'd commandeered. From the stadium came muted applause, but no heads turned. *Careful*, he thought, *they'll hate the truth*. . . .

'. . . Yes. What does it say, Tah Ti?'

The Guard's voice was breathless. Tah Ti smelled his sweat.

'The blind giant told me,' said Tah Ti, speaking deliberately to the Guard alone so that others had to crane to hear, 'that with a measure of wile he gained secret entrance to Baethnan, to the very vault where the book is kept chained. And he read part of the book. And, for all of his training and single-minded purpose, he was blinded in the reading of it. He told me nothing of how he escaped, nothing more of himself. But' – Tah Ti raised his head and his voice – 'of this time he said : *We live in the time of the Divine Mutant's return. The return will be signaled by the discovery and animation of the thirty mumen by a foolish ruler. The Mutant will be born again in the hill beneath the city of Phadraig. Then the whales and dolphin-folk will gather at Miir's delta; it will be the time for the Zuni Bird to sing for all to hear – if the people in their confusion do not choose to destroy themselves instead!'*

And before the crowd's fury broke, he shouted : 'That was six months ago! I thought him a charlatan for all his

strangeness. Then the mumen were rediscovered, Khassam
had them revived. Now he marches with them to Phadraig.
The mumen are the servants, the limbs of the Mutant! Now,
tonight, I tell you . . .' His voice was drowned out in bedlam.

Waving fists obscured Tschea's view, and Tah Ti disappeared from her sight as the disturbance grew.

'Scaremonger!' a woman screamed. 'Throw him in the
Pit!'

'He's right! He's right! Last night I dreamed I saw a . . .'

'He's mad, he's overstepped the mark this time. Get him!'

And Tschea was carried with the angrily frightened crowd
as fights broke out, as voices all around cursed, shouted, or
cried in confusion. A squad of bleak Guards pushed roughly
through, seeking Tah Ti, using long staves to thrust people
aside and clear a way. But the Boaster was gone.

Tschea found herself struggling so that it was all she could
do to keep her feet. She sensed only that she must get out before the gigantic general fear overwhelmed her self-control
– before she abandoned herself to the night's emotion. The
desire was compelling. Wasn't chaos all they could expect
from the coming days? Why fight to escape this first taste
of it? Why not be seized by it and learn to float madly,
second by second, hour by hour?

Nevertheless, she fixed her eyes on the heights of the
Tarasse and struggled toward it, so that eventually she was
on the Inila Way, one of a huge number of people streaming
back into the city, her dress torn, her shins bruised, her
body aching and tense. Limping slightly, she left the Inila
Way and entered the Tarasse grounds by an unguarded side
gate. And instantly she was in a different environment.
Lantern-lit rock gardens, silent save for the splash of foun-
tains, mounted up to the base of the Yeki House. The great
complex of sculpted heights loomed above her, the sloping
roofs like the scales of an animal sleeping against the dimness of the moon, the crowning combs of stone needles (the
grandiose affectation of a previous White Feather) like rows
of spinal spikes. She had no eyes for it as she mounted past a
sparkling rosewater fountain to the high doors of the Yeki
House. She passed through dim halls, up wide stairs, along
endless branching corridors. It took her nearly twenty

minutes to reach her own apartment in the Tower of Elu on
the northeastern side. She met very few people on the way,
for almost everyone was still at the Oval. Of a sudden
exhausted and wanting to sleep, she came to her own door
halfway up the spiral passage. She entered, thinking of
Namahon, Nikosner, Baethnan, Tah Ti, the Divine Mutant
... thinking of a bath, then sleep.

Instead, she found Hilgo waiting for her.

5 : The Small Hours

The signalman atop the southern flank of the valley squatted
by his fire and talked to himself for company as the night
wore on and the Oval emptied. 'What's going on?' he muttered again and again. 'People running in the streets, but like
a mob, not a festive crowd.' And he wished for the setting of
the moon which, in his view, had never risen properly, but
done no more than insinuate its ghastly presence. He had
many hours to wait yet; there would be no sleep even if he
wished it. The fire blazed beside him, and from time to time
he stoked it up quite automatically. And always he returned
to his crouching above Ussian, his eyes seeking for familiar-
ity. But tonight it seemed like an alien city, not his home at
all.

The Jerezid Consul, Chimalus na Yaahnem, had been
moody and restless ever since deciding not to attend the
Celebration. The decision had come at the last moment when
he was already dressed up in uncomfortable silks, cummer-
bund, decorations, and ridiculous bejeweled, fur-trimmed
headgear. His wife and his secretary had both tried to dissuade him from such a rash refusal; however, his mind was
made up, and he threw them both out of his office, where
he was making a pretense of work with papers. His wife
retired, sulking, to bed; his melancholy private secretary,
Sholee, was more persistent.

Now, much later, Chimalus was striding through the

Consulate like a caged bear. Sholee scurried after him, attempting to calm him with appropriate texts from the venerable Jerezid Dogmas.

'The wise man does not strive for understanding,' he panted.

'He lets understanding fall on him like the dew
He is a still pond in the heat of battle
Like the dawn he rises when it is time to rise
Like the birds he sleeps when the world is dark. . . .'

None of this was having the least calming effect on Chimalus, who half suspected that Sholee (who was surely in Clarai's pay) was doing it only to irritate him. Bursting back into his high-ceilinged office with Sholee at his heels, Chimalus whirled around, red-faced.

'Spare me this nonsense! Give me common sense, or go away! Clarai plans something. I sense it in the air tonight. Cuinneale has built up Guard-strength beyond the limits allowed by the Compromise; they've timed it well. Khassam's far away, and he stripped the lands of men for his army. If there were a rebellion now ... how could I go to such a false Celebration when the atmosphere speaks of rebellion? Tell me that! Tell me what to do, Sholee, you're a *man* of Ussian!' He threw himself down on a tapestried couch, glaring.

Sholee was used to the Consul's rages. Unblinking, he folded the embossed book away beneath one red-and-blue-checkered arm. 'First, sir,' he said crisply, fingering his long nose, 'we lie down and we order our minds. Then we consider the situation which we suspect has arisen. Then we make our decisions, with discretion, discernment, and tact.'

'Yes, yes, yes!' Chimalus sat all angles and uneasy bulk in his silks, his heavily bearded face pugnacious. 'I suppose you're right. But I will not play Clarai's games! I cannot match her slyness!' He breathed heavily. 'Yes, we will talk about it. First, get me some wine!'

'No wine, sir,' insisted Sholee smoothly. 'The doctor said ...'

'The doctor, the doctor,' Chimalus grumbled. 'Let him cure me of Clarai, then I'll know he's not her quack.

Then ... get me goat's milk. ...'

Sholee bowed and went without a word, his sleek center-parted hair gleaming in the yellow lamplight. *Greasy*, thought Chimalus, watching him through the closing door. *He knows the subtle games. He thinks of himself as a dictionary which guides my dipping.*

The thought was mordant. He was simmering, uneasy of Clarai's web. It was difficult to know what was going on about him, for he suffered a surfeit of conflicting information on every subject from agents he couldn't trust. Three years of his life he'd wasted here in Ussian, the fifth such Consul to preside here since the signing of the Compromise thirty years before. He'd never understood why Khassam had appointed him, of all people. He was a soldier, not a diplomat. The appointment was either a drunken error, a precaution, or an unpleasant joke. His vanity demanded the truth of the second possibility. 'Three years ago I commanded five thousand men,' he murmured heavily, staring at the wood-paneled wall. 'I dared to stare Khassam in the eye: that was my mistake. So he sent me here, well out of the way, to flounder in sophisticated games. Here I command a household of smiling rogues with Contract on the mind, and useless paper soldiers all bribed by Cuinneale. Here I command no respect, I'm a straw man, and they call me Clumsy Peacock.' He laughed harshly. 'A bear become a clumsy peacock – that's sorry for the bear, particularly when he finds himself in a den where he has to sheathe his claws and play games he cannot understand!'

The door creaked.

'Your goat's milk, sir,' said Sholee, holding out a mug.

Chimalus jutted out his chin, and silk rustled uncomfortably.

'Curse the goat's milk. I don't want it.' He looked curiously at his sad-faced secretary. 'The politics can wait. Sit down. Now tell me. You have a Contract with a Green Feather, Sholee. What exactly does she ... admire in you?'

Taking a chair, Sholee sat down, then answered.

'I carry a particular recessive gene, sir, for which she was looking. She wishes to produce a homozygous condition in her planned Unique – she also possessing this recessive gene, sir. She is a talented artist. I am honored to Contract with her. She will go far, sir.'

'Do you *love* her?' asked Chimalus, tugging at his tight collar.

Sholee expressed incomprehension with the briefest of motions.

'Sir, there is no room for romantic myth in creative artistry.'

'God help the child,' Chimalus declared fervently.

'Sir, the Unique will be better equipped than most. We plan ...'

'Doesn't a mating of recessives constitute a crime against the unborn?'

'The Preconceptuals have approved every stage including dates for conception and birth as suggested by the Leapers; the pregnancy will not begin for another two months, but it is best to get these bureaucratic details out of the way,' Sholee explained without any smugness.

'The Preconceptuals ... you slipped them a little ...'

'Not at all, sir.' Sholee took no offense. 'They congratulated us on the artistry of the preconception. *A daring hint of mutant piquancy* was the phrase used in official approval.'

Chimalus grunted, glowered. It was so hot that he was sweating freely.

'I call it inhuman. So – can you analyze Clarai's hold on me?'

'No, sir. Irrational emotions are not my province.'

'You mean you know nothing of people – from the gut. Sholee, you amaze me. No advice at all? Couldn't it be witchcraft?'

Behind drawn curtains wide windows were open. Chimalus heard distant shouts from the streets as Sholee answered, his pale eyes quite steady on the Consul's prematurely lined features.

'Witchcraft being no more nor less than the exercise of natural potencies, sir, I suppose your hypothesis is possible. But I am no expert on the subject.'

Chimalus suppressed anger. 'What are her intentions?'

Shrugging, Sholee folded one thin leg over the other.

'She is White Feather. Her creative career is over. It's quite normal for White Feathers to dabble in politics. Since the Jerezids – us – are at hand as natural competitors, it's hardly surprising if from time to time she takes it into her head to bend the spirit of the Compromise, to ... test the direction of the wind. ...'

Chimalus stared narrowly. 'Is that all? What about the buildup of the Guards? What about the rumors?'

'What rumors, sir?'

Sholee's face was as blank as his voice.

Chimalus, instead of pressing further, went to the nearest window. Looking to his left he could see half of the Market and the Kuwa Quarter beyond, while before him were the Consulate walls and riverside streets, and to his right he could just see the lower side of the Tarasse.

The streets were full of noisy, aimless crowds.

'Come here, Sholee. Tell me what you make of this.'

Sholee crossed the room, and looked down from the window.

'Celebration runs its drunken course, sir,' he said, too carelessly. 'Soon the street will be empty and tomorrow ...'

He found his shoulder grabbed by a very strong grip.

'Celebration,' said Chimalus sarcastically. 'And tomorrow. And no rumors. And Clarai is simply playful. Sholee – you are very good. Now bring me bedding. I will sleep in here tonight.'

This was done. Chimalus bedded down on the couch with the windows open, the curtains drawn back. He composed himself to sleep. No sleep came. His sense of danger was alerted. Through the window he could see how the moon struggled to penetrate the murky night with its reflections. He felt kinship with it. Here he was in a city where his natural superiority was not appreciated. He felt free only when out in the woods, hawking or hunting on the miserably small allotments where such barbaric pursuits were tolerated. Ussian! Eventually, suffering from a stuffed-up head, he fell into restless sleep.

He was awoken abruptly. The room was light: it was dawn.

Sholee stood over him. And, around Sholee, six armed Guards.

'Sir,' Sholee insisted, 'Clarai requests your immediate presence in the Tarasse. It is very urgent indeed.'

Chimalus, blinking and heavy-headed, saw the leather-helmeted Guards. He wondered what had happened to his own so-called guards.

'So I see,' he said, sitting up slowly. 'So I see.'

Hilgo was the last person Tschea wanted to see tonight.

He rose slowly from the cushioned depths where he'd been lurking in wait. He was tall, his magisterial brow was imposing, but his face had begun to sag. She could see that he'd been drinking. She stared without any greeting.

'I've been waiting for you,' Hilgo ventured in his pleasant voice.

'So I see.'

'I knew you wouldn't want to stay at the Oval.'

'You know me well. Hilgo, I'm tired.' And she brushed past him toward an inner room, beginning to undress as she did. He followed, and caught at her arm.

'Yes, I know you much too well!' His anger surprised her. It was unusual for gentle Hilgo to raise his voice. But everyone was behaving unusually tonight. 'Tschea, it's three years now! My wife and family wait for me at Ghillechly, many months distant. How can I return home with an un-fulfilled Contract? I'd be laughed out of town; my business would certainly suffer. And how can I stay longer? She'll divorce me in my absence. I've waited long enough! Still you dither and make excuses. The first year you had the Preconceptuals pull my entire glandular system to pieces to make me more fiery. Last year you made me play fiery music every day; I gave you rousing stuff which left you cold. Now you still maintain the time is not right, and you say the Leapers agree. I'm a patient man. But this is ridiculous. Now we hardly speak, let alone touch each other. I think you doubt me because you don't know what you want. And I don't think you ever did. I was speaking with Tschan today, we agreed on a lot of things, we ...'

Tschea, who had stood still throughout his tirade, swung around so sharply that his grip on her arm was broken. Her hair tossed in his face. 'You're quite right!' Her voice was sharp, edgy. 'Our Contract was a mistake from the very first day I let myself be persuaded to sign it. I think you have no fire – and you see me as a stamp of success to parade back home in Aquinte. A fine art, this is!'

Hilgo scowled, but didn't attempt to grab her again.

'I came to Ussian for a Red Feather Contract,' he said, 'a Red Feather Contract I have, and I cannot leave until it is fulfilled.'

She nonplussed him completely by breaking into laughter as she entered a tiled alcove with a bath sunk in the floor. She stripped off and threw away the tattered remains of her yellow dress. She was running hot water as Hilgo advanced behind her, without eyes for the bruises forming on her shapely legs.

'The damage you do to my pride. . . !'

'Listen, Hilgo,' she requested almost sadly, turning to place her hands on his shoulders, standing so close that he could feel her warmth, smell her perfume, look on her with angry desire while she held him off with words. 'Let your pride know the truth. Nikosner's back in the grasslands. It's said that the Divine Mutant is reborn, that our world is about to be torn apart. Nobody knows what is going to happen. It could be' – and her hazel eyes were briefly bright – 'that this is the time when the Fifth Element flowers. But who knows? All I know is that I'm tired, and that I was caught in a riot outside, that I am going to take a bath, and then I am going to sleep.' There was finality in her voice as she turned and bent to the bath. Hilgo's eyes followed the flow of her full breasts, the line of her thighs as she climbed into the circular bath. She looked up. 'You can scrub my back if you want to, you can stay the night if you want to, but let's have no more talk about our Contract until we know what's happening in the world.'

Hilgo sighed heavily, and he looked crestfallen.

'I will never hate you,' he said magnanimously, soulfully, 'whatever wrongs you do me.' He began sponging her back abstractedly. 'I know I'll never fully understand you; your mind moves in places I've no wish to know about. As for what you say about . . . about what's happening . . . I can't comprehend it. It makes no sense, it's irrational. . . .'

'Yes,' Tschea agreed lazily. 'It's irrational.'

She was almost relaxed in the hot water; she was even glad of Hilgo's company. Her eyes drifted around the mural walls, over the mythic scenes amid which she'd lived for thirteen years. A'Yaya was portrayed in one panel, a man with luminous eyes and a golden aura.

Tonight, she realized, her apartment seemed almost alien. She could not forget what Tah Ti had said. The Divine Mutant. Hilgo was right. It made no sense. But if the rumors had any substance at all, then it was life in the Tarasse which no longer made any sense.

They went to bed, made desultory love, fell uneasily asleep. Tschea tossed and turned all night. And she had a very strange dream: a dream of music which was felt, not heard. She dreamed that she stood on the misty mudbanks of the delta where the Zuni Bird lived, and the alluring music pulsed inside her, transforming the mudbanks so that she seemed to be standing in a beautiful garden. Amazed, she drifted in this garden of music, aware of many thousands of people nearby. She saw Namahon, and a tall man who struck chords of memory; she called out but they would not turn. And there was another man, more real than any of the others – a man with a wild red shock of hair, a vulpine face with dancing eyes. He played a scarlet instrument: it was he who made the wonderful music, he who had created this preternatural garden. In her dream the tears flowed down her cheeks, for this man was going deep into the delta where she could not follow. But for one moment he turned ... and she saw one eye where there had been two ... one immensely powerful eye which seized her, which whirled her down a black vortex, which spun her into awakening. ...

She awoke feeling utterly disoriented. Sun was streaming through a window onto the bed. For a moment she didn't believe that she was in the Tarasse with Hilgo snoring beside her. The painted walls, the domed golden ceiling above the bed, the familiar furnishings, the blue-carpeted floor – everything looked unreal. Stiff, she got up and padded from one room to the next, here touching a brass vase of chrysanthemums, here an inlaid ivory table, here a beautifully carved wooden chest. But everything seemed insubstantial, as if veiled from her eyes, as if ordinary reality were being supplanted by the buildup of an inner pressure – pressure which had resulted in the terrifying, fascinating dream. She stood at the window through which sun streamed and looked down at the glass-covered Winter Gardens which surrounded the Tower of Elu, looked past rooftops and spires at the city beyond. What was the meaning of the dream? She found herself reluctant to examine it too closely; she'd carried a dizziness from it into waking, though the eldritch music was gone altogether. But, Namahon, walking in the garden ... and the red-haired man whose two eyes had merged into one which had swallowed her ... she still felt swallowed. Leaving the window, she dressed quickly, carelessly, without regard for her appearance. Hilgo she left asleep in her bed. Let him sleep as long as he could; she held no grudge against him, only against the circumstances of their pointless union, which could not be nullified until it had borne Unique fruit. Another of Cuinneale's Formalist innovations. Was it redundant now?

Tensely expectant, she descended the spiral passage to the foot of the Tower of Elu, half surprised to find herself doing this morning as she always did. Reality hadn't shivered into fragments during the night; the earth had not opened up and swallowed them; as usual she was going to take breakfast in the Hlih Hall. And soon Namahon's disappearance must be discovered. The Celebration had provided an excellent cover, but now it was morning, and Namahon would be expected at Shaper classes like all other Uniques in his age-group.

What could she claim? That he'd run away? Possible. That the Cyclones had abducted him? Perhaps.

Passing beneath the Winter Gardens, she came to the Hlih Hall with a wary expression. The Hall was almost full, which was unusual, and there was a babble of conversation, which was even more unusual at this time of day. Tschea paused at the entrance. She could see that few people were eating; they were talking excitedly, their faces showing strain. She saw Tschan and Kryle at a nearby table with others, but they hadn't noticed her entry, so she passed them

by. Ignoring the privileged corner at the far end where the
Red Feathers usually congregated around a single table with
twenty-five places, she chose a table so far occupied only
by a young Green Feather with whom she was on friendly
terms.

Melanoe's blonde hair was uncombed, and there were
rings beneath her eyes. She spoke excitedly the instant that
Tschea joined her. 'Have you heard? Tokace's dead. Just
after sunrise.'

'Tokace? Dead? How?'

Tschea was surprised and not surprised. Into her mind
flashed a picture of the wizened Leaper whose Red Feather
mother had been cast out of the Guild for her negligent
cruelty in giving birth to him.

'His heart – he saw something too terrible . . . a vision. . . .'

'What was it?'

'Only Clarai knows. And Cuinneale. They were with him.
Now they're in conference. The Jerezid Consul is with them.
And the Guard Commander. It's about . . .' Melanoe paused
and searched Tschea's face. '. . . About those rumors, you
know, the—'

'Yes. I know.' Tschea, staring at the food on the table,
realized she wasn't at all hungry. Her head was throbbing
with a sense of imminence almost painful in its intensity.
She got up again.

'Where are you going? Aren't you going to eat?'

'No.' Tschea shook her head. 'I'm not hungry.'

'Neither am I,' said Melanoe. 'I don't think anyone is.'
Her voice was anxious, and she touched Tschea's arm.
'What's happening, Tschea? You know the Leapers. What's
this . . . this influence everyone's talking about?'

'I'm sure we'll find out soon enough,' Tschea answered,
leaving.

She wanted to go to her children. But Cassa, Flath, and
Larene – aged nine, six, and four – were segregated with
Uniques of their own age under Shaper supervision in different areas of the Tarasse. She couldn't see them until later,
when the first instruction periods were over. None of them
had Namahon's degree of intuition or insight, and frequently
she attacked herself for not loving them as much. Soon it

would be known that Namahon was missing. She would have to act carefully. She decided to claim that the Cyclones had abducted him, to play the distraught mother.

At least in part this was what she believed.

But Tokace was dead. What had killed him?

She went to talk with a Leaper friend in the Hinapa Galleries.

6 : Clarai from the Streets

It was nearly dawn when Clarai returned to her suite in the Tower of Naka'es. She was disturbed by the reports of Nikosner's return, by the riot which had taken place outside the Oval because of Tah Ti's fantasy, by the manner in which the Celebration had petered out so emptily. And Cuinneale hadn't been his usual self. Hearing of the disaster which had befallen the Opa Theater, she'd ordered Ahnem to be brought to her.

'They have already left,' Cuinneale had murmured, smoothly enough. 'I sent them on their way with an escort, for they were only adding to the confusion.'

And he'd stared at her unreadably, unblinking, his eyes like mirrors, his hands folded and hidden inside wide sleeves.

What's he up to? she'd wondered secretly while nodding curtly.

When the Celebration was over, she was taken back to the Tarasse in her gilded and gem-studded carriage, having briefly consulted with Cuinneale and Abramel, the Guard Commander. There were still many people about in the city, and they were not cheering as she passed. The Celebration had died – or perhaps it had aborted naturally. Electric with sense of impending crisis, she came alone to her rooms, leaving orders with the Darsans at her door that she was not to be disturbed unless something out of the ordinary happened.

She expected it. She waited for it. It was useless to try to sleep. She took a bath. She lay down. She got up and paced her lofty rooms as light grew in the east. The White Feather waited ... alone....

Clarai from the streets was growing used to being alone.

Increasingly she had grown to like her isolation, to have these large rooms to fill with her own abundant personality. But such power as she had was a poor substitute for her earlier life. When she'd scuffled from the streets and risen up the ranks of the Guild, past Tschea ... that was living. Now she was a symbol – public property, without claim to her own being, expected to display herself.

She lay on cushions piled against a mirrored wall and studied herself. Her face was tight. She found it increasingly difficult to recognize herself. Only her face was still her own – a famous face, in full maturity: powerful, mobile, still firm and regular, suggesting a gusty natural spirit allied with strong natural drives.

But ... her body. Only she knew how much time and discomfort the creation of the White Feather display had cost her. She had almost foregone the 'Privilege' as an outmoded ritual ostentation, before Cuinneale had persuaded her to take the tattoos upon her election. Now she couldn't help but feel that her flesh and blood no longer belonged to her. The tattoos so drenched her with a fixed traditional identity that she was growing progressively estranged from herself. Why had she taken Cuinneale's advice? Of course, she knew. She would never have become White Feather if not for Cuinneale. Cuinneale. She didn't love him, she didn't hate him, it was impossible to have any feelings for him at all. He was Cuinneale, a mysterious being of unknown background who had become Chief Shaper, now the spirit and prime mover of Formalism, insisting that the glorious and ancient art of the Tarasse should be reduced to a code of genetic rules and behavioral regulations. He had the power.

Formalism seemed to attract many who needed an order to make life explicable in this time of uneasy doubts. The Formalists were not her sort at all, but alliance with them was a pragmatic necessity. Of course, she was supposed to hold herself above all doctrinal wranglings, was supposed to

mouth and display as her predecessors had mouthed and
displayed. But Clarai felt the need to ... give a lead, to ...
ensure respect for her position in case people felt she had
not deserved it, in case they felt that Tschea should have
been elected instead. There were many such people in Ussian, and some in the Tarasse. Fortunately, the agents of
Cuinneale and Abramel knew about most, if not all, of them.

She resented Tschea. She resented Tschea's relative youth,
and the way that Tschea had come from Schroun with
wealthy backing and all the social advantages. She resented
the way that Tschea had ignored all the customs of the
Tarasse and had risen so rapidly. She resented the woman's
arrogance, freedom from doubt, and continued resistance to
every attempt to force her out of her completely untenable
Red Feather position. Tschea, who had sold herself to nobody, was a rebuke to Clarai from the streets, Clarai who'd
fought every inch of the way until Cuinneale took her over
with words murmured in her ear.

Now she was White Feather ... but ...

Clarai gazed at her long brown fingers, her fleshy, deep-
lined palms, at the patterns of her arms. The glowing maze
of weaving flame and flowers was beautiful.

But not Clarai.

Shrugging off her white robe, she gazed sadly at herself
in the mirror. Her shape was still good, though her waist was
thicker than it had been. But all the natural wrinklings of
age were concealed by the fantastic decoration of her tattoos. Her breasts, still deep and firm, were forever coiled up
in the purple-gold spiralings of the Sacred Dragons, their tails
linking at the back of her neck. Her back and sides were engulfed by coupling beings, explosions of color, chains of
petals. A red and yellow mandala expanded from her navel,
her thighs were an interlocking cluster of many-colored
stars, her legs were lush with intricate designs which flowed
down to her feet. She was a spectral field, a map of myth and
tradition, and tonight it dismayed her more deeply than
ever before. She dashed clenched fists into the cushions,
appalled by the enormity of the stereotyping which she'd
accepted.

'I was better off on the streets,' she whispered fiercely at her trembling reflection. 'There I knew who I was and what I wanted – what I thought I wanted. White Feather was the goal – but not this cage of color!'

Stiffening, she broke off. She felt so strange, so nervous! The mirror depressed her, and she donned her robe again and left the room for another. Dawn was growing through the windows. But she was sure that much more than dawn was about to break. The Leaper warnings, so vague ... the mad tale of Tah Ti, who was not to be found ... Cuinneale's abrupt dismissal of the Opa Theater ... the failure of the Cyclone Grand Master and the Jerezid Consul to attend the Celebration ... the atmosphere of the city.... It was so difficult to think and she realized that she was feeling lonely, that she wanted company now. She thought of and rejected every one of her current lovers. None of them meant anything – they were playthings. She crossed deep carpets to a voice-tube in the nearest florid wall, called the Shaper on night-duty in the dormitory for Uniques aged eight to ten.

'Have Wanunch sent here ... immediately....'

The tinny reply was censorious, and she couldn't believe it.

'He's asleep, he shouldn't be ...'

'Who do you think you are? Send him. I'm his mother!'

Simmering with anger, she stopped up the tube without waiting for a reply. She went back to an eastern window and watched the growth of light over the valley, thinking furiously about the rumors that she was trying to control the mind of her lastborn, that her creative humility had been drowned by lust for power. Tschea's rumors, she was sure. Clarai knew that her artistry wasn't yet beyond trial – and her position with it. She was judged as closely by the behavior of her Uniques as by her own qualities, just like any other member of the Guild. It wasn't unknown for a White Feather to be demoted because of the unpopularity of her offspring. So far, her nine children were recognized as outstanding human beings, but increasingly she found herself worrying about their diverse activities. Her Uniques. Her children. How clinically she was forced to think of them! Eight of them were beyond her reach, adult or nearly

so, in other lands or at least away from Ussian. Only Wanunch was still in the Tarasse, now ten years old. She paid
him more attention than she'd paid any of the others, gave
him guidance and love, and showed interest in the way he
thought. She knew that many believed she was turning
beautiful rainbow-skinned Wanunch into a receptacle for
her own anxieties. Was a mother's love forbidden? Who
cared what they thought? She had Cuinneale's support, and
people were reluctant to speak out against the White
Feather.

Cuinneale. Who was the gray ghost? Did he feel love for
anything or anyone beneath the sun? If only she could
separate herself from his dictates; his grip had grown much
too firm. . . .

Now light was streaming through the open windows, and
the eastern horizon was growing red and gold. The night
was fully over. The new day was beginning. Where was
Wanunch? Were they defying her orders?

The bell sounded at her door, two rooms away.

She went to it, swiftly, biting on her lip.

She opened it herself.

But Wanunch was not there.

Instead, behind the two tall female Darsans on guard, she
saw two frightened men with the servant red-tattoo on their
foreheads. They carried a litter on their shoulders.

Tokace was writhing on the litter.

The strangest of the Leapers was only twelve years old,
but he was already senile, with blue veins wild all over his
slack, wrinkled skin.

Clarai's predecessor, Inila, had nearly ordered Tokace's
destruction at birth on the grounds that he was too mal-
formed to live. Other Leapers had scanned the infant mind
and read evidence of the abnormal clairvoyant talent. Tokace had lived. Now he was old.

Now his eyes were starting from his head, his body was
humping and heaving on the litter, he was croaking about
some terrible battle. . . .

And Clarai realized that Tokace's agony spelled the death
of all familiar reality.

Part II : The Divine Mutant

7 : The Mad Musician

Six days later. Afternoon. At the eastern end of Lake Bhykan, Schroun's sullen avenues cooked in a humid haze. The
town at Miir's northeastern neck was gripped by the same
nebulous fear which was spreading across all the lands.
There was little movement in the geometrically planned
districts which stretched down to the reed-fringed verge of
the lake. The lake was supplied by underground water and
by the streams which, in the rainy season, tumbled down
from the ocher ramparts of the Scarp plateau farther east.
From the other end of the lake, the Bhykan Gasche flowed
sluggishly west to Lake Tardenoisse, which it joined at the
port of Alyss, passing through a variety of forests, plains,
and swamps on the way.

At her cluttered desk in the Guard Office in the Colena
District, Tschenner was swamped by work. The senior
Guard had just received word that the White Feather would
be visiting Schroun late next day, accompanied by all
twenty-five Red Feathers, by twenty of the Purple Feathers,
plus Contractuals, Uniques, Patterners – by what sounded
like half the Tarasse College. One of the College's Darsans
had come into Schroun at a full gallop despite the heat,
bringing the unwelcome news. The Darsan, a proud woman
with the blue-gold Tarasse tattoo on her forehead, had been
arrogant and peremptory. Giving the minimum of information, she had demanded a meal, a bath, and a fresh horse.
She had just left in a hurry without giving thanks for any
of these things, leaving Tschenner uncharacteristically furious. The Darsan had *ordered* Tschenner as Schroun's senior
Guard to arrange an appropriate welcome – to coordinate
catering, security, and all the rest of it. It was beyond
Tschenner's understanding. Such a visit was not only unprecedented, it was illegal. What was going on? Had the Jerezid
Consul given the White Feather leave to make a tour of
Miir?

Or did Clarai know more than Tschenner about the
rumors?

Tschenner didn't want to think about the rumors. She
had more than enough to cope with as it was. The harvest
had failed here like everywhere else, Schroun was full of
unemployed red-tattoo bondsmen who were getting drunk
and making trouble. The fifteen Guards had their hands full
– and the rumors were making things worse. The air was
not sane, it was pregnant with calamity. Tschenner couldn't
concentrate on anything today; she felt like giving up and
going back to her Hearth to sleep off her pounding headache. She was a handsome crop-headed woman in her early
thirties. But now she sat at a desk wearily massaging her
temples and staring out the window of her office. The sun
was a smear above these rocky eastern uplands, the surface
of the lake was burnished, the water seeming more like
molten metal than water. Usually from this window she
could see clear across Miir as far as Tardenoisse, but not
today. Today, there was no visibility, no energy – just sodden lethargy, bad tempers, and the rumors of unhinged
reality. Everyone was behaving so strangely. The normally
placid people of Schroun were plucking hate and dissent
from the overloaded atmosphere. For six days now it had
been like this, growing only worse all the time. Walking
from her Hearth to the office this morning, she'd overheard
querulous conversation everywhere. Angry, she had
stamped into the office to hear the red-tattoos gossiping
superstitiously when they should have been sweeping the
floors, washing the walls, doing the work for which they
were fed and sheltered.

'I dreamed my brains were stolen,' she'd heard one say.
'Pecked out of my head by a huge silver bird with glittering
eyes.'

'Mine was much worse than that,' another had claimed.
'I was petrified by a single giant eye staring from a blazing,
horrible sky. And lost in the eye I saw thousands of men,
all dead, in the remains of Jerezid uniforms. Khassam was
there, drooling, and the mumen were dancing around him,
singing and laughing like demons!'

'The mumen!' a third had whispered. 'The Warlord

should never have revived them. The legend warned that only the Divine Mutant's reincarnation could control the weird creatures. But he wouldn't listen....'

'No,' the first had said, 'Khassam thought himself the re-incar—'

Tschenner had heard enough. She burst in on them and slanged them in no uncertain terms. They had been resentful and insubordinate.

'What if it's true?' one of the red-tattoos had demanded. 'What if Khassam's dead and his army's destroyed by a strange new conqueror as the stories say? What if the Divine Mutant is reborn? Will you still expect us to sweep your floors?'

Disdaining to answer, she'd slammed her door in their faces.

'Don't you have dreams like the rest of us?' another had shouted after her. And she'd heard their frightened laughter.

Now it was late afternoon, the Darsan had been and gone, and she'd had more than enough.

Dreams, insubordination, the White Feather's visit, the weather ... where would it all end?

Mopping her forehead, she focused on the lettered plaque which hung on the cream-painted wall beside her.

Stillness and Tranquility Set Things in Order in the Universe.

That was what the plaque said. Today she derived no comfort from its wisdom. It was too hot to think, there was neither stillness nor tranquility in the air, nor in her mind. And Clarai was coming, acting as if she knew that the Jerezids had been swept aside and their power (nominal though it was in these southwestern regions of their empire) had been annulled. Tschenner sighed, pushed papers away, poured herself a glass of water from the jug on the desk beside her. Nothing made any sense. She felt so tired, and there was work to do – but she didn't care. She felt rebellious. Why should she have to do it all?

The knock at her door was repeated twice before she heard it.

'Come in!' Her voice was irritable.

A perspiring male Guard led in a middle-aged man whose

lined forehead bore the blue tattoo-mark of one free to hire out labor service to the best bidder. His sackcloth tunic and trousers were covered in dust, his face was tubby, his eyes were haunted.

Tschenner froze. She felt an incomprehensible premonition.

'What is it? Who are you?'

The blue-tattoo stared, his mouth slightly open.

'My name is ... Lunth. I come from the mines of Tatung by the Scarp. I've brought you a mad musician.' His voice was husky, strained, and his eyes shone oddly. Tschenner felt tight inside, uncomfortable in his presence. He gestured vaguely, jerkily. 'He's tied to my donkey. He's all yours, and I wish you the best of luck with him.... He is mad with a madness beyond understanding ... now I feel unsound inside ... my life is ruined, my friends are lost because of him. I wanted to kill him myself, but my sense of ... justice – Take him, it's your duty to lock him up ... examine him, but don't let him play his ... his music. I was hospitable to him, oh, yes, oh, yes....'

Tschenner stared as his voice trailed away. He stood there by her desk, his eyes went briefly blank, then he began shivering. He jabbered about a noise-machine, scratching himself, then he recollected his senses.

'Come and see him. He's unconscious; I've taken care to keep him that way ... I took pity on him ... hah! Mind you don't make the same mistake – come, I'll show you, he's outside, tied to my donkey. It's your duty to lock him up ... he's mad, he has a noise-machine, but he's unconscious, tied to my donkey....'

Tschenner felt too shaken to stop the man repeating himself.

She followed him outside the office to the tethered donkey.

The emaciated body tied over the back of the flea-bitten donkey seemed harmless enough at first sight. But, almost reluctantly taking the peculiar scarlet instrument which the badly disturbed blue-tattoo thrust at her, Tschenner realized that she was uncomfortable, that the cells of her body were crawling – that she was confronted by something which she did not understand. She stared at the figure of the mad musician. He was wrapped up in a tattered blue cloak, and she couldn't see his face. She wasn't sure that she wanted to see his face. She held the curious instrument as if it might bite her. It was scarlet, with a flat, solid body, and a curving fretboard, so that in outline it resembled a figure 6. The fretboard was about five inches thick at the point where it joined with the body, diminishing to scarcely more than an inch at the neck. The instrument was unstrung. A row of metal knobs was set low on the body, the scarlet finish and intricately filigreed decorations of which were scratched and specked with dirt – and blood. It was unlike any musical instrument she'd ever seen.

She looked up. A small crowd had gathered. The blue-tattoo was shivering. The instrument was heavy, and she laid it down on the street.

'Is this the noise-machine?'

Lunth nodded violently. 'So much noise you cannot imagine! It tears the mind to shreds!'

The crowd muttered. Tschenner frowned.

'Come inside and tell me what happened,' she ordered him.

Lunth was reluctant. 'I would rather not remember.'

'Do as I say! You brought him here.' Tschenner could feel her temper rising. Peremptorily, she called out red-tattoos to unbind the unconscious stranger and put him in a cell. Knots were untied. The man slumped from the back of the donkey, slid to the dusty street, the tattered cloak fell away from his face, his body. His face was like a white hatchet framed in a tangled, ruddy furze of hair, his cheeks were sunken caverns, and beneath bloodless lips his sprouting beard was a wiry ginger. He wore a black tunic with cat's-eyes of some luminous material stitched to his chest. He was dragged inside. Tschenner, picking up the scarlet instrument, indicated for the blue-tattoo to follow her back into her office. Lunth followed uneasily.

'Now,' she said when they were inside. 'Speak.'

The sun baked. It was six days since Tokace had died.

And it was two days since the haggard stranger had left

the sunburned hide and arid gullies of the Scarp plateau. Too exhausted to remember how long he'd been trudging, he came to Miir without baggage save for the scarlet instrument slung from his back beneath the tattered blue cloak. His mind was dull with starvation and a sense of flight from something forgotten, something too overwhelming to risk remembering. But within him were powerful energies which could not be contained much longer. He had a dim suspicion that they'd already experienced their first release, with the result that he'd fled, as though physical distance could reduce his mental distress.

He'd come stumbling down a deep and bare ravine past reddish boulders as huge as houses. In the distance, forests and fertile plains stretched to a sparkling lake perhaps half a day's journey distant. Beyond the water the sun was setting, great swaths of orange light drenched the countryside before him, blazed on the sandstone cliffs behind him, burned on his dust-masked face. The light was rich, the landscape full of beauty and variety, but he could appreciate none of it. He was locked inside an ugliness which transmuted beauty into mockery.

His worn boots dragged down the dusty slope and he was stiff as he came out of the ravine to find himself overlooking a single-street community in the western lee of the crumbling cliffs. He stopped dead at the sight. People. The taste in his dry mouth was foul. People. People were hateful. But he couldn't avoid the community. His body demanded food, drink, sleep. Like it or not, he had to enter the place. He lacked any energy to consider alternatives. The community lay right in front of him, and he could offer no resistance as his aching feet brought him down into the single wide street which sloped gently toward the sunset. The place seemed deserted. The buildings were rough and single-storied, of undressed stone; their doors and windows were black, irregular holes. Nothing moved, not even animals. The sky was empty of birds. He'd shuffled down the street, eyes casting lackadaisically, right hand on the hilt of the dagger at his belt, his thoughts turbulent and disconnected. It was an unreal ghost town, a perfect reflection of his own frame of mind.

The buildings had started to swim. He'd stopped moving; his strength was all gone. His legs had given way. He'd collapsed.

For a moment before passing out he'd been aware of a tubby face looking down at him. The face had been full of concern but, to his wounded mind, the concern was derision.

'... I've been caretaker at Tatung for the last ... twelve years,' Lunth told Tschenner, his eyes casting around the office. 'I do ... did ... all the work aboveground while the miners were in the galleries underneath. I was going about my duties when I saw him come staggering down the street.' His eyes clouded. 'If I'd known what was going to happen, I'd have overcome my weak nature and killed him on the spot.'

'But you gave him help?' Tschenner probed.

Lunth nodded.

'I ran out when I saw him. I saw his eyes for just an instant before they closed. That's when I first wondered about his sanity. You ... you haven't seen his eyes yet.' He shook his head. 'Anyway, I took him to my room, laid him down on my bed. He was covered in cuts and bruises. And he made me feel all uneasy inside, even though he was unconscious. I paid the feeling no attention ... and there was his noise-machine. I thought he must be a songmaker; it's – it's not the sort of thing a casual vagabond would own.'

'Unless he'd stolen it.'

'No ... I don't think so.' Lunth was shivering again, and his voice was grim. 'He could certainly ... play it. But ... that was later. Then I was hoping that when he was recovered he could ... entertain us. Life can get boring at Tatung. We're there six months every year, before the rains flood out the mines; we have no women, or—'

'Yes, yes, I know; this office grants your license.'

'Of course. I forgot.' Lunth was gripping his hands together.

'Go on.'

'Well, when the miners came up I showed them this ... this stranger, and the noise-machine. Nobody had ever seen anything like it. Some of them wanted to get rid of him; they said he made them feel unhappy. But I, idiot that I am, said we had a duty to be ... charitable. And ... and he was unconscious all night. I let him have my bed and I slept on the floor.'

The blue-tattoo started rubbing his forehead feverishly. Tschenner waited without interrupting, and she was breathing quickly.

'Late in the night he started to mumble like a ... like a bad-tempered ghost – in General Synthetic, but more like the Old Tongue ... the way they speak it at Phadraig. ...'

'Phadraig?'

Lunth nodded violently; he too seemed short of breath. 'Yes. I don't know what he did to me. I was scared ... and next morning – that's yesterday – everything seemed ... changed. It was as if the air were scratching me. My temper was bad. One of the donkeys bit me ... the day made me angry. I couldn't get the stranger out of my head, and I kept going back to see how he was.' Lunth bit his lip. Tschenner found the gleam in his eyes quite frightening. 'And about the fifth or sixth time I went back, he was awake. His eyes were open. ...'

Lunth's teeth started to chatter.

Tschenner found herself unable to look away from him.

The stranger had awoken into a claustrophobic hell. He lay on a bed, too weak to move. Raw colors flooded his perception with each leaden palpitation of his heart, his head was a crazed balloon afloat on gaseous fantasies, and his vision was obstructed by screens of mental static and retinal imagery. What had happened to the burning sky, the endless plateau? All about were blank whitewashed walls, closing in on him like waves of liquid concrete. Above was a sagging roof, with great cracks running the length of the cross-beams. He could hear the beams cracking, and soon the entire oppressive weight would cave in on top of him, crush out his life. He couldn't escape. He couldn't call out. He was mute. His memory was blank. His fear was total. Life was a conspiracy to bring death.

He'd shut his eyes and tried to hide inside his head.

But the internal pressure was even more agonizing.

Then the door had opened, and a devil-face had loomed above him.

The same derisive face which had looked down on him as he'd lost consciousness before. It pinned him down with its evil pretense of friendliness. A wide mouth bloomed open above him. Meaningless sounds echoed too loud inside his head. He'd grimaced, twisted, fought to escape, but they had detonated inside him.

Lunth managed to continue after a while.

'I spoke to him. My . . . voice seemed to hurt him. I told him he had to eat, and I gave him gruel, but he thought I was trying to poison him. I told him I was his friend. I asked him who he was; I showed him the scarlet instrument; thinking it might prompt his memory. But he wailed like a baby and turned away, started rocking in a fit. It . . . it shook me up, and I was . . . angry. He started shouting about – about *the eye* glaring in his head.' Lunth swallowed; he was quite pale. 'Then he sat bolt upright, and gave me a look of such hate, like a . . . like a hungry wolf. And his hate filled me, so I was shivering, and shouted back at him. . . .' His teeth were chattering again; his eyes went distant.

There was a knock, then the door opened.

'Get out!' Tschenner shouted. 'Don't come in!'

The door shut, harder than was necessary.

Tschenner leaned over her desk. 'Can you remember what you shouted?'

Lunth nodded, jerkily. 'I accused him of ingratitude. I asked him what he was. And he laughed, so I almost hit him. And he was panting like a dog, his face was . . . flooded with color – no, not color: it was more like a *glare*, something eating his flesh from inside. Then he said—' Lunth swallowed, shut his eyes. 'He said: *"Let me play you music, then you might learn what I am, and so might I!"* And I – I felt challenged, or something. I had to accept. I told him he'd play to everyone, and if we didn't like his music, maybe we'd kill him. Then I couldn't look at him any more. He was eating me up inside. I locked the door on him. I don't know what I did for the rest of the day. I think I was

half out of my mind. Then the miners came up, and I
told them the stranger was going to play for us all....'

Lunth stopped. The office was like an oven. He panted for
breath. Tschenner found she couldn't look away from his
eyes, his face. His description of the glare inside the stranger
applied to him. She felt dazed, almost unwilling to continue
listening, but compelled to do so. A shiver coursed up and
down her spine; she was excited, nervous.

'Yes,' she said, against her will, 'then what happened?'

Lunth was wringing his hands in distraught passion.
There was fear in his round face – and an odd slyness
which both chilled and fascinated her. 'Oh,' he whispered,
looking sideways at her, 'do you really want to know? You
shouldn't want to know. Really, you'd do better by not asking me to talk about it. I *know*....'

And he giggled, so that Tschenner shut her eyes, flinch-
ing inside. 'Tell me!' she insisted tightly. 'Get on with it!'
Opening her eyes, she saw frightened glee in his face.

I feel sick, she thought. *Why am I listening to this madman?*

'Well,' said Lunth, starting to speak very quickly, 'not
everyone wanted to hear his music, but I said I was sure he
was a genius. I persuaded them. I was determined he was
going to play, don't ask me why, it was necessary, it
gripped me, and I ... I convinced them. So when everyone,
all seventy of us – when everyone had finished eating in the
hall I went for him with three others and we brought him
to the hall. We set him up on a table by the fire at one end.
His face was so strange, he was smiling and looking scared,
eager and reluctant to play, shivering and tapping his toes
on the table, grinning like a wolf. A lot of the men were
suspicious, uneasy, they thought he was a warlock, and the
air was very strange, they protested. But I told them that
if we didn't like his music then we could easily stop him
playing, and that sounded sensible, so I gave him the scarlet
machine, and the strings for it which I'd found in his cloak,
and ... and ...'

Lunth was now so pale that Tschenner was sure he was
about to faint. He was having difficulty with his words; he
was gripping and ungripping his fists compulsively, leaning

forward over the desk at her. '... then ... then he started speaking. His voice was a high shiver; he said his music would break our minds into places we'd never been. He laughed, mad, mad, and I didn't ... the – the others tried to stop him ... but too late ... he was – he was moving so fast. When they grabbed for his ankles he jumped back, and then – and then his fingers came to the ... the strings, and ...'

Lunth's tongue jammed. The memory of agony raged in his head; there was no way for it to get out of his mouth. He could only shake his head as the events of the previous night rushed once more into a horrifyingly close focus. He was again in the crumbling communal hall beneath smoke-blackened timbers, in an atmosphere thick with smoke and the smell of roasted meat, where torches guttered fitfully from wall-brackets and threw flickering shadows across grimy, dubious faces. The air vibrated with tension, and he stood there in that instant when the mad musician's fingers had swooped down to the strings. . . .

And again, the sound of battle exploded inside Lunth's head.

Unaware of doing so, he screamed. The door burst open, and three Guards who'd been listening outside burst in to subdue him. He wasn't aware of their hands; he was taken on the torrential sound again – sound which split his mind apart, showed him the heights and depths of himself, which he'd met only in dreams but never in consciousness. A glaring sound, a piercing scream which knifed his mind and lit it up too bright to bear, a rumbling roar which shook apart his bowels and plummeted him too deep for his human understanding to comprehend. He was being shivered apart.

Tschenner stared with horror in her eyes. The blue-tattoo was shaking so rapidly that his features seemed blurred : his mind was obviously not in Schroun at all. The Guards stood back from him as he went crawling on the office floor in mime of his behavior the night before, oblivious of obstacles, heedless of painful collisions with tables, chairs, walls, the door. For he was trapped in the hall, writhing, shuddering on the floor, without any way to escape the onslaught

which was tearing his personality apart, his glassy eyes passing straight through Tschenner to the mad musician who
danced behind the wall of sound, the mad musician whose
fingers lashed the scarlet instrument in an ecstasy of alien
possession. Again, Lunth was crucified on the vicious battle-
music, upon the transmission of the madman's experience,
caught in the destruction of former assumptions and
identity. For a full ten minutes Tschenner's office was filled
with Lunth's groans and imprecations, with his futile efforts
to block out the noise exploding through the ears of his
memory. And then the torrent slackened. Through his tears
Lunth saw the dancing puppet-madman droop, and all about
him he saw the miners shaking on the floor. Then there was
silence in his skull, the piercing light was gone, and he
sagged, his face like crumpled gray paper.

Tschenner and the Guards saw him with horror in their
eyes: though the experience of the music was no more
than thirdhand they had felt it inside themselves; Lunth's
agonized vibrations had jarred their minds. After a further
while Lunth managed to prop himself up. He looked about
with a haggard, dreadful expression, he opened and closed
his mouth, and he shook his head in utter weariness.

Tschenner shivered. She looked at the scarlet instrument
which she'd stood up against her desk. So innocent it
looked. . . .

One of the Guards helped Lunth back into a chair.

When his gasping had subsided to a more normal breathing, Tschenner asked, in a raw and exhausted voice: 'Then
what?'

Lunth's whisper was scarcely audible. 'People so feeble . . .
all lying about . . . crawling . . . me shaking under a table . . .
and the madman standing like an empty shell in the . . .
silence . . . a knife . . . someone threw a knife at him, just
missed . . . then others going for him, zombies, no control of
bodies. I . . . I crawled at him, on hands and knees, wanted to
extinguish him . . . but . . . he escaped . . . ran off downhill
into night. . . .' Lunth sagged, his mouth open, eyes drooping
half-closed.

'Then – then how did you. . . ?'

'. . . On feet . . . miners . . . wanted to kill me, all mad,

minds flaming. Some chased after him, forget what ... what
they chased. I ... I took donkey from stockade, slipped away
– can't remember, but must have, because here I am ... here
... Schroun.' Lunth licked his lips; his eyes alone seemed
alive. Behind him hovered the appalled Guards. 'After time
I was alone in the night, below tree-level ... and I heard
music ... coming from ruins on top of a ... knoll. Thought
at first it was music in my head, then realized: couldn't be.
Visions in my head so awful, this music I heard was beautiful, and sad. Crept closer, up to ruins, very tired. By light of
moon I saw him sitting there, playing ... music. Just ...
music, a melody which was gentle. I think he knew I was
there. I listened from shadow.... After a time he stopped
playing, and he started talking to himself. He was telling
himself who he was, very carefully, very sad. Said he was
... Liam, from Phadraig ... said he was empty, and that he
belonged to someone called ... One-Eye. Said he'd lost his
soul, and didn't want to live, because now he was a killer,
because he'd abandoned his friends, and hated them, and
that this One-Eye made him do these terrible things. I think
he was willing me to kill him. He sat so still even when I
sent a stone rattling down the hillside. I came up behind him
with a rock in my hand ... he didn't try to duck when I
brought it down on his head.... Now ... here ...' Lunth's
whisper trailed out completely.

'Why didn't you kill him?' asked Tschenner in a very low
voice.

What might have been a smile touched Lunth's ashen
face. 'Don't know ... maybe this One-Eye has taken me as
well.' With difficulty, he raised a hand to tap his head.
'Maybe One-Eye is a new disease, maybe the mad musician
has infected me ... perhaps I am infecting ... you. Are you
shaking inside? Can you see a glare in your head...?' And
he giggled.

Involuntarily, the Guards moved back.

Tschenner's blood froze. Lunth's eyes ...

'Quick!' she snapped in sudden fear. 'Get him out! Get
him on his donkey, get him out of town!'

Lunth stood, slightly unsteady, but he stood without support.

'I go,' he said, 'you keep my friend, the mad musician. . . .'

And he left the office, leaving four very disturbed minds behind.

Leaving Liam from Phadraig unconscious in their care.

Lunth could see no future ahead of him. He felt weak, drained. From time to time during the day waves of dizziness had flooded his head, accompanied by a bright glare which seemed to dim out his external perceptions altogether. He got as far as a lakeside tavern. As evening fell he was drinking steadily, adding his story to those already circulating. Later, he became involved in an argument which developed into a fight, which he lost. When he came to the next morning he found he'd been robbed of the donkey and his few possessions. He found it difficult to care. The problem of his own life hardly seemed important anymore.

8 : The Cell

Liam from Phadraig awoke in the cell as the sun was rising. He had no memory of how he came to be inside it. His headache was vicious. He cursed automatically and felt the enormous lump on the back of his head. His bushy hair was matted with dried blood. Gradually, he opened his eyes and squinted at early daylight which was flooding through the barred window set high up one white-plastered wall. The cell was cramped but clean, and admirably free of bugs and damp. The pallet on which he lay was all the cell contained apart from a water pitcher and a bucket for waste. When he remembered what his feet were for, he stood on unsteady tiptoe beneath the window. He could just see the tops of slate roofs across the street. He could hear activity : carts trundling over cobbles, the stamp of ordered feet, a whistle being blown in the distance, a clock striking six, querulous voices beneath the window on the other side.

He sat down and took stock of himself.

Cloak, boots, and sirena were missing, along with belt and dirk.

He checked for the pouch tucked inside his shabby leather trousers.

It was there, and the tinderbox inside it.

His black tunic was torn, caked with mud, but the cat's-eyes still glared from his chest with irrepressible spirit.

Most important of all, he knew who he was; for the time being at any rate he was in possession of himself. But there was no guarantee that the state would endure. He sensed it would take very little to tip him headlong back into the insane glare of One-Eye's dream. He must not think about it. There were huge blanks in his memory, and he feared to think what he might have done during those blank periods.

His mouth tasted foul. He drank deeply from the pitcher. The warm water slaked his thirst, but did nothing to solve the foul taste. He felt dirty and uncomfortable. He sat. Nobody came. He grew uneasy. Eventually he lost his temper. He grabbed the metal-hooped bucket and hurled it at the locked iron door. The deafening clang enraged him further, so that he took up the bucket and struck the door repeatedly until the whole cell was reverberating. 'Cretinous morons!' he howled. 'Let me out!'

There was no response. He was weak. His fury died. He brooded.

He remembered awaiting the blow. He was surprised to find himself still alive, and to a certain extent disgruntled. He had hoped the blow would solve his most pressing problem, that of his being an involuntary agent for the one-eyed mutant infant. But suicide was not really his style. He snorted. Perhaps death would not have been a release, in any case. For all he knew, the Mutant operated on the after-death planes as well. It seemed quite likely. Anything seemed likely. At any rate, here he was, still alive, still self-identifiable. The blow had not been fatal. Just now, the blow was the center of his shredded memory.

Before it? After it?

Dreams and images and vague realities, mixed up through time and space. Partings, forgettings, insane rememberings. The battle. The endless journey across the top of the Scarp.

Exhaustion. Delirium. Madness. The flight, the blow. A bony donkey, though that was vague.

This tiny cell, so hot though the day was young.

One-Eye. The Divine Mutant. The infant of a thousand names.

'Why?' he demanded. The ceiling stared back. 'How?'

He shook his head, disgusted by the uselessness of his questions.

'Forget it,' he ordered himself hoarsely. 'The answer's plain. We were fools.' He cracked a knuckle disconsolately. 'That I can recall.' He cracked another knuckle. 'Thought we were on a holy mission, saving a prophesied life from Norm Purity.' A third knuckle went. 'The prophecy warned us, but we didn't want to know, we just wanted to get out of Phadraig, and we used the infant as an excuse. But he used us – he used all of us – he fooled us and he fooled Khassam equally. *I heard the mumen laughing!* I saw how they danced with joy at being reunited with their lord and master. Well, I suppose a thousand years *is* a long time to wait. They danced, and One-Eye dreamed, and the army tore itself to pieces, and the Company too....' He heaved a great sigh, and stared at the wall for several minutes. 'Of course,' he muttered at length, 'the infant couldn't have all of us dead; he needs us to spread his dream, his crazy dance. Who's responsible? Us of the Company? Or Khassam? Or everyone?' He spat at the wall. 'Academic! We were all ignorant idiots, and now we reap the rewards.'

One-Eye. He could clearly picture the infant. The smooth skin, olive-yellow, the single eye where the bridge of the nose should have been. An abyss down which sanity and love had plunged, an abscess riding in his mind. His agitation began to grow, his head felt hot, and he could sense the glare encroaching on his consciousness from deep inside his own psyche where he could not tread. Fearing himself, he stood. He felt energetic, not at all weak, and though his body hurt he no longer noticed it. He began to stalk the cell, caught by the eye which glared inside him, spinning continually on his heel as if he might pluck it out and dissociate himself from it. But he and it were one; it afflicted him only when his mood admitted it – and the more it was

admitted, the more dead he became ... he knew it very
well. Struggling for self-control, he lay down on the pallet,
and he concentrated on relaxation, which only made it
worse. The cell became vague; he couldn't resist the scorch
of his own imagining. His head stormed with myriad
images: they seemed to flow from what he could only con-
ceive of as the Mutant's eye – like a third eye which completely drowned the perceptions of his own two eyes, a
third eye over which he had no control. There was no way
for him to tell whether the images were the subjective
phantoms of his own captured imagining, or whether they
had some absolute validity of their own and were being imposed upon him. Lying on the pallet in a cell in Schroun, he
lived through many other situations; that was all – and they
were real. As real as anything he'd ever called real.

He was sitting at a table in a gloomy basement tavern in
Phadraig, arguing with two men: one was sleek, stout; the
other was gaunt and black-bearded. 'A joke is all there is!'
he insisted aggressively. 'Our lives are jokes! Patrick wants
us to pursue the escaped woman to protect her and this one-
eyed child, a mutant prophesied!'

Elsewhere and when, he saw and heard Patrick Cormac
raging at them in a snowtree grove in the Wastelands:
lying on a pallet in Schroun his mouth was speaking
Patrick's words even as the door of his cell was being opened
and Tschenner entered.

'The child's a change,' Liam/Patrick shouted, 'a signal, an
unknown direction, which will kill us or lead us to new
perceptions – but Phadraig is the past, it's a corpse, it's dead!
Cling to ...'

A rough hand shook his shoulder. He swung to meet the
face of a handsome woman who had appeared from nowhere in the middle of the grove. On either side of her were
two coarse, red-faced men with red tattoo-marks on their
foreheads. It was one of the men who held him back, so that
he feared he'd be pushed against the nearest of the beautiful
but deadly poisonous branches of the crooked white snow-
trees. What was going on? Where had these people come
from, where were his friends of the Company gone? 'Careful, you stupid louts!' he shouted, enraged, gesturing at the

nearest of the branches. 'Don't you know they're poison-ous?'

Frowning, Tschenner stayed calm with some effort. Clarai's visit was only hours away. And now she confronted the mad musician. By all rights he should have been as weak as a kitten, but he radiated a potent energy which she found as inexplicable as his delusion. She considered his sharp, cadaverous face. He struggled against the grip of the red-tat-toos who were holding him back against the wall of the cell. Where did he think he was? What was poisonous? What should she say to him?

'Where do you think you are?' Her General Synthetic was precise.

Liam stared at her, furrowing his brow.

'I'll be in my grave if you don't tell these idiots to stop pushing me back against the branches! Where do you think *you* are?'

One of the red-tattoos was shaking with fear, but the other was firm.

'You're in a cell in Schroun, in the land of Miir.' Tschen-ner couldn't keep the tremor out of her voice. 'There is a *wall* behind your back – there are no branches.'

'If you say so,' said Liam, 'but what have you done with my friends?'

Tschenner couldn't follow him, and she felt very disturb-ed.

'What do you see there?' she asked, pointing at the win-dow.

'The sky – what else?'

'What's between you and the sky?'

'A window?' he hazarded. 'Bars?'

'Yes!' But Tschenner was doubtful. 'Are you sure you see them?'

'Of course! Do you think I'm crazy?' He laughed sharply. A cell? Yes, he was in a cell. It hardly mattered whether the walls were walls or poisonous snowtree branches. Confusion swept him. Images wavered. He shook his head. Miir? Yes, Miir. He slumped. What was the matter with him? He could have sworn. . . . He groaned.

Tschenner, seeing the change sweeping over him, tried another, more aggressive tack: 'You come from Phadraig?'

'Yes. Why don't you tell these morons to let me go?'

Her face was thoughtful, then she motioned the red-tattoos back. They retreated thankfully, exchanging meaningful glances. Liam massaged his arms and glared at them.

'Phadraig, eh? Tell me: is it true that insemination there is artificial, paternity is secret, mothers are killed if their children are judged to be deformed?' She examined him. 'Did you flee from Phadraig? Or were you expelled? And what's this mad music you play?'

Liam said nothing. Tschenner didn't know how to deal with him.

'Is it true that Khassam is dead?' She shot it at him.

His eyes widened. He could read her doubt, and it amused him.

'Yes, and unmourned,' he agreed, his whisper grisly. 'A new time's upon us now. The Divine Mutant's alive again ... with his mumen.'

'You're mad!' she snapped, paling. 'Your mind's split!'

His gesture was bored, his tone, offhand. 'Two heads are better than one. Is your mind whole?'

She had no reply. There was threat in the eyes of the red-tattoos.

'I read your worry,' he hissed. 'You're afraid I'll infect you. Sanity's impossible to define when madmen challenge your definitions. Certainly, I'm mad. And I'm the first of many.' He laughed. 'You can expect thousands more like me. You'll have to learn to think in new dimensions.' His face clouded. 'And you won't find it pleasant. There is no way you'll keep One-Eye out of your minds.'

His voice was sad, mocking, certain, challenging.

'We could have you killed, or incarcerated forever.'

He shrugged. 'Do what you please,' he said, as if it were a matter of no interest at all. 'I died at the battle,' he added casually. 'I am no longer Liam the Songmaker. I saw the mumen dance, and One-Eye entered my head. By all means, kill me. It will make no difference. The Mutant has entered many heads. He will enter many more.'

Tschenner felt discomfited. She could find no appropriate response.

His eyes ... pale, penetrating, with a dancing mockery in them ... Tschenner could take no more. Turning abruptly, she left the cell.

Leaving unveiled fear and threat behind them, the red-tattoos followed her, slamming the cell door behind them with unnecessary violence. Liam didn't move. He felt nothing at all. To be thoughtless and motionless after the agonies of the past seven days should have been a luxury, except that the idea of luxury had ceased to have any real meaning. He sat against the wall, waiting for whatever should happen – for a change in his mood, for a new storm of overwhelming images, perhaps for his execution. They were scared. It wasn't surprising. And they hated him. He could understand that. It simply wasn't important. He was a vehicle. And if there still existed a part of him which resented this, then presently it was quiescent. Liam the Songmaker had been capable of resentment – Liam the Songmaker had been swift, witty, impulsive, eccentric, derisive, talented, sentimental, loving, and spiteful by turn. Now he was One-Eye's creature, and though there had been moments since the battle when his own character had come through, there was no continuity to them. If there was a way out of the madness – as good a word as any, he supposed – he had yet to find it. He was waiting on circumstance, circumstance engendered by the alien inside him. Circumstance the night before had decreed that his possessed mind should direct his nimble fingers to unleash the full horror of the battle upon the miners, to convert them into the mutant dream as he had been converted. As thousands of others had been converted.

Seven days. Seven days since the few members of the Company Chatachain, fleeing Phadraig with the infant, had been taken over by the 'infant' and directed into Khassam's advancing army. And so One-Eye had been reunited with the mumen, and the mumen had danced. Their patterns had charged the army into cannibal violence, the infant had fed on the energy thus released, had dreamed it straight back into the chaos, had planted himself in the vacuumed minds of the survivors, had left them staring numbly at their bloody hands as huge silver predators flapped down from the sky to feast on the dead and wounded. Now the survivors were spreading in all directions, carrying the spores of One-Eye's reality with them, and he was one such survivor. Khassam's army was dead, and so was the Company Chatachain. The six left alive of the Company had tried to stay together afterward, had started across the Scarp plateau, but they had simply lost touch, drifted apart, isolated from each other. Now here he was. In a cell in Schroun, in Miir, to which his feet had taken him. Waiting.

Head aching, belly mumbling spasmodically, he dozed into the afternoon. Gaily striped flags were being strung across the street outside his window. They were quaint. He wasn't interested. For a time, he sank into a near-emotionless nostalgia. He went back fifteen years, to when he had been nineteen, when he was Songmaker to Patrick Cormac's newly formed Company Chatachain, when they roamed the Wastelands north and south of Phadraig, carefree. To when he'd discovered the ancient scarlet sirena in the ruins of a sorceror's stronghold on Comrie Isle, far to the south. To when his music had been acclaimed, to when he'd played with beauty, passion, harmony, humor. To the great days, when the Company drove Kalnakill's hordes into the Burning River and saved Phadraig.

The great days. The late days. The dead days.

Later in the afternoon, with the sun baking directly through the window, he grew giddy with the heat, and threw off his tunic. His body was black with bruises, and utterly emaciated. Time went on. At length the door opened again, and one of the red-tattoos brought him a bowl of mushy porridge.

'Food,' he barked, banging down the bowl, turning away.

'Wait!' Liam jerked a thumb at the window. 'What's going on?'

'White Feather,' the dull man grunted. 'Comes to Schroun tonight.'

'You don't sound happy about it,' Liam remarked, teasing.

The red-tattoo bristled. 'What are you raving about?'

'It must be to do with Khassam being dead,' said Liam through a mouthful of porridge. 'How would she know?'

The door was slammed a second time, more violently than the first.

Later, when the sun was in steep decline and it was much cooler, another madman was thrown into the cell with Liam. He was a dirty, gangling Yellowbelt from Phrenge, and he had one ear missing. His face was pitted by smallpox, his greasy hair was ponytailed down his back, and his eyes were grief-stricken and demented. Liam shifted uneasily. He felt colors inside his head, and heat growing. He looked away. But the Yellowbelt came and grabbed Liam's thin shoulders in both hands. 'Glass!' he gabbled, his voice high like a child's. 'We're all made of glass! If we fall down we'll shatter. Your panes need washing, but I can see into you. Don't hide from me; you were also at the battle!'

Liam grew rigid. The glare was mounting in his head, washing away his former equanimity. He refused to answer. The Yellowbelt only gripped him harder.

'I know you can hear me, you can see me, your panes aren't that dirty! You have no compassion. You don't care if I do shatter into fragments. The Mutant has cracked your panes, you have no pity. Speak to me and give me compassion, I demand it!'

Liam couldn't suppress his fury – he was his fury. He glared at the Yellowbelt's dislocated features, at the verminous remains of the man's yellow uniform.

'Remove your vitreous hands from my shoulders or I'll shatter you into many thousands of fragments!' he hissed.

The Yellowbelt shivered, but his grip tightened and his knuckles cracked.

'Rogue, do you hear that?' he wailed. 'My fingers have splintered! How can I let you go? I can't feel a thing!'

Liam wrenched violently, but the hands stayed glued to his shoulders.

Hate spewed out from him in a bloody aura. He prised at the long fingers, but they were set like concrete. He hit the Yellowbelt in the stomach. The man toppled backward to the floor, taking Liam with him. He lay rigid and grotesquely poised in his former standing position, one leg bent up in the air as Liam struggled to free himself.

'Maniac!' howled the Yellowbelt dismally. 'You're breaking my windows! I'll smash you up!'

Liam succeeded in tearing himself free at the expense of a clawed shoulder, and he fell back against the wall as the glare incinerated his self-control completely. The Yellowbelt's rigidity collapsed into jagged, hysterical laughter which pierced Liam through; Liam felt the laughter as an attack by cruel glass needles. The Yellowbelt appeared to him now as a coruscating interflow of vitreous surfaces and shards, a monster to be overwhelmed. Roaring up blind courage, he threw himself upon the glittering creature, upon the much larger man, somehow seeing the glass-man as the glass-man saw himself.

The lunatics grappled physically through their fantasies, each doing his best to shatter the other, each locked in the mutant dream which had fallen impartially yet subjectively upon them, each in reaction transmitting and affirming the hold that One-Eye had laid upon them.

The distortions of their imagination led to misdirected blows: their bodies were so weakened by days of deprivation that they pummeled each other without damage until exhaustion intervened and they fell apart.

Bruised and bloody, they lay side by side and semiconscious as the sun went down and Clarai came to Schroun with her caravan, her fading ambition, and her mounting fear.... Clarai – and Tschea.

9: The Caravan

It had been an ordeal watching Tokace's experience of the battle.

Clarai had called for Cuinneale, Abramel, and for scribes to write down the substance of Tokace's broken ramblings. Wanunch had come, and she had sent him away. With Cuinneale and swart Abramel she had watched the tormented Leaper grimly as he writhed, as he babbled of the terrible energies currently being released far to the east, on a slope

beneath the southern rim of the Scarp Plateau. Two ancient,
complementary forces were joining to achieve new union –
the Mutant the hub, the mumen the spokes. The critical
mental mass of this union was unendurable; it was crushing
Tokace even as thousands of soldiers slaughtered themselves
in forced self-sacrifice to the celebration of the weird mumen and their ancient master. Then, with the sun rising
bloody on Ussian, the Mutant's eye beamed into the survivors and scorched them. In that instant Tokace was
shriveled – and thankfully, for his life had been a burden.
His heart gave out, and he died.

And Clarai realized what she must do. Of a sudden, she
was very calm and sure. It had happened – such a rip in the
fabric of familiar reality was clearly beyond repair. She had
to act before fear and confusion overwhelmed them. If
Khassam could fall so easily, what guarantee was there that
any traditional order could survive the coming days? She
was not optimistic. Nevertheless, she decided she must do
what she could on her account, assert the authority latent
in her position. She must show herself to as many of Miir's
people as quickly as possible, establish an image of calm
authority as a bulwark against the approaching madness.

For once in his life, Cuinneale seemed dazed, as if only
just realizing that the Leapers had not been lying, that an
event had occurred which almost certainly left Formalism
in ruins. When she told him that she intended to tour Miir
immediately, and that he must organize the caravan and the
journey's itinerary, he merely nodded, hands as ever wrapped discreetly in the sleeves of his robe.

She sensed that there was fear in him.

'There is danger in such a journey,' he'd murmured. 'Nikosner . . .'

'His return's no more than a symptom,' she'd replied
briskly. 'We will take an escort of fifty Darsans. Nikosner is
a vulture by nature. He will not attack where there is great
opposition.'

Then, she didn't know that she was still thinking in the
old dimension. As yet she had no new perspective to think
any other way.

'Very well,' Cuinneale had agreed, features blank. 'I take

it you'll want me to remain in Ussian and look after the—'

'No. You'll come with me. Abramel will remain here in charge.'

Cuinneale gave Abramel a pointed look, and the dark man protested : 'But I have no experience of government. . . .'

'You'll do as I say,' said Clarai.

They were uncertain. She had reacted faster. She dismissed them, and sent for Chimalus. She told him that she was taking over. She told him to advise all Jerezid personnel in Ussian to acquiesce with her coup if they didn't want to be thrown in the Pit like common criminals.

She told him that Khassam was dead, but he didn't believe her.

'I knew you were plotting rebellion !' he bellowed.

'There's no rebellion,' she snapped icily. 'Only disaster.'

'This is one of your games. If—'

'Choose ! Submit to me, or go to the Pit !'

Proud, Chimalus damned her and chose to go to the Pit. He was taken away by Darsans. Few of his underlings elected to join him. Clarai gave orders to those who'd been in her room when Tokace died that they were to say nothing of what they knew. On that day she was full of energy, determined that she was no longer going to submit to being a figurehead. Action was the only antidote to the fear inside her, the fear of being changed into something else.

That evening she addressed the Guild in the Hlih Hall. She told them that Cuinneale was organizing a tour of their land, the Red Feathers would accompany her, and those uppermost in the Purple ranks. When she heard of Namahon's supposed abduction by the Cyclones, she had no time to consider it. The caravan occupied her mind, and the politics of her present situation.

Would Cuinneale accept the about-turn in their relative positions? It seemed he would. He showed no sign of resentment; he organized the caravan with his usual efficiency. But Cuinneale was secret, and Clarai knew he'd bear close watching. As for Abramel, leaving the city in his uncertain hands was a risk. Abramel had never been more than Cuinneale's puppet. Perhaps it was time to enflame the Guard Commander's personal ambition with a brief taste of personal power, and thus reduce Cuinneale's influence over him. It was a risk, but now there was nothing which wasn't. Everything was wide open to new influence.

All day, the city was full of talk and agitation, Tah Ti was reported everywhere but seen nowhere, and Clarai was told that the symbol of the Zuni Bird had been chalked on the outer wall of the Tarasse by some unknown artist. Everywhere there were mutterings that the Divine Mutant was come again, and that reality was about to dissolve, and that Clarai's sudden actions were based on the sure knowledge that this was so. How else could she have gained the courage to act as she was acting? Imprisoning the Jerezid Consul, overriding Cuinneale? It was Cuinneale's apparent acceptance of the situation which people found most bewildering. Was he biding his time? Was he nursing some scheme which would undercut Clarai in the fullness of its time? Or was he so shattered by whatever Tokace had told them that all his long term resolve was snapped, just like that?

The long caravan climbed slowly out of the valley early on the day after Tokace had died and took the north road through the grasslands. Teams of black oxen pulled the gilded carriages; horses pulled the heavy covered baggage wagons which went behind. Mounted Darsan archers accompanied the caravan. Messengers rode out in front to warn each approaching community that Clarai was coming, and asked for news of Nikosner's whereabouts. But the black mage had not been seen since the unexpected attack on the Opa Theater, as if that single assault constituted his signature on the situation.

It took a day to reach the southern shore of Tardenoisse. The caravan's zigzag progress through the agricultural communities in that fertile area was greeted with complaints about Nikosner's return. Clarai assured all and sundry that Nikosner would be dealt with. Her assurances were doubtfully received. And whenever Nikosner was mentioned, Cuinneale's face was blank. She wondered what was on the gray ghost's mind.

The caravan progressed up the lake's eastern bank, bypassing the Zaidam Marshes and the Cyclone College at Dulankir, its length greatly extended by casual followers –

mostly restless people too disturbed by the rumors to remain still in one place. The third and fourth days were soft and full of sun. Clarai watched the countryside as the caravan passed ancient ruins of enigmatic structures, stone circles, earthmounds, and barrows which had been piled up in the distant past. More than once during these two days she had the uncomfortable feeling that the landscape had been ... constructed. In places it seemed too regular to be natural. But more important things were on her mind. The caravan was possessed by an undercurrent of nervousness. And a storm blew in across Tardenoisse on the fifth day as they came to the northwestern port of Alyss, and the streets of the sprawling town were drab, wet, gray.

It was during the interminable official banquet in Alyss that night that the first portentous ugliness occurred. Clarai sat at the head of a horseshoe table laden with food and drink. Wanunch was to her left, a local dignitary sat to her right, and the Guild-members were spread out down the arms of the table. Red and purple feathers nodded in the fragrant yellow light of the tapestried hall. The local entertainment was as pleasing as the food and wine and it seemed that all was going well, though the Opa Theater had flatly refused to appear.

But when the evening was well advanced, a wild-eyed man burst into the hall past the Darsans on guard at the entrance. He wore the remains of Jerezid uniform, he brandished a sword and radiated a repellent energy which set the Darsans back on their heels. Single-minded and tireless in his delirium, he had been running for days, had run west until he'd run right into the waters of Tardenoisse. With water still dripping from him as he raced up between the horseshoe sides, he leaped up onto the table in front of Clarai, knocking food and drink aside as he did. And he transfixed Clarai with eyes seeming much larger than ordinary human eyes. She and everyone else in the hall — Tschea included — were quite unable to move as he ranted in a high, hoarse voice:

'Futile, spineless people! Eating and drinking as if time and the world itself belonged to you. Fools! The Mutant grows in you all, I bear his hungry cancer, and the dream is spawning in every land. Stuff yourselves, enjoy yourselves while you can, your days are numbered. Soon you'll see with eyes like mine. Look! See your future selves! See—'

A Darsan recovered. An arrow sprouted from the madman's back. With windmilling arms he crashed forward over Clarai, and his glazing eyes jellied her soul as he died. His ragged corpse was dragged away. The banquet broke up amid an atmosphere of sour fearfulness.

Next day, the caravan turned southeast and followed the sluggish Bhykan Gasche into the woods to Danaimon, home of the Fire-Dancers who praised Vaira – their personification of the Fire-Essence which they claimed to be the underlying creative principle of the universe.

Clarai brooded all day. Alyss had been a disaster. After the madman's death, the City Council had denied the necessity of uniting under her lead. They'd questioned her motives, resented her advice, and openly blamed her for Nikosner's attack on the Opa Theater.

She wasn't the only depressed one. Nobody was happy. Doubt had infected everyone, and it was growing impossible to conceal it. The way the madman had vibrated ... it made them shiver ... and where was Nikosner? Only Cuinneale appeared to be unaffected, silent.

And Tschea, still half-caught in her dream of the redhaired musician, was unhappy to be traveling away from the delta. She had come under suspicion. Few believed that Namahon had been abducted. She'd argued that she should stay in Ussian in case Namahon returned. Clarai had insisted otherwise, with a narrowing of the eyes and a sideways glance at Cuinneale. So Tschea had come. She shared a carriage with Tschan, Frith, and Urseen (all Purple Feathers), with Hilgo, Kryle, and the Contractuals of the other two. She'd ignored them all the way. She wasn't surprised by what had happened in Alyss. But she was tense as the caravan approached Danaimon. The red-haired Fire-Dancers ... was the man of her dream among them? What was the meaning of her dream?

The Fire-Dancers didn't welcome the caravan, and Tschea saw nobody who fitted her memory. No madmen had come to Danaimon yet. The Fire-Dancers were aware of

more than one influence spreading, they were evolving a
new dance to express the Mutant Change, and they were preparing for a vital journey to the southwest ... every man,
woman, and child.

They entertained their unwanted guests politely, though
frugally.

And when one of them bluntly told Clarai that she
should be at the delta instead of traipsing around Miir toward disaster, they didn't fail to note the flicker of hatred
which crossed Cuinneale's face at mention of the delta. But
nobody from the caravan noticed it.

And when the caravan had left next morning, the Cyclone
adept of the Inner Vortex who was with them came out of
hiding.

The caravan left the river and climbed from the woods
onto sere moors. The day grew hot and very close, and the
land about was shrouded in haze. Fearful arguments were
increasingly common as the sweating ox-teams drew the
carriages down toward Lake Bhykan. The Darsans rode
half-slumped in their saddles, sweating in their full gear of
blue leather cuirass, conical helmet, quilted trousers, too
lacking in energy to brush off the droning insects which
swarmed and bit as the caravan reached the lakeside not far
from Schroun. The waters were gelid, metallic, without a
ripple in the setting sun.

Tschea was silently fretful. Danaimon had been a frustration, and Schroun was the last place on earth she wanted to
visit. She couldn't bear the thought of leaving the carriage
and exposing herself to the people of this town, which
wasn't really her home town at all. She decided that she
wouldn't move. As the Darsans led the caravan into the
town, relations in this sixth carriage were particularly
strained. While the others were making last-minute adjust-
ments to their dress and appearance, Tschea lay in a velvet-
cushioned corner with a flagon of wine, her face obstinate,
her expression distant, so that the others were exchanging
looks of annoyance. The tension in the air here was great. It
was dark now, the sun was an hour gone, but the air retained the heat of the day.

The baggage-wagons were left by the lakeside. The Dar-

sans led the fifteen carriages up a wide avenue to the Great
Hall in the Yelin Square. The avenue, the white-cobbled
square, and the facade of the pillared gray Hall itself were
strung with bright flags, but the waiting crowds were sullen
and unenthusiastic. The Darsans took up watchful position
about the perimeter of the square. The crowds muttered and
pointed as the ornate carriages clattered in, to draw up one
by one before the marble steps of the Hall. Torchlight glimmered on the sweating black flanks of the oxen, on the
paintwork and gilded designs of the eight-wheeled carriages.
A hornblower in blue-gold uniform rose from his carved box
on the convex roof of Clarai's carriage.

For a moment he stood there, poised in torchlight.

Then he sounded three short, sharp blasts.

The hard-faced team-master jumped down from her oaken
booth high at the front of Clarai's carriage. She opened the
dragon-crested door in the side of the carriage. Behind it,
Clarai was waiting in her tattoos.

Clarai was apprehensive, filled with conflicting emotions.

She stepped down and out to meet the welcoming delega-
tion advancing from the Hall. There was a ripple of unenthusiastic applause. The doors of the other carriages opened.
Some seventy others came out.

In the sixth carriage, Tschea showed no sign of moving.

'Clarai will notice if you stay here,' warned Tschan.

'For my sake,' implored Hilgo, magnificent in white fur,
'please.'

Their own team-master had opened the door. Frith and
Urseen had already stepped out in the company of their
Contractuals. Kryle was waiting for Tschan. Hilgo was
hovering above Tschea, picking at his manicured nails.
Tschan's shoulders were hunched impatiently in the deep-
plunging, full-length dress brocaded with white flowers.
Tschea stared at the half-empty flagon of wine. Her head was
throbbing, not just with wine.

'I'm staying here.' Her voice was hardly audible.

'You're a fool!' Tschan scolded. 'You're in enough trouble
already. Nobody really believes your story about Namahon's kidnapping. If it weren't for this crisis, you wouldn't
get away with it. Why make matters worse for yourself?'

'She's trying to help you, Tschea,' Hilgo insisted.

'This is your home town, Tschea; people here love you!'

'Tschea, you have a duty to the Guild. You—'

Tschea stared up, her eyes blazing.

'Get out, the pair of you!'

Tschan shrugged coldly. She turned abruptly and left, Kryle taking her arm, leaving Hilgo with a burning face.

'I've never been so humiliated,' he ground out. 'Sometimes, you—'

'Stop pretending!' Tschea insisted with loathing. 'These games are dead. You can sense what's happening as well as I can.'

'That's just what you want to believe!' Hilgo was trembling.

'I don't want to believe anything. I know it! So do you!'

'I know nothing of the sort. I only know that you're impossible, you take pleasure in hurting me, you are antisocial and arrogant!'

Tschea felt an intense desire to drive him away forever. She stood, went to a box, and pulled out a ribboned scroll.

'That's my Contract,' said Hilgo, suddenly perplexed, doubtful.

Smiling, she slowly tore it in two, watching his eyes widen.

'That *was* your Contract,' she corrected. 'Now go away, back to wherever you came from. I don't want to see you again. Shoo!'

Hilgo stood bemused.

More than half-drunk, she laughed.

'But, you can't—' he began, raising a plump white hand.

'Get out.' Her voice vibrated with ugliness.

Hilgo took a step forward, angry, astounded.

'This is a breach of Contract. You'll be thrown out of the Guild!'

'*Get ... out...!*'

Hilgo deflated. He wheeled and left the carriage without a word.

Tschea stared at the torn halves of the Contract. It was done. What a relief. Doubtless he'd run straight to Clarai with his accusations. She didn't call him back. It didn't matter. There would be no more Contracts, no more Guild. That had been obvious since Alyss, and everyone sensed it – even if as yet not everyone had admitted it to themselves. She no longer cared what they did to her. Her spontaneous action had briefly reduced the pressure of the ugliness mounting inside her – an ugliness she associated with the burning eyes of that madman in Alyss. A general and malignant growth from which nobody was exempt, the wave of the immediate future. A feeling which was stifling her mind, driving her to dismiss all former preoccupations as unimportant and redundant.

Her dismissal of Hilgo was no more than a temporary relief. After some minutes were past the oppressive weight had returned to roost in her mind. She grew restless. She couldn't stay in this stuffy carriage a minute longer. Nor could she bear to go near the banquet. She hated the thought of all those peacock people sitting in there around the tables, pretending. She laughed out loud. How futile people could be in their self-deceptions ... herself included. Minute by minute the world was changing, existence was being reformulated, somehow it was growing to mirror that wildness which she'd always carried in her mind. Somewhere, not far distant, was an anarchic ecstasy she was eager to embrace. Her pulse was rapid, her palms were damp, she felt almost nauseous with a strange excitement.

Donning a hooded cloak for disguise, she slipped out of the carriage and clung to shadows while she checked the situation in the square. The square was only partly lit. Some curious citizens were poking around the carriages, and she saw a boy gouging his initials with a knife into the woodwork of one of them; somehow this delighted her. Other people were shifting, murmuring in uneasy groups, pointing at the lit windows of the Hall, at the aloof Darsans ranked by the Hall steps. Keeping to shadow as she slipped past the carriages to the side of the square, Tschea picked up the apprehension and cynicism in the air. She overheard the conversation of several young men and women who lounged by a water trough; they were dressed with style but without joy or conviction.

'They caught another madman this afternoon.'

'Yes, a huge man, a Yellowbelt who thinks he's made of glass.'

'What about the one they got yesterday?'

'You mean the red-haired one? I hear he drove some miners crazy with demented noise which he forced from a strange scarlet instrument. . . .'

Tschea, like a ghost nearby, felt her heart leap. Her dream . . .

'Tschenner the Guard says he comes from Phadraig.'

'Why didn't the miners kill him? Why give him to us?'

'Maybe because he drove them mad.'

There was nervous laughter. Tschea felt as if her head might explode. Feeling fated, she let her feet take her away toward the Guard offices, to the cells. She remembered where the Guard offices were located. She slipped past a tavern in which the caravan's team-masters were drinking. She moved quickly, her mouth dry, quite certain that she was about to confront her destiny face to face. There was only one way to find out the truth of this change, this madness with which she was infected already. From a madman. Perhaps he had seen the Divine Mutant with his very own eyes. The terror she felt was delicious.

Not having the slightest idea of what she was going to do, she came to the Guard offices with her cloak drawn tight and her face deep in the shadow of the hood. There was nobody about in the wide street at this western end of Schroun. She paused only a moment before rapping on the iron-hasped door. There would be a minimum number of Guards on duty here because of Clarai's visit. Probably underlings. Could she bribe them, could she. . . ?

Light shone through a spyhole as an inner lid was flipped back.

The light was occulted by an eye. The door was opened.

Not knowing what she intended, she stepped inside.

She didn't know that Hilgo had followed her.

When, having herself eaten nothing, Clarai advised Tschenner to have all madmen killed on sight, Cuinneale interrupted for the first time since the beginning of the tour. Leaning across the white-clothed table, he placed a

slender hand on Clarai's arm and suggested that perhaps it
would be a better idea to take some alive for study by the
Patterners, in order that they might get to the root of the
madness before it was too late. He spoke persuasively. Clarai
stared at the white hand on her arm. She had hardly ever
seen Cuinneale's hands. It was rare for him to remove them
from his sleeves where they lurked in concealment. This
action in itself impressed her with the seriousness of his
suggestion. If Cuinneale felt driven to expose his hands, then
the times were surely changed.

'... Let the Preconceptuals dissect specimens to understand the physiological and chemical causes behind their
behavior,' he insisted quietly, so quietly that his voice was
almost drowned by the background murmur arising from
all about the crowded, restless Hall. 'Let the Leapers have
some in order to analyze the psychic elements of the
change. And the Shapers must examine the behavior of these
madmen. Perhaps then we can arrive at a common denomin-
ator, perhaps we can isolate the roots of the change con-
fronting us before we ourselves are overwhelmed.'

Clarai regarded him doubtfully, suspiciously.

But Tschenner laughed.

Tschenner felt sick and uneasy inside; she was haunted by
thoughts of the mad musician, and by the fantasy of the
Yellowbelt who thought himself made of glass. And, though
she was reluctant to admit it, she had to recognize that
she herself was changing already. . . .

Her laughter was harsh. Clarai and Cuinneale stared.

'And how will the examiners isolate themselves from the
effect of those they examine? How will they know that
their conclusions aren't the product of their own changed
minds? Set eyes upon these changed people and before you
know it you are changed yourself!'

Clarai remembered the eyes of the madman in Alyss.

Across the table, Cuinneale gestured smoothly; his eyes
were black hollows.

'There are ways and means,' he insisted. 'Measurements
can be made, objective tests can be carried out, and there
are techniques to compensate for the admitted relativity of
the situation.'

Tschenner shrugged.

'At the cells in the Guard office here,' she said, her voice rapid, 'we have two such madmen. You're welcome to them.'

Clarai was afraid. She couldn't reveal her fear.

'Very well. Take us to them.'

'But the banquet is not yet over,' said Tschenner.

Perhaps there was a hint of mockery in her voice.

'I'm not hungry,' Clarai answered.

'Nor I,' murmured Cuinneale. 'Take us. Now, please.'

So Tschenner conducted the White Feather and her chief adviser from the Great Hall to the Guard offices, and Tschenner's mind was in a savage state. She was more than willing to deliver up the madmen to these people from Ussian, she was happy to know that Clarai and Cuinneale would themselves be infected just like she was. Her emotion was strong, violent.

The Guards were gone. So was the madman from Phadraig.

There was only the Yellowbelt, snoring on the floor, doomed.

Fury broke out. Tonight, Clarai could feel panic nibbling at her mind. Nothing was going right. Cuinneale was re-asserting himself. Now a captured madman was at large again, suggesting that mere physical incarceration was no bar to those whose minds were changed. She called three Darsans, ordered them to set out after the escapee, and not to rest until he was captured and killed. She spoke the word 'killed' with a flat emphasis at which Cuinneale blinked. The three Darsans waited until search-parties had turned Schroun upside down without result. They rode west into the night, choosing that direction at random. Now robed against the predawn temperature, Clarai was in a state of barely controlled anger which Tschenner's attitude did nothing to improve. Tschenner did not seem disturbed by the disloyalty of her own Guards; she seemed fatalistic, almost amused. Clarai reiterated her insistence that all madmen should be killed on sight, and Cuinneale made no protest.

At this point there was no reason for Clarai to associate

the madman's escape with Tschea's absence from the banquet. Perhaps, had her mind been functioning more efficiently, she might have connected the Red Feather's well-known predilection for musicians with the fact that the escaped madman was a musician. But neither she nor Cuinneale made any such connection at this time. Hilgo did not appear to tell them of what he'd seen. Furthermore, Tschea seemed fast asleep when the others of her carriage got back near dawn, drunk and foul-tempered.

Fresh outbursts of chaos near dawn added to the confusion. The futile search was diverted by the irruption of more madmen into the area. A wild Mountainman of Kor who'd served in Khassam's army, his greased hair splines in jagged disarray, climbed a gabled roof to rant terrible nonsense. A disturbed crowd was attracted – none had slept that night – before Guards and Darsans arrived together to shoot him down. On the outskirts of the town three ex-soldiers from Purplefield broke into a corn warehouse, murdered the middle-aged caretaker, and raped his wife. Two Darsans died before the crazed soldiers were overwhelmed, howling to the last from their barricades that the Avenging Orphan was terrorizing their minds and forcing them to commit awful crimes.

The nervousness and irritability of the townsfolk grew with every passing minute. As dawn rose, a crowd gathered to throw stones at the carriages parked in Yelin Square. Clarai found herself conferring with Cuinneale, who showed no emotion as he advised that it would be sensible to cut out the rest of the tour and head back to Ussian. He showed no emotion, yet his tone was odd. Clarai had no option but to agree. She was no longer sure of her own mind. Her motives for making this tour now seemed vapid and foolish. Any further delay and they'd be overwhelmed by Schroun's increasingly querulous population. The madness was accelerating; the people of Miir were losing their customary mildness and good sense. And who knew what was happening in Ussian? It might be in turmoil already. Why hadn't she fled to Mantrim? Or to the delta? Though, of course, the myths were rubbish. Yet the Fire-Dancers hadn't thought so. Now it was her duty to return to the Tarasse – at least, she could think of nothing better to do. She felt gnawed by defeat, inside and outside, actual and incipient. And the Tarasse with its walls and mazelike structure was virtually a citadel – not that she'd ever thought of it in such terms before. Her brain was flustered, seemed to be on fire; she was surrounded by confused people who magnified her own confusion. Only Cuinneale appeared to be cool.

Though when she asked him what would happen if they met Nikosner – whose whereabouts were unknown – Cuinneale's eyes flickered away, and his mouth tightened. Was Cuinneale afraid?

Amid mounting confusion, the caravan prepared to leave for Ussian as the sun rose over the ocher ramparts of the Scarp to the east. Flustered women, nervous Contractuals, crying Uniques, and stiff-faced Patterners climbed into their carriages while the team-masters hurriedly harnessed fresh ox-teams. A crowd of onlookers jeered, Schroun's few Guards made no effort to hold them back, and it was only the threat of the Darsans which ensured the caravan's safety as it departed – in such a rush that several people were left behind. The baggage-wagons tacked onto its rear as it came out of Schroun.

Nobody had thought to check these wagons during the search for the escaped madman.

10 : In the Gulf, on the Wagon

Exhausted, Liam had drifted through crushing hallucinations while the Yellowbelt wept. Then hideous trolls came to drag him from the cell. They had violent auras and burning coals for eyes; they emanated fear and loathing. He was dumped on the stone floor of a windowless room. A woman's sandaled feet swam inches away – delicate feet, with toenails painted yellow. The shape above was vague – cloaked, hooded, casting an ominous shadow over a wall and half the cracked plaster ceiling. An oil lamp guttered on a low wooden table beside her. Presently the woman seemed to him less substantial than her wavering shadow. He could feel his energy building. Then there were voices, and they struck him.

'Out. Leave us alone. Go.'

'What? You must be mad!'

'He'll harm you, he's possessed.'

But the protests of the red-tattoos lacked conviction. The unknown woman was shivering with excitement, radiating energy they couldn't face. Why were they risking their lives, their souls? They were only too happy to retreat as she advanced on them, crowded them out, slammed the door.

The finality of the slam vibrated heavily through Liam's head.

Tschea turned. She felt dizzy, she was breathing fast. What was she doing? How had she persuaded the guards? And the madman's red hair ... it was he! She sat, and she looked him in the eyes....

Two wide eyes met two which were narrowed, puffy with bruising.

Tschea's heart hammered, and she felt the energies building.

Two eyes. Wry, illogical – and intense.

So intense. They caught her, stilled her breath. The whole room was wavering, fading away. Energies were shuttling back and forth between them with a sudden unstoppable ferocity. The thin man stirred with electricity; he raised himself up on his hands and brought their eyes closer. His cavernous face was flooding with prismatic colors. It was as if wells had burst deep inside him, as if they poured out a corrosive energy burning away his flesh. Now his face was phosphorescent, and filled with bewildered wonder echoing hers.

For the boundaries of her face were dissolving. Instead of a face he saw a flickering field of spectral energy. Only the most tenuous of material envelopes confined this field, and even as he watched it, too, was burned away, so that only two eyes were left to shine out like beacons. Finally even they were dissolved and transformed, so that he was being bathed in the aura of one brilliant eye – in the light of a consciousness which was surely under the same sign as himself! In the colors he read so many of the same characteristics! Moody quickness, surging yellow and violet, a being too agile and impulsive for her own good – just like him. And intense. Yes. Their frequencies twinned along so much of the arc! And she was familiar. Not in terms of current personality, but in a more timeless nature.

They saw each other.

Astonished recognition met amazement.

Transformation continued. Tschea forgot time. Now the prismatic brilliance of the madman was extended in aura so strong that she was enveloped in the tent of it. And he in hers. It was an open connection. There was only mutual doubt in the way. Neither had ever seen like this before. Surely the energies were too high and fast to control. It was too much to believe. There was too much doubt to be resolved. They couldn't hold it. They both looked away in the same instant. Looked away so briefly, their eyes flickered to the reaffirming floor and bounced up again.

Two eyes saw two eyes, and flesh and blood and bone—

The oil lamp glimmered. Now its light was the greatest light. The shadows wrapped themselves around Liam's head again. The woman's face was a crescent moon, her straight nose the terminator. Memory of the former state faded quickly into mundane sight and confusion. And Liam lost his place. He was somewhere else as well.

'Wait for the fields of waving grass,' he mumbled; 'there the black one will attack!'

She opened her mouth. And he slapped his face.

'This offends my natural vision!' he snapped, his face suddenly sharp, and bitter with his situation.

Tschea's features mobilized into passionate insistence, stuttered out under pressure. 'It *is* natural vision. Natural – to the Fifth Element!'

They double-took each other, no longer sure what they meant.

'... You ...'

'... Who... ?'

'... Why come here? What are you looking for?'

'... My dream! You'll play new music on the delta....'

'Dream? Dream? Nonsense!' He tugged violently at his drooping moustache which was now almost beard, and his face was strained with fury. She didn't move back, she couldn't. 'I'll play nothing anywhere,' he hissed. 'The Mutant has opened me up like a barrel of fish to the sun; my elements stink so unpleasantly that my new music converts all who hear it into gibbering apes!'

There was a knocking at the door. Impatience sprouted through Tschea.

'Idiot! Why cling to what's lost and gone? Hear that? You must get out. They'll kill you. You must come with me to the delta.' She leaned forward, lightly touched his forehead with a fingertip. 'You hold your own solution; there's sublimity through this madness....'

Liam let the finger remain; he was shivering with the strain of self-control. He felt no anger toward her, rather a strange closeness, but he couldn't answer for the Eye. 'There's chaos,' he whispered. 'Little enough of Liam is left to call his own, but that little does not care to inflict the sublimity of chaos on people who will suffer enough now that the Mutant has come, thanks to idiots like myself! Now remove yourself before I do you worse harm.'

Tschea's finger returned into a gesturing fist. 'Don't you see? This new way is how we're meant to see! The Eye was always in us....'

'It's too much, and too soon!'

'We can ride out the flood – and hear the Zuni Bird sing!'

'I thought I could ride it,' said Liam quietly, shoulders slumping. 'I thought that for nearly three days. Then the strain of thinking grew too great, and I forgot. Now you remind me. At first, I thought I could ride it.' His eyes were drained of energy. 'When you came in here ...' He shook his head. 'When I was dragged in here, you were changed already. But recently. Another day – and I guarantee – you'll forget your dream. There's no stability in the glare. We're like tops sent spinning. Once in a while there is no wobble and the rotation of the mind is smooth; just for a moment I can be here and tell you it is hopeless.'

Even as he spoke he felt his head beginning to spin. He sensed something – something which had happened recently

– but he couldn't catch it; moreover, the woman was leaning at him again, the mobility of her face was fascinating,
and her anger was resonant.

'This is the time which A'Yaya foretold,' Tschea hissed
stubbornly. 'We must go to the delta and there we will know
how to see!'

'Oh – your dream!' Light-headed, Liam laughed sarcastically.

'Yes – on the morning of the battle.'

His curiosity was reluctant, distant. 'So you know about
the ... massacre....'

'You were there.' A pleading note followed her certainty;
she touched the tattoo on her forehead with a sudden motion. 'Did you ... see the Mutant?'

Liam bared teeth in a macabre grin, and he hunched up
thin shoulders. 'I have carried him in my arms!'

Tschea suppressed a shiver. He looked like a death's-head.

'You're scared,' he panted, 'yet you keep on sitting here.
Are we going to spend the night together? Introductions! I'll
tell you my name if you'll tell me yours!' There was a
frightening light in his eyes.

'We've got no time for games!' Tschea rushed her words,
conscious of time. 'And I don't need to know your ... yes,
what's your name?'

'No, you tell me your name first! I insist you take prece-
dence!'

She struck the ground with the flat of her palm. 'Stop!
Or you'll die.'

His grin remained.

'It doesn't matter.'

'They'll come to kill you....'

'They're welcome. It's no escape – for them.'

Tschea crouched. 'You're being futile!'

'I *am* futile.' Liam opened his mouth with melodramatic
lunacy. 'In a minute, I may be filled with heroic purpose,
who can tell? It's your bad luck to meet me in this present
state.' His face fell. 'It may be my bad luck as well.' And
he laughed jaggedly.

She bit off any reply. She stood. She stared at the wall. She
ignored a second knocking at the door. She had to get him

out, though he was quite intolerable with his act of uncaring self-abandonment. But what if he was right? What if the change grew too overwhelming and she forgot as well? She could still walk out and pretend nothing had happened. No, she couldn't. It had, and it would. There was resolution at the delta. No logic explained her certainty; now this made it more certain. Here was the musician. And something had happened above recall. Here he was. Tricking and separating himself. So smugly sure he'd lost his faith and soul. Now staring at the floor as if he might vanish down the cracks, willfully unwilled – it had to be so! Coercion was the only answer, whatever harm this might do to potential benign circumstance. She'd have to smuggle him to Ussian first; she couldn't leave her children to confusion. Smuggle him somehow. What was she thinking? Her head was whirling. Voices were jabbering in her skull. She had to act before . . . before what? He wouldn't help. Like a sack of rags again. Masochistically exulting. What a game to play! Had he learned it, or was he improvising? Contemptuous, she went to the door, opened it.

The red-tattoos were right outside.

'One thing more,' she demanded before they had a chance to utilize their already open mouths, 'and for this service I'll pay you a substantial reward – myself. Now listen.'

She shut the door behind her so that Liam shouldn't hear what she had to say about him. No telling his change of mood. She overwhelmed the red-tattoos with a torrent of incisive suggestion and command. She played on their confusion. Already, she understood it very well.

While Liam sat unmoving and bleak in the mind, savoring a cold landscape, looking away from the low red sun-eye of passive, rejected hope. He was trekking into the northlands, he was endless days out in the wilds, and his supplies were low. There was no life here, just the invisible currents that sluggishly tendriled the atmosphere and breathed the bleakness into him. There was nothing.

Then coal-eyed trolls swooped down from the sky and grabbed him.

And a cloaked arm which sprouted yellow sponge instead of a hand.

The sponge enveloped his face. It was soft and cool. The cool became cold. He breathed icy fumes.

A chasm opened up in the ground at his feet. He fell down into a vast black gulf where strange elementals gibbered and vibrated, where the thought-gas drifted as thin but omnipresent as hydrogen between the stars. Here he was dissipated.

Until the gulf closed in to become a jolting, stifling blackness.

Hilgo didn't go to Clarai, not even after what he saw.

Disgracefully ejected, he'd stamped furiously up and down between the empty carriages, confused by his altogether too fair-minded reluctance to be the cause of her downfall. He'd never loved her character, but he respected her fighting qualities, and he didn't want to run to her enemies and bleat. And it was possible she was right, that their Contract was now an irrelevance. What was he thinking? She'd insulted, hurt, and rejected him, why should she go unpunished?

He couldn't make up his mind, he was still lurking irresolutely when Tschea left the carriage. Curious, suspicious, he trailed her to the Guard offices. She went in, and he crossed the street, a dim-lit but bulky spy who came to a window and heard her excited, imperious voice. Doors slammed. There was silence. He contemplated climbing through the window before rejecting the idea as ridiculous. He found he was shaking quite violently. Vacillating, unable to think, he let instinct take him to the back of the low, squat buildings, where he crouched behind a pile of chopped logs. Instinct led him right. Soon a door at the back had opened. Two burly men, momentarily framed in yellow light, dragged into darkness a limp figure with a sack over its head. Tschea followed, holding a curious scarlet instrument. Hilgo crouched lower as they passed the other side of the woodpile. The men were remonstrating nervously, and he heard Tschea's reply.

'Forget the Guards. Forget Tschenner. Forget Schroun. Get out while the going's good. Go to the woods. First, do this for me, and you'll be paid as I promised.'

They'd gone swiftly through backstreets to the wagons by the lake, Hilgo following with suspicion aflame. He saw Tschea entering a wagon, saw her leave the captive with the wagon-master. She spent several minutes with the wagon-master. Then he followed her and the two men down to the lakeside. Though there was no light to see how she paid them, he could well imagine. Of course, it was none of his business, but jealousy bloomed nevertheless. He crouched behind an overturned boat and generated complex schemes of revenge, generated a mental violence formerly quite alien to his equable disposition. He'd killed her a million different ways by the time she came back past him, alone in the night, striding rapidly.

He stayed where he was, crouching silently.

Now I will tell Clarai, he decided.

Instead, his feet ran him to the nearest tavern. Perhaps he meant to take the smallest of drinks to settle his mind, but it was redweed he found himself asking for. He had never tried the popular plant before. It opened him up to the ferment of his head. Talking to the air, he staggered through growing predawn crowds and out into the vibrating night. He crawled up through the briars on a hill outside Schroun as the sky surged into turbulent motion which shredded him. He lost consciousness. He'd chewed far too much redweed. He was quite unaware as the tavern-keeper and two cronies, who'd followed him up here where there was nobody else, methodically stripped him of rings, necklace, money, and his coat of white fur. They left him.

'He's alive.' The tavern-keeper laughed. 'I wouldn't kill a man.'

'He's mad anyway,' commented another; 'anyone wearing a coat so thick on a night like this must be out of his mind.'

They were nervous themselves. The dawn was growing, as lightly fingered as they. And the streets were full of clamor.

The sun was high when Hilgo came to, with a splitting headache. He was slow to realize he'd been robbed. When he did – then, like Lunth, he hardly cared. He plodded back into Schroun. The caravan was gone. Something in him had changed overnight. The desire for revenge was all he had.

Tschea had betrayed him – and the Tarasse – and people!

He set out on foot after the caravan, not stopping long enough to realize that in all the confusion he could easily have stolen a horse.

Like a brightly segmented centipede with forty-five Darsans as feelers, the caravan crawled southwest toward the populous agricultural region this side of the Boribet, past wind-flattened fields of corn, through ancient groves of oak, elm, and candletree, across languid rivers flowing to Lake Bhykan, through thatched rural communities whose people shouted nervous questions. The caravan didn't stop all day, and the oxen and horses labored in the heat as the ceramics town of Tsarsa was bypassed.

Clarai was intent on reaching Ussian as quickly as possible. Who knew what Abramel had been doing in her absence? That was a rash decision! She insisted on speed. The ornate carriages were clumsy, never built for speed. The day was humid and without a breath of wind; the sun was a cooking smear that boiled tempers up and threw friends into hot disputes which flared, then died of exhaustion. There was strain in every carriage.

Tschan, who hadn't managed to visit her Hearth, refused even to look at Tschea. Nothing had been said about Hilgo's disappearance since the leaving of Schroun. Tschea had muttered briefly of an argument, of Hilgo screaming violent imprecations before stamping out into the night, not to be seen again. 'And good riddance!' she'd added. All day she remained sphinxlike and remote, dreaming through the carriage window at the searing sky, gazing at the intolerably bright smear of the sun as if she sought blinding. The others whispered among themselves. What was she thinking about? She didn't speak.

It was hard to believe she'd done what she'd done. Perhaps her memory was another dream, she thought, no more real than this journey, which was more and more a sweating fantasy as the day broiled on. From time to time she worried about the end-wagon, and about what would happen if it were searched before they came to Ussian – if they came – and about the consequences of Kanlo's nerve breaking. The blue-tattoo wagon-master was not the most dependable of allies.

A dream? The illogic of her remembered actions suggested that this was likely, while what she recalled of the madman's behavior reinforced this likelihood. Her mind roamed strangely all day long. The red-haired madman of her dream, the wild musician with such burning eyes ... her heart raced to think of him. What did she hope for from him? Did she believe that her dream might become real? And if it had really happened, why had she done it? Was she already so crazy that she hoped for a love much greater than any she'd known with Algon? Or was she so filled with hate for the Guild that she hoped to destroy it by smuggling the insane musician into the Tarasse? And what of herself? Why hadn't she fled in the night like the Guards she'd bribed?

Tschea no longer knew herself. The questions tangled up her mind all day long. As for Hilgo's disappearance ... Hilgo was just another question. Where had he gone to, would he return to strike at her ...?

The hazy sky gave no answers.

The wagon-master of the terminal wagon, Kanlo, was so worried that he could hardly think at all.

Kanlo was a thickset young man, a taciturn redweed addict, a blue-tattoo with no other desire than to get through life as easily as possible. Now he had gone and made life exceedingly difficult for himself. All day long he sat at the reins of the team of four horses, frequently casting uncomfortable glances into the dimness of the wagon behind him, half expecting an ominous shadow to rise up from the baggage at any minute....

The wagon was covered by canvas stretched over a rectangular wooden frame; it was filled with Tarasse baggage. The madman was well concealed beneath the baggage, drugged unconscious, bound in a sack.

He could do no harm.

Kanlo didn't believe it.

He was mad to have accepted Tschea's alluring bribe.

But Tschea was very beautiful, and he'd never before had the chance to make love with a Red Feather. Moreover, she'd promised that if he succeeded in bringing the madman undetected to the Tarasse, he'd get the chance to make love with her many times more. Now he wondered how he could have been such a fool. Not even the pleasures of Tschea's elegant body could make such a risk worthwhile. Of course, he'd been up on the weed when she came secretly to his wagon during the night. She'd been accompanied by two jittery red-tattoos who'd held the unconscious man. Kanlo had been alone beside his wagon, dreaming by a crackling fire, gazing at the stars and wondering what life was for.

Her insane proposition had brought him down to earth.

Evidently, he hadn't come down far enough.

Usually, he could handle emergencies quite neatly on red-weed.

Now he looked back on the night with fuddled bemusement, striving to understand what had possessed him. Tschea had used all her considerable powers of erotic persuasion, but surely they were not sufficient reason for agreeing to participate in such an idiotic scheme. She'd assured him he'd have no trouble. It was simply a matter of keeping the man drugged and of holding on to him in Ussian until she got in touch. He remembered protesting. She'd drawn him inside his wagon to talk about it. *Nobody else need know,* she'd assured him; *you're the only wagon-master here, all the others are in the town.* He'd been suspicious. Why the secrecy? Why the hood over the captive's eyes? Did he have dangerous eyes...? Was he one of these madmen? Tschea had calmed his fears most seductively. She'd assured him that the man was solidly unconscious and would remain so for a long time. She gave him a vial of cloudy liquid, a drop of which, she said, would renew unconsciousness instantly. He'd accepted it doubtfully even as she'd helped him off with his trousers. Later he'd found himself lying back with gratification, nodding stupidly at her instructions. He'd examined the scarlet instrument with fascination; now it was buried next to the ... madman. For mad he was sure the man must be. Tschea had left in haste with the red-tattoos, assuring him that he'd be all right so

long as he kept the captive hooded, bound, and unconscious
... so long as ...

So long as he didn't look into the madman's eyes....

Near dusk, the caravan passed from woods into the
bleakly impressive Boribet, where no birds sang. On all
sides great mica-flecked slabs lunged upward for hundreds
of feet; they hung poised over the narrow, gloomy pass like
drunken sentinels. The Boribet glittered; the light was ambi-
ent, peculiar. The team-masters shouted loudly, bravely,
their calls echoed back. And Kanlo wished the caravan
could make greater speed. He felt utterly threatened, by
twisted nature and twisted minds. His short hairs prickled.
Soon the madman must recover consciousness.

Soon Kanlo would have to administer the drug from the
vial.

He wasn't sure that he could bring himself to approach,
much less touch the dangerous stranger. He was terrified of
infection.

11 : The Black Mage

Liam surfaced into bondage. His cry of anger reached his
mouth before discovering the gag. There was no glare, only
the remains of vertiginous nausea. Everything was black,
and he couldn't move. Information came from ears and
nose. The creaking of wheels, the sound of hooves. Fabric
crinkled when he twisted his head. There was a choking
smell of flour, and rough fibers rubbed his face. He made no
deductions, for he wasn't curious. Curiosity was futile. And
memories proved nothing – they hurt as much as curiosity.
Memory. There had been a cell, and a crazy man who
thought himself made of glass. Memory. A strange and
energetic woman whose eyes had burned, whose eyes he
had shared, so that briefly they'd flowed in a mutual space,
in a knowledge which was quickly forgotten. Now he forgot it again. So much was lost, it didn't matter. If hope

wasn't yet entirely defunct, then it ought to be.

However ... something unresolved was irritating him. Something about the woman's eyes, echoing things he had forgotten. She'd called him an idiot for clinging to what was irrevocably lost; she'd insisted that his days of music weren't yet over. Something stirred inside him, a rejected memory. Now he had it! Abruptly, he was back in that somber night in the wake of the battle. The six of the Company still alive were struggling up through the maze of tunnels leading to the surface of the Scarp plateau, following the route which One-Eye and the mumen had taken already. They found themselves on a ledge above a black lake in the peripheral shadows of a greenly luminous grotto. They were lost, divided by despair. And Liam took his sirena, and sang a soft love song. One of the others demanded to know how he could sing about love at such a time, and Liam replied:

'Because we're stuck in the very bowels of misery, my friend. What else can we do that's profitable?'

What else? But he'd forgotten, given way to despair. In despair he'd rejected her insistence that they could win through. In consequence, here he was. Bound up. Being 'saved.' She hoped he could come through his deadness of heart. And he had forgotten how to hope. Now he tried to move. Several times he tried, but each time he abandoned the unequal struggle. In time, the jolting motion ceased. He heard a fire crackling, a river rippling, an owl hooting. Night. His bondage was intolerable. He could hardly breathe. The glare rose, fury came, and he forgot his exhaustion. He struggled against the knots binding him, the weights pinning him down; he writhed like a snake....

Hands were fumbling with him.

The sack was being raised. There was a lessening of blackness. He smelled garlic breath through flour, and the sweat of fear. Fingers tugged at his gag. As soon as it was half-loose he twisted his head, and he bit hard, viciously. He heard a muffled, frightened curse.

Then the sponge was on his face again.

He fell back into the gulf.

*   *   *

The caravan stopped for the night by the banks of the Bulanshe, west of the Boribet. The Bulanshe, which flowed southeast from the Zaidam Marshes to join the Naenshe some fifty miles east of Ussian, marked the halfway point of the return journey. Clarai would just as soon have continued all night through, but the oxen and horses were exhausted, and the passengers in the carriages were so bad-tempered that a rebellion seemed likely. Besides, as Cuinneale reminded her, the night was dangerous. There was no knowing Nikosner's whereabouts. Far safer to camp by the river, to eat, wash, and sleep soundly with the Darsans on guard. So this was done. The carriages were drawn up close beside the wooden bridge with the baggage wagons spread about them as additional protection.

Kanlo didn't join his fellow wagon-masters around the fires which were soon burning. Fortunately, he had the reputation among his fellows of being a solitary dreamer, so that nobody was surprised by his refusal to join them. Besides, tonight there were many people on the caravan who didn't feel gregarious, who felt oppressed by company. So nobody paid any attention to Kanlo, nobody noticed how much more nervous than anyone else he appeared to be, how he sat so restlessly by his wagon, how once he scrambled up into its interior, to reappear a minute later all white and shaking as if he'd seen a ghost.

The only person who thought about Kanlo was Tschea, and she didn't dare to approach him. She sat by the river and stared at the gurgling waters as the light faded and the heavy night descended, and the grass of the riverbank was where eventually she tried to sleep, along with many others who couldn't bear to stay in the carriages. Meals were eaten in near-silence. There were a few desultory attempts to play music, but there was no laughter.

While the Darsans patrolled the semicircular perimeter of the encampment, Kanlo sat up all night nursing his fear and his bitten fingers. He had hoped that he might feel better once he'd summoned sufficient courage to approach the madman and administer the drug: the reverse proved to be the case. He shook all night. Sleep was impossible. He feared that if he fell asleep he might wake up a different being altogether. In this fear he wasn't alone.

For the second night running, few people slept. Sleep evaded even Cuinneale. The gray ghost lay beneath Clarai's carriage all night long, examining his emotions with cold surprise. He wasn't used to emotions. Now they nibbled at him more strongly every night. And not just emotions. Other sensations hovered on the edge of his consciousness – disturbing sensations, half-memories of matters forgotten ... matters connected with the distant past, with the time before he'd come to Miir from the north, twenty years ago. He was no longer sure what was happening. It was obvious that the order he'd sought to impose on his life and on the lives of others was failing. What could be salvaged? No answers presented themselves. Instead, there were wraiths, delusions, fantasies. The face of Nikosner figured prominently. Nikosner was the only being whom Cuinneale feared. It was fifteen years since Nikosner had been expelled from Ussian for murdering his wife, and five since he and his marauders had been driven out of Miir. Now the black mage was back again. And he hadn't forgotten how Cuinneale had ruined his life. Nobody else knew. The secret had been well kept. Cuinneale didn't fear the Mutant. It was Nikosner he feared. During the last few years, Cuinneale had succeeded in forgetting Nikosner as he'd risen to power. Through Formalism, Cuinneale had succeeded in forgetting much which once had troubled him.

But now the Mutant madness was ruining Formalism, and Nikosner was back in the grasslands. Cuinneale felt that he was fated. Tonight, old ghosts haunted him. He lay beneath the carriage, unsleeping, turning a small pocket mirror over and over in his white hands. The mirror. He had carried a mirror for as long as he could remember. He'd gained his greatest inspirations from its reflections.

But his experiment on Nikosner had been a failure.

And tonight, in the darkness, the mirror reflected nothing.

When dawn rose, there were only forty-three Darsans left. Two – both men – had deserted during the night. Nobody was very surprised. And there had been a murder. The Contractual of a Purple Feather called Sairee was discovered floating face down amid bulrushes at the side of the river. There were stab-wounds in his back. Sairee had vanished. Nobody knew anything about it, or if they did, they were keeping quiet. Clarai raged. The assembled company heard out her exhortations in silence. She felt increasingly undermined, and she stamped into her carriage, giving the signal to get under way. It was hot already as the carriages and wagons trundled over the wooden bridge and made lethargic progress southwest toward the grasslands. Many chose to sweat out the journey atop their carriages rather than swelter inside them. Tschea was among them. Often she gazed from the sun-smeared sky back at the wagons which followed. She could make out the distant figure of Kanlo only when the caravan curled around bends of the open, unbanked road. She felt like weeping and couldn't understand why. The immediate future was such an oppressive question mark; the familiar games were dying, and perhaps she was more attached to them than she'd supposed. But the image of the red-haired man was constantly on her mind. She felt helpless. If her scheme worked and Kanlo brought him safely to Ussian, then what?

By midday the grasslands were visible in the distance as a green, apparently solid wall which marched along the horizon. Now Ussian wasn't more than five hours distant. Nobody felt safe. The thought of Nikosner preyed on their minds. When, where would he strike? Given the growth of chaos, it seemed unlikely that he would let the caravan pass safely through. Surely he must attack, simply to attack. And the air was stifling, heavy clouds were growing out of the hazy sky, and thunder threatened.

Kanlo, still at the tail, was stiff and sick with worry. The madman hadn't moved since the evening before, since receiving the second dose of the drug. Perhaps the dose had been too strong. And the captive hadn't eaten. What if he were dead? Of course, that would be the best thing all around. Tschea would be furious, and there would be no more loving from her. All the same, it would be the best solution. . . .

The caravan came to a halt at an agricultural hamlet near

the lip of the grasslands. Smoke still curled up from several gutted buildings. There was blood in the dust of the road. Scouting grimly with drawn swords and notched arrows, the Darsans uncovered a young girl from her hiding place nearby. Clarai and Cuinneale listened as, sobbing, the girl told them how devilish monsters on horseback had swooped out of the night to gut, murder, and abduct. She described an ebony-skinned man with a hook nose and the scream of an agonized animal. Cuinneale's lips went tight. A quick emergency conference was held with the Darsan lieutenant. The girl was incapable of giving rational information but, when asked in what direction the raiders had departed, she pointed with a shaking finger to the southeast. There were bodies here and there. There was no time to give them burial. The caravan was rearranged. Clarai's carriage was placed in the middle for greater protection.

Kanlo took the opportunity to duck inside his wagon. There were no Darsans about to watch him through the open back as he started to turn back the concealing blankets and bundles. He was fixated by thought of the madman. At that moment the wagon-master of the wagon ahead came to talk with him. The wagon ahead carried several kegs of explosives picked up in Schroun. Kanlo concealed the madman just in time. It was some minutes before the other man returned to his own wagon. Kanlo ducked back inside. Again, he turned back the blankets. The madman was utterly still. Trembling, Kanlo felt for a pulse. It was there, and stronger than he had expected to find it. *Better give him another dose*, he thought, *and tighten up the knots – they look loose*.

He was given no time. Even as he went to his jacket for the vial the caravan was jolting into hasty motion, and he was being left behind, and angry voices were shouting at him. Darsans were galloping back down the line to take up defensive positions at the rear. A swarthy, unshaved face ducked inside the wagon even as Kanlo covered up the captive and was scrambling back to the reins without having administered the drug.

'Wake up,' the Darsan snapped. 'We can't hang about!'

'All right! All right!' Kanlo was breathless. He was

shivering, and his face was flushed. The Darsan had no time
to investigate Kanlo's curious behavior. Besides, the Darsan
was thinking about deserting. It was obvious that everything was falling apart. Reluctant, he took up a position
with others at the rear.

The caravan approached the grasslands with the carriages
hemmed by wagons. Ten Darsans rode out in front, ten protected the rear, and others were distributed along both
sides.

The Darsans seemed frail protection to Tschan, who was
on the roof of her carriage with Tschea. Neither hearth-
sister had exchanged words for over thirty hours. Now
Tschan's apprehension made her forget her anger.

'Will we get back safely? Oh, what's happening? What's
going on?' Her voice was strangled.

Tschea gestured sharply at the threatening sky. And she
remembered what the mad musician had said: '*Wait for
the fields of waving grass. There the black one will attack.*'

Her face went bleak. Tschan was scared by her expression. 'I'm getting back inside,' Tschan muttered frantically
to herself. With clumsy haste, the Purple Feather descended
through the open hatch, leaving Tschea alone on the roof
with the grasslands only minutes away.

Tschea remained where she was, gazing at the fields and
gentle parkland about and behind. She could see no motion
in the darkening landscape. The grasslands grew closer.
There was as much safety up here as down below: there
was no safety at all. She felt incapable of thinking conse-
quentially. Reason and memory were overcast by the lower-
ing atmosphere. The night of the Harvest Festival belonged
to a defunct reality. Her dream of the delta had become so
vague she could scarcely recall it, let alone continue to
attach importance to it. Endless inconsequentials webbed
her perception, endless doubts and questions were pricking,
hurting, disrupting her.

Perhaps the madman was right. Perhaps nothing mattered.

The front line of Darsans rode cautiously into the grass,
followed by the first of the wagons. The road here was little
more than an unrutted trail, initially wide enough for two

carriages side by side, but quickly narrowing as it penetrated deeper into the grass. The tough-stemmed growth was
constantly being hacked back; keeping the roads through
the grasslands open was a continual job for hundreds.

Now there was a puff of wind and the great green sea
rustled ominously. Sighing like an army of sad departed
souls, its overhanging tips nodded under the deepening
thunderheads as it swallowed the caravan. As the White
Feather's carriage entered the green jungle, Clarai was trying to soothe Wanunch. His rainbow cheeks were smeared
with tears.

Cuinneale sat opposite them, thin white hands gripping
the edge of his embroidered seat. There was fear in his expression.

He could sense the proximity of his fate.

And so could Nikosner. The black mage was feverish
with anticipation as the caravan drew close to ambush. He
could smell the collective fear. He fancied he could pick out
the sour tang of Cuinneale's emotion from the general
emanation. Fifteen years he'd waited! Now there was only
a screen of grass to separate them. And the Darsans. But the
time was his. The plan was laid – he knew about the munitions wagon. His scouts had trailed the caravan from
Schroun. The Darsan deserters had been captured, tortured
for information.

He'd been waiting here with thirty horsemen concealed in
the grass, waiting motionlessly, muscular hands gripping the
pommel of his saddle. He was small, powerful, dressed all in
black on a coal-black horse, his waxed black hair shining
like his tight-stretched skin. A gleaming rock-crystal was set
in the middle of his forehead – the bone had been cut away
to accommodate it.

Now half the caravan was into the grass. Nikosner's men
were ready for his signal. He could hardly contain himself.
Behind him, his two lieutenants saw how he trembled.
They exchanged taut glances. One was a huge yellow-haired
man with a mutilated face. The other was scalp-locked,
rawboned. They'd followed him from Kor, where the vision
of Ussian burning had first seized him. They held drawn

swords. They'd wanted to attack head-on the moment the caravan had been reported in sight; that was their instinct. Nikosner had insisted otherwise. And Nikosner awed them.

Now the waiting was as unbearable as the pressure of the air.

Nikosner's shaking was growing more intense.

The god-fit seizes him again, thought the rawboned one anxiously. *May he vent it on his enemies, and not on us. . . .*

Kanlo licked cracked lips. Soon his wagon would be swallowed up in the ominous grass. He was sure that the sky was about to spill something more fatal than a thunderstorm.

He'd forgotten about the madman tied up behind him.

Liam's eyes were wide open beneath the sack.

He was awake. He was filled with energy. He could sense the threat of the sky, the disquiet of his captor, and he could sense watchers. It was time to abandon negativity. While drugged in the gulf he'd had an experience that gave him direction. What he'd felt was a stabilizing commitment ... if he could hold on to it. He flexed his bound body, searching for his limbs, for the position of the knots. Returning feeling was an agony, pins and needles running him through. He continued his slow flexing until his blood coursed more freely. Then he began a methodical attack on the knots of the cords which bound him. The terrified man at the reins a few feet away was paying him no attention. Beneath the sack, beneath the blankets, he worked patiently on the cord which bound his wrists. It was difficult, for his fingers were still numb. But now he felt internally coherent. The worst of his mental struggle appeared to be past, leaving him only his physical incarceration to overcome.

I'm not the Mutant's puppet, he thought, *and I'm not who I was*. The glare was gone. It had been a derangement of his own energies, unrecognized as such, occurring whenever he'd fought to force himself into the mold of a former personality – a personality which he'd confused with his very soul – a dead personality incompetent to cope with present necessities.

His mind was lucid, and he felt no need to question his sudden change of attitude. His songborne flight while in the drugged gulf ... he'd think about it later. Now his hands were almost free. The attack was almost due. Where was the lady who'd rescued him? Who was she? He'd have been dead by now if not for her intervention – and she wouldn't have been so determined if not for the dream of the delta which she'd talked about. The Zuni Bird. What did the Zuni Bird stand for? Was there a connection between the Zuni Bird and the experience he'd just had? Now his hands were free, and he attacked the rope which bound the sack around his arms. The delta. Circumstance indicated the delta as a destination for both of them. He wondered if she remembered her dream. She was right – sanity was possible, sublimity too.

The wagon was almost into the grass. He picked faster. Still Kanlo didn't notice. Liam heard the storm grumbling, felt the pressure imbalances of the disordered atmosphere. And he sensed Nikosner waiting in concealment, sensed a mind controlled by imperatives unknown to itself. He sensed ... presences watching, presences connected with the outlaw who lay in wait. For Nikosner radiated a manic ecstasy which Liam felt clearly in the instant that he was free. Then ... Nikosner screamed. ...

12 : Cuinneale's Fate

Demented, the scream sliced from the grass through the gloom and into every head the length of the caravan. Eyes started wide, bodies hit floors as the Darsans wheeled, nocking arrows, uncertain. The thick penumbral air was riddled by shrieks, by the drumming of hooves, by hasty commands and the bellowing of oxen. Heart hammering, Tschea sprawled flat on her roof.

Clarai was astounded by Cuinneale's reaction. Even in her own fear she was amazed by his metamorphosis from gray ghost to abject human being. His emotion was naked, and she saw him for the first time as Wanunch bawled, as the grass waved, shook, as Nikosner came howling at the head of his band. They burst out onto the trail at a dozen points. Clarai saw two go down immediately, hit by the only accurate arrows in the Darsans' hurried flight. Disordered blue-gold clashed and closed with the motley brigands who came slashing with two-edged swords, but the brigands had the momentum and the certainty, and blue-gold fell back.

Nikosner led his men straight for the rear wagons; he disdained the carriages altogether. Bewilderment. Was looting his only objective? Crouching, Clarai couldn't believe it, and she saw that Cuinneale couldn't either. The carriages had stopped, and the teams were in confusion. A wounded horse was screaming. The heavy air was filled with ringing, cursing clamor as the brigands surrounded the munitions wagon in front of Kanlo's.

Kanlo had dropped the reins with shock at the mind-tearing pitch of Nikosner's scream, and he was still sitting frozen as a huge lizard-faced outlaw came at him with sword raised high. A Darsan arrow missed the outlaw and hissed into the wooden frame by Kanlo's head, but the outlaw was diverted by another Darsan the instant before his sword could take Kanlo's head. Kanlo snapped into motion. He dived backward into his wagon in panic, and the wagon shuddered and half-left the ground as a whinnying horse backed into it. A fallen Darsan was crushed beneath a wheel as the wagon plunged down again. Steel rang all around as Kanlo turned, gasping, scrabbling for cover, meaning to burrow deep.

He saw, and he howled with horror.

He saw a white-matted specter rising from the baggage, saw a frightful face in which only the eyes weren't hoary, and they burned with an inhuman intensity. Kanlo threw up his hands, started backing off, the physical danger behind forgotten in the face of this threat to his soul. Outside, the struggle was fierce. The master of the munitions wagon was dead, his skull split by Nikosner's sword. Nikosner was at the reins, for the raiders had succeeded in turning the wagon and its team. Kanlo appeared backward at the front of his wagon as the raiders whipped up the munitions wagon against a wall of desperately fighting Darsans. Heavy drops of rain began to fall. And a thrown knife sprouted from Kanlo's back. It stopped him. He arched up straight and stiff amid the melee of bucking horses, clashing swords, and twisted faces; his eyes and hands jerked up to meet the start of deluge from the blackest of heavens. Lightning forked into the grasslands to the west. For an instant everything was frozen, outlined in electric blue.

From her rain-drummed roof Tschea saw how Nikosner lashed the wagon-team against the Darsans. The wagon was parallel with Kanlo's, and momentarily she saw Kanlo, standing crucified through the angles of cleaving swords. Biting her lip, she raised herself up. What of the musician...?

Then the violent tableau lost its freeze and disappeared as rain poured solid from the murk, drowning even the clamor of the fight.

Kanlo fell forward into his wagon, hopelessly grabbing for the knife. His sight was fatally clear through the murk as he fell. He saw the madman grab up the scarlet instrument, saw him dive from the back of the wagon past trampling hooves into the safety of the grass. Unable to reach the knife in his back, Kanlo lay against the empty flour sack with blood in his mouth. Flour. Now he knew why the madman had looked so hoary. He would have laughed, but he died as the sky growled and broke with a crash; he died, damning his own stupidity.

Hard-pressed at the reins of the munitions wagon, Nikosner saw the red-haired madman dive from the wagon. For an instant as the thunder crashed, the madman turned and looked at Nikosner through the rain, through the failing wall of Darsans. And each recognized in the other an enemy in some conflict which neither as yet fully understood. Their eyes clashed briefly. Then a falling body intervened, the Darsans broke, and Nikosner had no chance to pursue the changed one from the battle.

Whipping up the frightened team, the brigand and his
men retreated, leaving eight of their number dead and
wounded along with fourteen Darsan casualties. The out-
laws disappeared into the rain. The wounded crawled on the
track which was already churned into mud as carriage doors
opened tentatively. The Darsans pressed the slippery pursuit, though several rode off in other directions, deserting.
And Cuinneale was among those who stood in the rain,
quickly drenched, peering into the murk. He was shaking.
Was it possible he might live? He couldn't believe it.

He couldn't see or hear a thing through the storm.

Then lightning speared again.

And his hopes were dashed by expectation amounting to
certainty.

For he saw how, hundreds of yards away, the raiders had
abandoned the munitions wagon to the pursuing Darsans.
He saw how Nikosner jumped from the wagon onto a horse
guided alongside by one of his ruffians, and how the black
mage galloped off. Then the murk descended again.

The Darsans closed around the wagon. The glow warned
them too late.

Their lieutenant threw herself at the pile of burning rags
which Nikosner had left against a powder keg's open bung-
hole. The explosion beat back the storm, blended with the
thunder crashing closer. It blew the remaining Darsans to
shreds.

Deep in the grass, Liam was whipped by agitated stems.
Wide-brimmed hats were blown off the heads of some
standing bowed in the rain. Clarai, her eyes misted by confused emotion, saw how Cuinneale was among those who
turned and fled into the grass as pandemonium broke out
the length of the caravan.

For the brigands were charging again with nobody to
stop them.

Nikosner was coming, howling high and audible through
the elements.

Something in his pitch froze minds, glued feet to splatter-
ing mud.

Several team-masters tried to whip up and get the caravan
moving.

There was no coordination, no room. The bottleneck at the narrowing of the trail was firmly plugged by two carriages grinding alongside a wagon stuck axle-deep in mud. The deluge grew more ferocious as the raiders came sweeping up the buckled, helpless caravan. They came howling for Cuinneale as lightning seared and thunder roared closer. Tschea counted more than twenty of the dark horsemen. They burst through the men and women caught in their path, and to her they seemed as elementally hostile as the spearing rain. They were riders of plague and death, appropriate to this time, with their dark and inchoate auras. . . .

Nikosner dismounted at a run when he came to the bottleneck. He grabbed a terrified Red Feather by the neck and jerked up her chin.

'Where's Cuinneale?' he hissed. 'Where's my lovely benefactor?'

Lightning struck close. The Red Feather saw what held her, and she was sick at the way he shivered. He slapped her. Trembling, she pointed at Clarai's carriage as thunder clapped. Dropping her, Nikosner went at a run to the carriage with five men at his heels, while the others remained on horseback, patrolling the caravan. The shaken Red Feather was helped to her feet by friends, and the nearest brigand didn't object. Again, some people were wild enough to hope. Perhaps Cuinneale was the only one Nikosner wanted. If they did nothing to offend the brigands . . .

As Nikosner came to Clarai, a young Contractual was being held from attacking the black mage by those in his carriage. The Contractual's eyes were mad with hate. Nikosner sensed the hate very clearly, but he paid no heed, and jumped into Clarai's carriage. The White Feather was sitting there with Wanunch buried in the folds of her robe. Nikosner scanned her coldly, and she flinched. There was no human warmth beneath those heavy lids. He was repulsively fascinating. He had a serpentine quality enhanced by the way he shivered as he bent, by the sinuosity of his hand reaching down to stroke Wanunch's beautiful skin, by the labored hiss of his voice. 'Cuin . . . neale,' he breathed, running thick, sensual fingers from the rigid boy to his mesmer-

ized mother as the sky flashed and bellowed. 'Where iss my
... long-lost friend...?'

The shuddering touch of his wet fingers grew an ache in
her head. She couldn't think, she couldn't answer, she closed
her eyes to his gelid black menace. Suddenly vicious, he
jerked Wanunch from her by the hair. The boy was much
too terrified to utter a sound when the knife-point pricked
his neck.

'... Say now ... what dir-ec-tion did ... the archfiend
take...?'

Clarai sat upright with fascinated eyes. The knife-point
twitched, cut a little. Wanunch was limp in Nikosner's
grasp. Nikosner's eyelids drooped lazily as Clarai struggled
to control her nerves. He shivered with an apparently un-
controlled spasm. The knife cut a little more. Blood began
trickling down the rainbow skin. With great difficulty
Clarai raised a leaden arm and pointed out the direction
Cuinneale had taken. Nikosner made her dizzy. The sky
flashed again. Nikosner considered her frozen face. His
mouth fell open. His teeth were perfect. He howled with
laughter. Then he threw Wanunch on top of Clarai, and
leaped out into the downpour as the sky crashed again.

Dazed spectators saw his men gather around him, follow
him as he stamped and staggered up and down, barking
orders, giggling under his breath. Half his men plunged into
the grass in the opposite direction to that which Clarai had
pointed out. He sighed enormously, rolled his eyes at the
teeming sky. His time was come at last. Fifteen days since
epileptic vision had indicated the return from exile – and
fifteen years since the seizures had first taken him, since
Ussian had expelled him. Now the world echoed his own
madness. The demon king he'd be, worshiped by thousands! In the seas of madness! In the great turbulence to
which he'd been prematurely condemned by Cuinneale's
ambition and inefficiency.

Cuinneale!

He was impatient for Cuinneale to be dragged from the
grass.

He shivered, grinned, scowled through the darkness and
the din, went lurching up and down the caravan with four

of his men behind him. Their dark moving shapes jerked frozen from one bright electric instant to the next. Many people cowering in carriages watched this strange procession, waiting to discover whether they'd be killed, raped, drowned, or burned first. Ussian was a forgotten unreality. Others stood like bedraggled statues in the rain, or lay where they'd fallen, or stumbled aimlessly as Nikosner came lurching past them like a prehensile drunkard, raving high-pitched idiocies echoed by his men.

Tschea hadn't moved. Plastered flat on her roof, she'd seen how Tschan had been knocked spinning by a charging horse, how Frith and Urseen had tried to comfort the injured woman. Tschea had felt nothing at all. Now she could hear screams from the grass, but they meant nothing. The hallucinatory unreality of the madness, the rain's drumming, the sky's charged flickering – she was numb. Now she could see Nikosner lurching past, his arms and legs gone wild. His senseless gibbering poisoned her mind with feral images, his violent shaking was infectious, and her teeth began to chatter as he passed below, as he capered through the storm like a clown, like a demon king with an entourage of aping jesters armed with bloody swords, shrieking jesters who broadcast fear and senseless words. Nothing made sense to Tschea; none of her thoughts could connect in this chaos. What had Cuinneale done? She couldn't think. She couldn't feel.

Then lightning revealed how Cuinneale was being dragged from the grass by two of Nikosner's men, just two carriages farther up.

Tschea stared emptily into subsequent murk as Nikosner scented his enemy. He turned. He howled. He ran to his revenge with a crab's scuttling speed. Cuinneale was thrown in the mud at his feet near the bottleneck. Nikosner kicked him in the ribs. Cuinneale rolled with the kick like a rag doll. He'd lost his direction in the grass, had almost completely looped back; he hadn't resisted the brutal capture. It was his time. He was being replaced. He knew it. Now, through a blur, he half-saw the dark forest of legs all around. Fate had caught up.

Panting as if the atmosphere held too little oxygen, Nikosner seemed less like a human than an elemental being. He gestured. His men went to chivy everyone from the carriages and wagons. Even the injured were forced into the spectator circle that formed around Nikosner and Cuinneale, near the bottleneck, pushing out into the grass. Several brief struggles took place before the circle was complete with nearly seventy overcharged people. Tschea remained on her roof. She hadn't yet been seen or remembered – by anyone.

Holding Wanunch, Clarai was pushed past storm-numbed faces to the inside of the circle, shaking her head with disbelief.

For the streaming murk above the circle appeared to be glowing.

From the steely wet grayness grew a pulsing, reflective luminosity, an aureate haze which was brightest immediately above Nikosner.

The brigand was shivering too fast to watch comfortably, and there was something hypnotic about his shivering. Clarai saw him squat down, saw him take Cuinneale by the jaw and jerk the gray ghost to trembling feet.

Cuinneale's eyes were taken by three – by Nikosner's two natural eyes, by a third, the rock-crystal set in the middle of his forehead. There was silence save for the rain as Nikosner stood shivering, still with his fingertips prodding up the soft flesh behind Cuinneale's jaw, mesmerizing the other man. Above his head the incomprehensible light grew and ebbed, grew again, stronger, brighter. The storm was moving away now. But nobody noticed it now. They were held by the slow execution.

Cuinneale ... his mind was gone into a soft, sickening spin.

For Nikosner's face was a shimmering mask, a gleam too fast to fix on, a misfeatured chaos ... was a mirror in which Cuinneale read his own death ... his rejection by those he'd served, half-unconsciously, for so many years. Through Nikosner's fingertips rippled the icy power of those who'd invaded him. Cuinneale's face was blank as Nikosner embraced him, at first almost tenderly, taking him tight in prehensile arms, taking him so that Cuinneale was shaken through with Nikosner's shaking, with violent images, suppressed memories, so that he hardly knew now that Nikosner was crushing the life from him.

They were so tightly merged that now they were like one shivering creature haloed by the strange gleams and flashes which darted and pulsed in the air above ... as if light from some other dimension were breaking through here, supplanting the natural light of Miir. Nikosner's men saw it, they saw how the slackening rain washed foam from his lips, how his features had melted together in an extremity of shivering: many of them looked down. The god-fit was about to break loose. He was about to drench them with his vision again. Many of them sensed that they were being watched. Others in the circle felt this. Spellbound, they couldn't move, though the atmosphere building was too tense and alien to bear. This sense of being *watched* froze them as much as the pitiless horror of Cuinneale's dying.

The flickering, reflecting light ... behind the thickening of the glow they sensed watchers, disembodied intelligences which studied them curiously and without compassion. Cuinneale felt them too, and half-remembered the days of his youth before he'd come to Ussian.... His face was purple, hopeless, and he stared desperately upward for a second before his eyes were recaptured.... The glow, now it churned with vague colors which slid in and out of vision; it hinted at shapes which changed and reflected off each other, seeming to take greater solidity with each reflection. Now not even Nikosner's men could resist the fascination of it. Some of them feared for themselves, and secretly they cursed the day they'd met Nikosner. For this fit was more intense than any he'd ever grown before, and it was still building....

Cuinneale was all but drowned in roarings, thunderings; in images of judgment and condemnation, while the glow grew thick and yellow as butter which greased smooth through every disordered mind, greased them with images of what had been and what would be; with the images of a future which nobody was in a fit state to reject as insane.

Tschea was flat on her roof, fifty feet away; the images

stirred in her mind and held her – they translated into her personal terms.

Cuinneale promised to make Nikosner a genius. Cuinneale gave Nikosner vision, gave him madness too. Fifteen years! Nikosner's still mad dog in glare of beast visions! Now times are mad, times are Nikosner's, times are One-Eye's. Who can resist the glare? Mad dog Nikosner pays his debts. Cuinneale rejected Nikosner. Cuinneale dies. Ussian rejected Nikosner – now Ussian must destroy and curse itself in sacrifice to the Mutant who is Lord in All. Cuinneale dies! Ussian dies! All is accomplished. See Ussian burn in One-Eye!

Then Tschea saw Cuinneale drop dead to the mud.

This wasn't why she cried out, involuntarily, at the same time as many other people.

For Ussian was burning above the grasslands.

In the air a great green emerald spun, rotated with sparkling facets, drew them into itself as it transformed into an unbearably gorgeous flower of flame. Nikosner howled. He fell to the mud beside his dead enemy with limbs and body arched; he began humping through the rain-spattered pools with eyeballs jerked up into his skull, shrieking up at the sinuous vision burning, ridding himself of the intolerable energy which fueled it, caught in commands beyond his knowing.

Faces frozen like gargoyles stared up as the spires and combs of the Tarasse took clear shape, banishing the twitching rain. The flaming city began crackling in every mind. It was a strange burning. The flame of it twisted high, but it seemed cold, and was tinged with the color of ice. In many it stimulated an immediate fierce joy; quickly it took up a mass of people on its implicit command. Destroy Ussian, sacrifice their city to the Divine Mutant – what other propitiation could there be? The watchers were forgotten as the lust to destroy spread from mind to mind.

Clarai shouted with joy to see her prison dissolving beneath crowns of transforming fire, and she longed to apply the torch herself. Horses screamed, oxen bellowed – they were trapped in their traces as the circle began to break up, as people fell into slavishly adoring imitations of Nikosner's epileptic writhings. He knew! He had the light! Others stood rooted, fighting the mounting fire of unwanted change inside them, desperately resisting the destruction of their wills. They fought. One by one, they succumbed. The glare grew too bright. The city flamed outside them, inside them; the reflections of innumerable cities flaming caught them in all angles and degrees ... reflecting from themselves, from the faces around them, from the sky ... from the forgotten, drowned-out watchers.

Soon, Nikosner was surrounded by beasts who scratched the burning air with him – their baying was sweet music. Projection of the vision was intolerable agony, and it tore him apart every time ... yet now his enemies fueled it with their own energetic imagination. They'd tear up Ussian, stone by stone, cursing every one. Converted, they'd convert the rest of the deranged population. Those trying to escape to the delta would be destroyed. The delta! The Zuni Bird – it would never sing! With Ussian converted ... turned over to the Divine Mutant ...

Nikosner could see nothing beyond the destruction of Ussian.

Beyond it lay blankness, darkness, without even reflections.

Then ... but before then, his revenge. So sweet! Enough!

In this bittersweet agony of conquest he'd forgotten the red-hair.

Why the thoroughness of the cursing and destruction, he didn't know. He knew it was necessary. That was all. He writhed around Cuinneale's dead body with his flip-flopping worshipers, ancient pains exploding, and the Green Emerald flamed from every one of them.

Caught up in the burning city, Tschea stood, was about to join the worshipers and submit herself to Nikosner's vision. She was in Ussian. Running its streets, past the cursed rubble of the Inila Way, falling through the dark burning ... an alien burning. For she felt the watchers behind the cold flickering flames: it was as if they waited for the completion of destruction, so that they might materialize. She didn't want to be in Ussian when that happened. Somewhere, fading inside her, was the feeling that Nikosner was hostile to everything she believed innately. And her children ... Cassa, Flath, Larene ... she was sure they were lost inside the doomed Tarasse. She had to find them – they must escape. But how, where? The road to the delta was blocked, the city was closed, and there was no way out. Her doubts were dying – she could no longer sense the watchers. Of a sudden, all she could think of was the sublimity of sacrificing Ussian to the Mutant.

With yellow dress clinging tight she jumped heavily from the carriage into the soaking grass. She turned toward the writhing celebrants, filled with a horrible delight which she could not resist.

She would have been lost there and then but for the hand which came from behind to grip her shoulder, but for the sharpness of the voice:

'Come away! It's not One-Eye he worships, not the Mutant who feeds him with power. I sense some other confusion, hostile to the delta! You are being used. We must get away from here. Now!'

Liam had watched from the grass. The brigand's eyes ... in them, Liam had sensed a dark possession. The brigand had seen him, Liam knew that, and he'd been tempted to flee immediately. But it had been quickly apparent that Nikosner could not spare the time or energy to chase him now. So he'd waited. Watched Cuinneale's death. Watched the vision grow. With a dispossessed Darsan horse already claimed, he was ready to ride off at any moment when he saw Tschea, standing on her roof, about to join the madness around Nikosner.

He'd thought swiftly. He'd decided.

So he came to her before she could join the writhers.

Her first reaction to his hand, his voice, was one of fury.

She swung to see the red-haired man. His pale eyes were energetic, and his hair was plastered. He led a horse. His grip on her shoulder was firm, and she couldn't break it. She struck out in panic, ineffectually.

'Devil! My children are burning! Let me be!'

'They burn in reflection, in fantasy – it's not real. Wake up!'

Now she half-recognized him. They argued. His insistences broke through, so she stood uncertainly, shivering, with the hideous worshiping going on so close.

'Who are you? Why do you want me with you?'

'Who are you? Why did you take me from Schroun?'

She was dazed. She touched her tattoo, shook her head.

'I don't remember,' she mumbled. 'I feel very confused....'

'You'll feel less confused once we're away from here. Come on!'

And before she knew what was going on, she found herself being hoisted up onto the saddle of the Darsan horse, a roan animal. Liam mounted behind her. Before she had a chance to object he'd twitched the reins; the scared animal was only too glad to take them away from Nikosner, away from the caravan.

Only two saw them leave.

One was wounded, a Darsan lying near the shattered remnants of the munitions wagon. She was dying. And when the burning city had drained from the clearing atmosphere, when Nikosner's fit was over, the caravan continued toward Ussian with its passengers spellbound, the Darsan was left to die. And neither Tschan, Urseen, nor Frith now remembered Tschea to realize that she was gone. The past was dead. They were no longer members of the Feather Guild. They were Nikosner's storm-troopers.

The other one who saw Liam and Tschea leave was Lonawi, the Cyclone.

He had his orders. He followed them, alone, and at a distance. He knew how little time there was, but he couldn't contact them. Not yet, and perhaps, not at all.

Part III : Liam and Tschea

13 : The Nature of the Change

And already before Nikosner came the Green Emerald was turned red and lurid. Abramel hadn't lasted long; neither had the order which he'd been left to maintain. In the first two days after the caravan left there were dozens of different riots which his Guards put down with increasing violence. Ussian's people were splitting apart in dissension (dissension about the rumors, dissension about everything it was possible to dissent about, including the cause of all their dissension), even before the first dizzy-eyed madman from the battle came to the city. He was a giant Yellowbelt, weak with self-mortifications, wild with fierce exhortations to repent, for a new kingdom was at hand. Hundreds heard him and felt him before he was killed; after that curious currents tugged at their minds, seemed to be shredding their physical substance, and they shook.

Then another madman came – and another – and another. On the third, fourth, and fifth days, the Green Emerald babbled faster and faster; hundreds of people were seized by a dancing mania, as if continual agitated movement was the only way to tolerate the new energy shaking inside them. The Guards, as influenced as everyone else, were impotent and soon had no control over the city.

Tah Ti emerged from hiding, began talking everywhere about the Zuni Bird, about A'Yaya's Tale. 'This is the awaited time! Go to the delta, now; go there and wait with the whales and dolphin-folk who sense it too! Go now, for great danger threatens; it's not wise to remain in Ussian. Go to the delta, the heart of Miir; join those who wait there already, wait patiently!' And by the night of the fifth day the white flash of the Zuni Bird was chalked, painted, scrawled, daubed everywhere. When they weren't fighting, dancing, or running wild, people now argued violently about this new strangeness, about A'Yaya's Tale and what it might really mean. Had Analee after all been a true herald?

Was this the time foretold? Certainly, it was true what Tah Ti said about the sea-creatures converging in the Bay of Whales. They seemed to be awaiting something. And there was nothing left to wait for in Ussian. Many took Tah Ti's advice and set out for the delta.

Many others didn't. Either they disbelieved, or they were incapable of listening any longer. For everyone was going crazy at once; after several days the arrival of more survivors from the battle was hardly noticed – their shaking was easily swallowed in the general shaking of the city. There were other warnings. Several Leapers had suggested that people should leave now; in Nikosner they sensed a threat of great magnitude, though they couldn't clearly read the nature of the threat. There was a general exodus from the Tarasse, many going toward Mantrim, the land of the Cyclone Colleges and independent communities.

Tschea's three remaining children were among those taken away.

On the sixth day after the caravan's departure, Guards on duty at the Pit at the eastern end of the city assisted the mass breakout by the two thousand who'd been locked up there since the troubles began. And Abramel was assassinated by his own men as the escaped prisoners surged through the city. Chimalus was ecstatic among them, peacockry and position forgotten, a warlike and wild-eyed bear. So Khassam was dead, the new conqueror was incomprehensible, the plague was beyond understanding, the End might well be at hand . . . but Chimalus was alive again in the mounting chaos of Ussian, even if his head raged senselessly, even if he had less and less idea of who and where he was. The ex-Jerezid Consul was among the thousands swallowed in the growing ferment, immune to the lure of the delta, losing all sense of space and time, caught in a gathering mental field in which imagination began to manifest nakedly, in which causality was fast losing all meaning.

Senseless crime quickly grew to epidemic proportions. Arson flourished, few warehouses went unlooted, food was soon in short supply, and disease began to spread. Mobs surged, and anyone suspected of being a Cyclone was lynched. The Tarasse was ransacked. Two Preconceptuals who'd remained behind bravely tried to tell the mob that the madness had a simple biochemical explanation – a reduction of the sugar supply to the brain, they said. They were lynched. Cults proliferated, and human sacrifices were being made to ancient, long-forgotten deities from the dark side of the mind as gangs went raiding in bars, in brothels, and in the houses of the wealthy. Bodies lay in gutters, many hid in darkened corners, petrifying and starving to death, frozen by the destruction of their world-views. Ghostly shapes were seen in the daylight air and were differently interpreted by the increasing numbers of shaking people able to see them; it was as if a myriad wild thoughts now took semi-material form for the instant of their duration. And by night the sky above Ussian flickered and glowed as if electrically charged by the collective energy released below.

So that when Nikosner brought the caravan to Ussian on the evening of the eighth day, delirious chaos was rampant: the city was a death-trap. Many already fled for the lesser intensity of the countryside. Many had gone west, to the delta, not so far away, where it seemed there was a chance that a different spirit might prevail. And it was not only from Ussian that people had gone to the delta: in many lands there were people who felt the magic lure of the southwest.

Many set out. Many never got there.

Some were sidetracked or killed along the way.

Others were drawn into the cursing of Ussian.

One-Eye had come to Zagrin, followed by many thousands. There had been no opposition, only fearful worship. Now the Mutant dreamed in the Chaguine Palace which the Jerezids had built, dreamed in the arms of an enormous woman with blue flower eyes, dreamed while the mumen danced around him in ceaseless celebration. The Mutant paid no attention to the disordered world outside the Palace. His act was performed, his dream was spreading, so there was no more need for his intervention. And he could not be touched or harmed until all people were agreed upon his true name. In the confusion he'd begun this was hardly likely.

So the Mutant dreamed of what went on in the lands, of other powers striving for advantages in the confusion caused by the coming-together of Mutant and mumen. Dreamed of how the chaos accelerated most quickly in the cities and large communities.

What was happening in Ussian was by no means atypical – until Nikosner came. If anything, the chaos in the land of the Zuni Bird was less virulent at first. Yet Miir faced a great threat.

What was the nature of One-Eye, of the Change?

Everywhere, thinkers speculated. A myriad theories proliferated in a short time before the chaos speeded up and the thinkers forgot what they'd been thinking about. Societies fragmented and fell apart in hours, days. It was incomprehensible. For there were no comets in the sky, the sun hadn't stopped shining, and the birds still sang. Only humanity seemed to be affected – in as many ways as human imagination could project. Flight served only to spread the contagion, for flight was only undertaken once the danger was realized, and in realization lay the dreadful shaking. People reacted according to their natures, their unknown natures. Many committed suicide in the first bleak despair of total alienation from themselves. Many hid hopelessly, from themselves, from the war-bands that rampaged everywhere. Some set out for Zagrin to pay the Mutant homage, hoping that thus they'd recover their balance. Others punished themselves and others for the sinfulness which had brought this catastrophe. Social barriers disappeared, the rich and respectable turned out to be as feral as all others, as the accumulated tensions of their lives exploded. And by the time Nikosner had reached Ussian, the populations of every former Jerezid land – except in parts of Lamassa – had begun to swarm like deranged bees.

Lamassa lay northeast of Phrenge, east of Spokane, west of Zagrin.

The human beings who lived in their dreary land were

caught up in as vicious a frenzy as humans everywhere else.

Not the Unmen.

The Hou'on sages had prepared their mirror-worshiping people.

Nobody had ever learned much about the Unman race. Not even the Cyclones were sure of their origin. Some said the Unmen had come from the skies at the time of the Great Forgetting, but it was more popularly believed that they'd revolved into this dimension from another earth — possibly in flight, possibly seeking living-space. Since the Middle Kingdom at least they'd occupied the northern part of Lamassa, living in half a dozen villages built on artificial lakes. They never traveled physically. Some speculated that their vibrations were different from those of humans native to this earth, that they couldn't materialize outside their own territory unless invited – or unless land was abandoned and cursed by those occupying it. But for hundreds of years they'd kept themselves to themselves, not communicating with neighbors, living in their peculiar fashion.

Their villages were connected with and surrounded by a geometric network of dead straight roads built to cross at places of natural energy and power. At every crossroads stood four of the great mirrors before which the Unmen were said to sacrifice themselves, perhaps in the belief that they'd be caught up to some higher plane of existence. Nobody but the Unmen understood how the mirrors worked or what they were. Another belief was that such ceremonies let the Unmen discard their bodies to take over the minds and bodies of human beings. They were feared. Tah Ti had often said that they were a race of doppelgangers, aspecting personalities of people alive in the world elsewhere. Who knew? The Unmen never gave clues. The forces of Kalnakill and Khassam had swept through Lamassa as through every other land; yet neither father nor son had ever quite shaken off the uncomfortable feeling that the Unmen only played at being conquered.

Now the Jerezids had fallen, One-Eye was come, and the Unmen had closed in on themselves. In the lake-villages they gathered in solemn communal trances, silent, austere.

At every crossroads the Hou'ons met naked in their Sevens.

And some people were increasingly sure that the Unmen were using the confusion of the Mutant's coming to win an invisible war which had been thirty-five years in the waging. A war which grew daily more open and obvious in the transformation of the change. A war to do with whether or not the Zuni Bird should sing through Miir....

The atmosphere at the delta was very curious. Though so close to the carnage of Ussian, though frightened multitudes were streaming past into the supposed safety of the Mantrim peninsula, the delta seemed to grant exemption from the general pandemonium.

Thousands of believers in the Zuni Bird were arriving by the hour to join those already encamped along the misty shoreline. Most were gathered amid the scrubby dunes between Naenshe and Lansalle. And they waited patiently, though scarcely silently, for increasingly they felt the presence which the delta emanated. It was like some vast subliminal pulse which went a long way toward neutralizing their confusion; many felt they were in a holy place. The local people watched the arrivals and felt the charged atmosphere; they whispered among themselves that the Zuni Bird was awakening. The colonies of birds knew it, and their continual raucous clamor was excited. And there was the congregation of sea-creatures in the bay – great schools of dolphins leaping and tagging each other in the bay beyond the outermost margins, whales which waited with a more leisurely dignity, and other intelligent beings of the sea.

So beings were gathering, waiting all around the dangerous expanse of mudbanks and clashing currents, many scarcely knowing what they awaited – though it was something other than panic-stricken hope which had brought them here. At night they saw strange lights flickering, drifting above the mudbanks, and the delta seemed to be alive; they listened to the roaring of sudden waves, and agreed they didn't want to be the first to venture out there in search of the Zuni Bird, no matter what ecstasies were to be won in the first light of this strange new time.

*   *   *

When it was known that Nikosner had come to Ussian, a new mood took hold of the thousands who waited. They sensed crisis, and it drew them together into the pulse of the delta. Somehow they knew that Nikosner represented an acute threat to the hoped-for awakening of the Zuni Bird.

It was that same evening, with great banks of cloud hanging ponderous over the Bay, that the Cyclones suddenly came among them.

Many adepts of the Inner Vortex came walking through the crowds, among the dunes and down the alleys of ramshackle encampments, openly declaring who they were, why they'd come. They moved with purposeful confidence as if welcome, dressed in unadorned white robes, talking with crisp directness to people who were at first unsure and suspicious.

'Nikosner works for a concealed enemy which is not the Mutant. If you have mirrors, destroy them now: we must learn to work together and fight for the Zuni Bird. If Ussian's cursed, we'll be lost.'

The Master of Baethnan came. He was a powerful man in his mid-forties, moving easily and thinking clearly despite the crisis. Several Cyclone Colleges were being attacked by mobs who blamed the brotherhood for the madness. Adepts were active throughout Mantrim and Miir, many incognito. The matter of Ussian would be decided in the next two days.

Namahon was with the Master. The boy was excited by the atmosphere, and he gazed eagerly at the misty delta and at the growing crowds.

'When do we start?' he asked the Master, his eyes shining.

'Tomorrow morning we'll go around the outer margins in a boat. Then we'll see what you can pick up.' There was a hint of affectionate pride in the Master's voice. 'The key point may have shifted since Analee's time. You must build up your concentration in the fashion I've taught.'

'But what about Tschea and the man with the songmachine?'

'They must commit themselves to the delta of their own wills.' The Master was stern. 'We'll know he's suitable if

and when he plays the delta-pulse. If he feels it, then we'll
open a Gateway.'

'What if they're taken over? Don't you care about
Tschea?'

'We can't risk infiltration. We must be absolutely sure
before we bring them here – or the Zuni Bird will not fly
through Miir.'

Proud but dubious, Namahon followed his father into the
crowds.

14: Visions in the night

The sun had been setting, splendidly golden, as the Darsan
horse carried the two of them northwest, from wide moors
toward lower woods and pastures where long-horned cattle
grazed. Liam was in tune. The world sparkled as if newly
minted. The sky was aglow, the breeze was zestful, and the
open land about was emerald, lemon, russet. He felt as
sharp as the tip of a pyramid, better than he had done for
many days.

Tschea was in confusion. Half in his arms, half in the
saddle, she was a sodden weight, shaking with cold and the
pain of drifting mind. Soon he'd have to find shelter and
make a fire before pneumonia was added to her troubles.
She was internally fragmented, almost oblivious of his
company. From time to time she looked at him briefly, fret-
fully, brushing ringlets of hair from her haunted face. He
kept talking to her. His own experiences were only a general
indication of her condition; everything was so subjective.
What to say, how to tune into each other? She was very
strange. He wasn't quite sure why he'd taken her. Perhaps
because she attracted him. Perhaps because she was at the
center of a growing mystery, one which tugged at his mind,
tugged at his body – to the southwest. It was difficult to ride
north – all his instincts strained against it. The natural lay
of the land indicated the southwest. But first of all he

wanted to put distance between himself and Nikosner. He wanted to find a place to think. For he was sure to meet Nikosner again. So he rode on down toward the pastures, holding her tight, speaking softly, projecting as much friendliness as he could.

'... Nikosner won't walk on the delta. He'll never hear the Zuni Bird sing. He saw your dream in my eyes; he hated me for it. When I was tied up in that wagon I had such a strange experience. I felt the power of this land. Do you remember me? Do you remember your dream? I'd be dead already if not for it. Don't be afraid. If my voice hurts or scares you, tell me if you can....'

She was shivering so violently he feared she'd slip off despite his grip around her waist. He sensed something peculiar coiling in her mind. He followed her half-focused gaze to a dead tree marking the upper corner of the pasture immediately before and below them.

She moaned. The tree was a malevolently beckoning skeleton, a magnetic doom which would suck out her jangled essence should her jabbering captor carry her too close. For she knew only that she was helpless, like a twig whirled along in a spring torrent; crucified in a chill dark universe which pulsed with meaningless energies, captured by a vulpine creature which possessed a noise-machine of incredible destructive power. She could feel it; it had a soul of its own, slung from his back. He was going to destroy her. She needed help. Deep inside her an ancient image formed, a warm memory mixed with more recent horrors. She began pulling it closer. As Liam detoured around the blasted tree down the green evening slope, his sharp face was uneasy. He could sense her mounting intensity, but not what was forming. He fell silent, remembering how alien the friendliest of words had been to him in the worst of the madness, a condition he'd left behind – presently, at any rate. Then he began to hum soothingly. She shivered faster against him.

His humming brought back a clear memory of his mind-flight above the ghostly night-world he'd visited in the gulf.

The night-world hadn't been altogether dark. It had been far below. He'd been carried safe above it on a rich, subtle vibration which had seemed to originate beyond him. He'd seen pulsing avenues of blue fire which ran beneath the surface of the planet like a grid. He'd seen ugly clouds of blood-red vapor floating between him and the surface of the alien world. The clouds had been living entities, malevolently awaiting his fall, the failure of the ethereal song which held him on high. Sure that the vibration controlled him, sure of his helplessness, he'd panicked. The smooth shiver of the song had transformed to an ugly glare, a rasping which threw him down. He'd begun to fall. Then it had come to him that he, all unconscious, was the singer, the maker of this song. And in this realization the fall had been halted. He was responsible for what was happening to him, responsible (somehow) for One-Eye's transforming presence inside him. Not in any way he could rationalize or understand. But the realization had been enough to pull him out of the gulf, out of the wagon. Now circumstances were changed. He was no longer fleeing the Mutant. He was in Miir, half-sensing a conflict in which he was already involved, humming softly.

The shivering woman paid no heed. He was shaking with her violent energy as their nervous horse carried them out of the sun and down through the long-grassed pasture. Curious cattle were gathering, and not far away several were rubbing against a single standing stone. The atmosphere above it seemed to flicker, as if a will-o'-the-wisp played there. The air was richly scented, insects droned, and the woods ahead were invitingly lush. Then Tschea stiffened convulsively. She jerked herself upright, almost tearing free, and she stared wildly.

'Algon,' she whispered in icy supplication. 'Algon....'

Liam sensed the shadows coiling out of her shaping mind....

'Algon!' This time she cried out loud, fearfully delighted. Liam's heart hammered, and their horse was dreadfully nervous.

For the shadows were thickening into shape, into the shape of another rider beside them. Cattle bellowed. Liam was all but frozen to see a bearded man glaring at him, trailing a smoke of incomplete imagining. All in black he was, riding a black horse, carrying a drawn ghost-sword, a semitransparent phantom more than slightly reminiscent of Nikosner. Through the phantom Liam could see how, thirty feet away, a restive bull was pawing the grass, debating whether to charge or flee.

Tschea called out again, her eyes wide and huge, and the ghost grew more solid, seemed about to attack as the bull decided to charge. Liam unfroze. He seized her head in both hands, jerked her eyes away from the phantom. The connection was broken. Horse and rider dissipated almost immediately, but misty remnants hung in the air for an instant as Tschea slumped. Their horse bolted without needing Liam's bidding; bolted just in time, for the shaggy bull was almost on them with its horns. It was quickly left behind. Liam was almost unseated. He gripped tightly with his thighs and struggled to hold Tschea, who was whimpering in complete desolation. Soon the lathered horse slowed down. Liam brought it to a halt near a belt of trees which were beginning to turn. Tschea stared at him with bewilderment, having no real idea of what had just happened.

Her eyes were enormous, lustrously beautiful.

'Algon,' she whispered fearfully, 'you're not Algon....'

Sad, he held her close, trying to reassure her.

'No, I'm not Algon. I'm Liam. The one you dragged out of Schroun. We're going to the delta – remember?' Then he asked, 'Who is Algon?'

She'd turned away, paying him no attention.

So they continued through pastures and belts of wood as twilight grew. And Liam was thinking that her image of Algon, whoever he was, was more than slightly warped by Nikosner's influence. . . .

Soon, having passed two ramshackle huts without having met anyone, they came to a wooded valley where Liam decided to spend the night.

Before it was dark he'd found a sheltered clearing at the bottom of a wall of rock. There was a small, dry cave in the rock; the clearing was protected by a thick screen of trees and brambled undergrowth, the insects were not too annoying, and a stream tumbled down nearby. It was ideal.

Tschea showed no interest. He helped her into the shallow cave. Tethering the exhausted horse, he took saddle and striped saddle-blanket into the cave. She was mumbling to herself, picking at her nails. She didn't even notice when he pulled her soaked dress off over her head before wrapping her up in the dry blanket. She lay huddled with the saddle for a pillow while he collected wood in the last of the light.

By the time the first stars were out he'd rubbed down and fed the horse; the fire was crackling cheerfully. He took her dress and spread it over a rock near the fire to dry. It was made of expensive material. With her manner and her clothes she was obviously an important lady – or *had* been, in the social sense. Now her importance was an ambiguous thing. He crouched beside her. She was asleep, in shadow beyond the flames, with just a tumble of disheveled platinum hair to catch any light. He felt how deep she was sleeping already, how deep, how intricately. He felt protective, also fascinated by her mystery, by her pride.

'You're a strange lady,' he whispered. 'How can I help you? How can you help me? I was never one for the ladies, but you are intriguing. Who is Algon, I wonder. What lies at the delta? I sense that you were an ... odd one ... even before all this began. With your dreaming, with your eyes which say you don't really know who you are ... you from Miir and me from Phadraig ... how can we understand each other with everything in flux?' Behind him the night murmured; above, a great dome of stars was growing from deepening velvet. His whispering was hoarse. 'Twilight's gone. Can you summon up your phantoms in broad daylight too?' He shivered. 'And what happens when everyone is projecting dreams into solid existence, all at the same time? What madness lies ahead?' Then he relaxed, laughed shortly. 'Probably we'll discover that all our deepest, most private, most guilty imaginings are exactly the same, the whole world over. Perhaps One-Eye will lead to us seeing through ourselves. If we don't wish ourselves to death first.'

An owl hooted. Liam stared around, up into the night. Black trees nodded slowly against the stars.

'What can you tell me, owl?' he called out. 'What are

these forces playing with us? What's going to be ... tomorrow... ?'

Then he gave the sky a mordant eye as he sat down cross-legged by the fire, and he tapped his head significantly. He wasn't yet in sane balance, and he knew the heavens knew it, and he winked at them. He wasn't hungry. He felt light, insubstantial, as if this new clarity were still anchorless and unconfirmed, at the mercy of chance and still-undreamed possibilities. Dreaming ... it was all like a dream. Had Phadraig ever existed? What had happened to his old friends? Were they perhaps dead already? Or were they perhaps beginning to find a way through the confusion? He shrugged. It was unimportant. Here he was, in Miir, on a still and soft night, with the sirena on his back.

The night was stealing into him as he fed the fire and watched the flames leap up. The hypnotic quality of the flames reminded him of the afternoon. What drove Nikosner? It was more than personal revenge. Liam remembered sensing the watchers. Almost lazily, he realized that he'd retained the sensation. He was sure he was being watched. Somehow, it didn't matter. He also sensed that his mental lucidity of the last few hours was fading. He was growing numb, as if the air he breathed were opiate. Feeling sudden thirst, he reached clumsily for the varnished wooden canteen which he'd taken from the saddlebag, fumbled with the stopper, dropped the canteen so that the water spilled away. The gurgling of the small brook nearby grew large and restful in him. Through it he faded into the night-rhythm, into an ocean of synesthetic currents, into the dance of the dark hours.

Miir breathed softly, darkly. The waning moon was away. The land was a living entity tending toward the southwest, and the pull was almost magnetic, as if every current on earth and air were orientated in that direction.

He became the woods about him; he embraced and became the slow dark world of the root-force beings in the earth below, primeval and enormous in their instinct lairs, dancing so ponderously, yet so perfectly according to their natures. He became part of the planet which pulsed har-

moniously in the heavens, receiving and creating according
to its nature, changing – always changing – with infinite
subtlety and unexpectedness, growing in a harmony which
included the disharmony perceived by its overexcited, self-
isolated energy transformer aspects. One of whom was
eventually standing by the ashes of a fire, head back, awe-
stricken face inwardly reflecting the argent light in the
sky.

For he saw seven great silver birds gliding luminously,
high, and from the northeast. They were star-dimming, star-
occulting, cold fires in the heavens which silver-toned the
earth and the motionless woods, their wings beating a
silence of utter completeness. Watching what he saw, he
didn't remember the predators which had descended after
the battle, nor the seven silver ravens which had appeared
to the Company on the Scarp plateau on the day after the
battle, urging them north after One-Eye. For the phantom
birds filled the sky this night; they approached the zenith in
a cross of four and three, exerting a curious and alarming
attraction on him. Their wings seemed to be beating inside
him. But then, when right overhead, they transformed into
a great wheel of spinning, spectral fire, with seven flickering
spokes and a blinding bright hub which drew him. Vaguely
he felt his shredded motes streaming up, up into the dimen-
sional depths of the hub.

Then he was in a curious place, an immanently beautiful
garden.

And walking beside him was a tall middle-aged man, his
face craggy, healthy, with piercing eyes. All about were
shrubs and blooms which shimmered with inner light,
varieties of flowers which he'd never seen; all about was
lightness and the sense of laughter.

'Do you know what is said of the delta?' he heard the
man beside him ask. 'It's said that in *two* dimensions the
delta is the culvert of Miir's triangle; that in *three*, it is
the apex of Miir's pyramid; and that in *four* dimensions, it is
the heart of Miir's people. But if Miir's heart is to beat again
as it should, then the correct music must be played at the
delta. If this does not happen, if Nikosner succeeds in cursing Ussian, then Miir's heart will bleed and Miir will die....'

Liam heard without understanding; he looked about in wonder. 'Where am I? Who are you?'

'This is the garden of Miir,' his informant told him, 'as it could be ... as it should be in everyone. This is the time for the garden to bloom, but instead it may wither. This is the delta. I am Algon.'

Liam had no words for the beauty about him. And even as he watched a rosy haze grew over everything, and he felt himself falling....

He found himself standing, shivering by the ashes of a fire, in a wood, beneath the stars which burned with a hard brilliance. What had happened? He'd been somewhere so beautiful ... now he forgot. And a very strange thing was beginning. The stars were speeding up.

First he saw them beginning to creep ... faster, faster, soon blurring toward their settings as the old moon rose. Then the east was a sudden fan, the sun was up and about the new day before Liam had finished scratching his head. By nightfall he'd realized he still existed; dawn caught him halfway through his blink of astonishment; the sun bulleted up and down to night which was day-night-day with leaves all shed and winter on its way with him still tuned to late-summer rhythms. Something twisted agonizingly in him as spring and summer flashed past. Through the hub. Disintegrated. He was wafted through vast fields of fire, circular fields which ringed and looped each other through a universe aflame with light and energy, a singing universe.... A universe which was a darkless eye, it looked on itself and lived in itself and bred its imaginings continually in forms existing for the duration of their imagination. A universe containing many conflicts, many songs, many possibilities.

A universe containing Miir, the delta, and the enemies of it.

And out of many possibilities emerged a situation in which Liam the Songmaker lay cold by the ashes of a fire, with a woman sleeping a few feet away, and he not so much as knowing her name.

Dawn saw him, curled up unconscious; dawn saw Tschea asleep.

Dawn saw Lonawi, watching from not so very far away.

And dawn saw three Darsans, tracking down the mad-man.

Tschea's sleep was deep, violent; she teetered on preci-pices, went on abysmal journeys which were forgotten upon awakening. In time light entered her sleep and drew her from it, into full day. The sun was dancing through leaves into the cave, dappling her pale face with moving patterns. She blinked in dull surprise. Groggily she reached for the glass of water on the table beside her bed. Her mouth was so dry. Her dreams ... so strange, with so much flame in them. She reached out. And touched a mossy wall of rock instead of the table.

Not yet realizing, she stretched out her other hand, ex-pecting to meet the head of Hilgo in bed beside her. In-stead she knocked over a metal canister which Liam had left there; it went rolling and clattering out of the cave and finally was stopped by Liam's body. He lay curled up in the dewy grass outside the cave, head in hands, eyes open to the sky ... wide open, but unseeing.

Tschea was fully awakened.

She saw the cave about her.

She saw Liam, saw the trees, the open glade, the sun streaming.

Disoriented and in shock, she started to unsteady feet. She looked at herself in bewilderment. She was dressed in a filthy blue-gold striped saddle-blanket, and her arms and legs were all smeared with dried mud. What had happened? She'd gone to sleep in Ussian, in her room in the Tarasse. Fantasies chased through her mind. Had the Cyclones ab-ducted her through the air in her sleep? Was she a prisoner? Or had she fled, had she lost her memory? She stared at Liam. Either way, what ... who was this pathetic bundle of rags all curled up and unconscious? So dirty and unkempt he was, yet there was an icy sharpness in his face, and the expression of one who'd been through fire and remained un-burned. She stood uncertainly above him. There was some-thing strange about him. Something which suggested she should try to revive him, not abandon him and take the tethered horse, which was cropping peacefully on grass at the edge of the clearing. The horse ... the two of them ... two? ... where was the third? The third? She looked around, suddenly distraught by half-memory, half expecting to see a heavy-bearded figure come stepping with open arms from the tangled undergrowth. Vague shadows swirled – but the morning sun was too strong for them. She shook her head. What third? What was going on? She was scared, and suddenly alone. Teeth rattling, she bent and shook the curled-up man by his bony shoulders. He rolled over; his eyes stared unseeing through her. She was gripped by fear, and she slapped his ginger-stubbled cheek. There was no response. Anxious, she felt for a pulse. It was there, it was steady – but slow ... so slow, so ponderous....

Then the open eyes below her focused and expanded in her vision.

She was aghast. Memory nibbled. Hadn't this happened before?

Frozen in her half-bent position, she watched as Liam raised himself stiffly to his elbows and shook his head with unexpected violence.

Dew-drops flew sparkling in all directions.

The horse whinnied; a pheasant whirred from the undergrowth.

He flexed his shoulders and stared at her; she couldn't move.

'How long have I slept?' he croaked. His accent was strange – General Synthetic, but more like in the Old Tongue, as spoken at Phadraig. 'A year? Two years? Or longer? Tell me the truth!'

She was bemused. Her brow furrowed, and she touched her tattoo.

At first when she opened her mouth no sound came out. Then – '... How would I know? I haven't ... met you before ... have I... ?'

Liam saw her. She was nervous and uncertain, but she was beautiful. As beautiful as the paradise to which he awakened. Every leaf of every tree about him shone with its own inner light. Layers of shimmering color spread from the trees up into the dancing air. It was a strangely beautiful dawn, this dawn of his return to the world. And the

energy in him! Before answering her, he felt for his sirena.
It was all wrapped up in his cloak beside him. Music!
There was music to be played! The music of the spheres,
of the flaming fields in space, of the Change!

He nodded his head, and he smiled so wide she feared his
face would split in two.

'Oh, yes. We've met. Yes! Let me assure you of that. You
saved me in Schroun – against what was left of my will –
and I dragged you away from your carriage when Nikosner
attacked the caravan. We rode here. And you were asleep in
the cave when the spaces took me. Such a very long time
ago!' He jumped to his feet and started pacing the clearing
with light-footed exuberance, tapping out quick rhythms on
his shanks, nodding emphatically at her where she stood
with the striped blanket wrapped tight about her and the
early sun streaming onto her confused but still-proud face.
'It's very good of you to have waited all this time for me to
wake up. You'll be rewarded. I'll take you safe to the delta
– I swear it!' His eyes lit up with childlike delight. 'Because
now I'm seeing properly! Everything vibrates and dances
with energy. Oh, it's so beautiful!' He threw his hands and
eyes up to the sky in graceful, grateful recognition of the
world's beauty.

Tschea followed his delighted capering with troubled
eyes. There were irritating hissings and whinings in her
head – it was difficult to stay upright.

'If it's as you say,' she said slowly, heavily, rubbing her
eyes, 'then I may have a memory to fit it. Then ... I can't
be sure ... it was last night I fell asleep in the cave, and
you've only slept for a few hours....'

Liam stopped; he turned on her with aggressive jaw as
she sat back against a rock beside the remains of the
fire.

'Oh, it can't be so,' he insisted. 'I'm sure we must have
slept for many years. Who knows how our natural rhythms
have been altered?'

Tschea felt stiff and dull. Nevertheless, she managed to
indicate the tethered horse.

'If that were true,' she said weakly, 'then the horse would

have been stolen, or would have broken away, or would have starved to death.'

Liam saw how she'd started to tremble, and he came to her with a concerned face. 'You may be right,' he said, 'and so may I. It may have been simultaneously many years and only a few hours.... So strange ... yesterday you dreamed a shadow into existence, last night I journeyed through many years, and now yesterday is long ago ... now you ...' He squatted beside her, laid a hand on her arm. 'Are you being troubled by ghosts again? Is your mind confused?'

His voice boomed in her head. She nodded weakly. His hand on her arm was comforting. He began massaging her shoulders and neck; his fingers were supple, expert, and brought her relief. 'Relax,' he said, 'remember I'm a friend, however things might appear. This is a bad time. But we'll come through. Somehow. Now sit still, I'll relight the fire. I'm sane – for the moment – I think. We'll steer each other to the delta. Yes? Now, I'll make something to eat.'

She didn't know what he was talking about, her head throbbed, but the sound of his voice was a help. He sounded kind, and she wanted kindness, she wanted to trust him. And while he turned away, quite abruptly, as if troubled by something he'd said, she stared at a blade of grass. It grew large and fascinating as Liam went to gather wood. A drop of dew hung from the tip of the blade; her vision was drawn into the expanded sphere of this drop, and in it she saw many sights.... She saw strange beings carrying a one-eyed infant along a glittering avenue in some distant, enormous city ... she saw a chaos of warbands, looters, murderers, saw them darkly ... she saw Namahon, and her eyes widened, for he was walking by the delta, and there were thousands of people there ... she was caught up in a multitude of simultaneous visions, and many made no sense at all, but of them all the most impressive was of a man and woman whirling, flaming, dancing in the sky – they joined, separated, fell apart, swooped together, and met so the whole sky in the dew-drop shook. And the man was red, the woman was golden ... the man's face was a mixture of past and present – it confused her deeply. For she felt strange tides inside, tugging her different ways at once. Then Liam's voice came distantly to her through all of it, and his prattle was like a rope connecting her with the clearing, with her bodily reality.

'... Oh, it's weird, I know, but there's beauty in it, just as you assured me. It warms the heart to see how nature glows. And you ... I sense your fear and confusion – but I can see brave colors underneath. We must all go through this chaos. You're strong, your soul won't be drenched, you'll be all right. Listen to the birds singing!'

And she drifted on as he got the fire going again. His voice was thoughtful. He could imagine the enormity of the visions she saw in the dew-drop. The eye came like that at first, like a flood – up and down, up and down. And this morning, though beautiful, was also slightly menacing. There were the watchers. And what had happened during the night? He was sure there was something he couldn't quite remember – something connected with the delta, something which made it more important than ever to reach the place.... 'These strange places were always in us,' he remarked. 'We're curious creatures. We create our own obstacles. Last night I was swallowed, this morning I'm a newborn babe, and tonight? Who knows? We'll find out. As for the moment, my belly grumbles when I think too much about the universe. Contradictions make for poor digestion. Fasting's excellent for visions – but too much of this spirituality is simply stupid. We'll eat.'

He began preparing a porridge as sun and fire together warmed her. Slowly she emerged from her spate of incomprehensible visions to see him stirring a mixture in a black pot, slowly, calmly.

'What's in there?' Her voice was doubtful, shaky.

'Oatmeal, salt, water, herbs.' He smiled. 'It'll warm you up.'

He continued stirring as she stood and slipped off the blanket without any self-consciousness. She pulled on the yellow dress with a worried expression. He looked up and nodded frankly.

'You're beautiful. I couldn't have made a better choice.'

'What do you mean?' she bridled. 'Who do you think you are?'

'I'm Liam, from Phadraig.' He smiled. 'What's your name?'

'Tschea.' Her voice was curt. She wished she had a mirror.

'Good. Now we'll eat. Then we'll start off for the delta.'

'The delta? Why? Who says?'

'You said.' He scanned her. She looked so uncertain, but she hadn't lost what he suspected was natural aggressiveness. 'You said that there we'll learn what everything's all about.' He frowned. Again, the hint of things not quite remembered. 'You said that there I'll play unimaginable music. I hope you're right.' He frowned. 'I thought you were talking of One-Eye's music. Now I'm not so sure.'

'Oh, One-Eye....' She shivered, dabbed at her tattoo. 'What is One-Eye? You've held him.' She broke off, looking cross and confused. 'Why do I say that? What do I know of you?'

Liam tasted the porridge with a fingertip.

'I told you that,' he murmured. 'It was a lie. In my frenzy I wanted to demonize myself in your sight. I never actually held him – though often enough I was next to the one who did. His mother was with the Company. Her name was Salamander. She was badly wounded in the escape from Phadraig, but she was still alive when I last saw her....' He was silent for a moment, studying the clear sky. 'Her mother was behind our escape – behind the infant's survival – behind ... all this. The old woman had foreknowledge of his birth. In Phadraig there was a forbidden prophecy about his birth, made two hundred years ago by Maelnagar the Maker of Outcries. They killed him for it.'

He shut his mouth, poured porridge into two wooden bowls.

Tschea couldn't understand. 'Why ... why did you want to save the creature?'

She accepted the bowl he handed her, found she was hungry.

'You told me,' he said quietly, 'that this is the time when the Fifth Element becomes conscious in us, that it's time for people to change. Perhaps One-Eye's not a demon at all. With the mumen perhaps he's more like a natural spur to

goad us into evolution – he takes no sides, he leaves it to
other powers to squabble in the confusion. Maybe the same
spirit which made us save him made you save me from
Schroun. Also' – he shrugged – 'we were ignorant fools. He
was a good excuse to escape Phadraig. We thought we were
taking him to sanctuary. We didn't know how powerful he
is – until he showed us. Now – eat.'

She did so. Then she began shaking with some new sadness.

Liam leaned forward, touched her forehead gently.
'What's the matter?' he asked. 'Do you think of
Algon?'

She dashed his hand away. Her cheeks were tearstained.
'*What's the matter?*' she mimicked savagely. 'Are you
now changed to such a perfection that you can patronize
and presume to lead me? Do you think yourself higher
than me? Do you think you've come through this ... this
madness? You – you who helped to bring it about?'

Liam sat back, saying nothing. Shivering, she glared at
him, her eyes sparkling with ugly energy. Their eyes met,
and held. Liam sat perfectly relaxed, absorbing her emotion.
Then she broke, she threw herself at him, sobbing fiercely,
pummeling him until she was breathless and exhausted.
'All your mad nonsense!' she screamed in his face. 'I've
abandoned my children, I've betrayed my friends! What
am I doing here? Am I so mad I must sit here listening to
your trickster talk about dreams of the delta? You're crazy.
You're not even going in the right direction – we've come
north, and the delta's to the southwest. And what's the
purpose of it? Why go there? Why go anywhere? My
head's spinning. All your melodramatic spiritual nonsense
about evolution makes things worse!' She stood, furiously,
fists clenched. 'I'm going!'

Liam also stood, apparently undisturbed. He slung his
sirena over his back, his cloak over his shoulder. He picked
up the saddle, and the striped blanket, and the sack of
provisions.

'All right,' he said. 'And I'm coming with you.'

Her narrowed eyes were hot and utterly miserable. 'I'll
scream to people that you've abducted me!'

'I'll scream to them that you're mad. Who will they believe?'

She looked ready to attack him again.

'I'll bring an army of shadows against you out of the air,' she threatened. Then she turned, began running to the tethered horse.

Liam followed, thoughtfully. Shadows ... the air was uneasy. The song of the birds was slightly muted now.

'Try to stop long enough to remember yourself!' he called out.

'I can't remember anything!' she shrieked back at him, pulling herself up onto the jittery horse without either saddling or untethering it. The animal whinnied and bucked fiercely and unseated her into Liam's arms. Angrily wrenching herself free, she ran off downhill into dense undergrowth and was soon lost from sight. Liam almost gave chase on foot. Then he checked himself. He soothed, saddled, and untethered the horse before mounting with thoughtful caution. For a moment or two he sat motionlessly and gazed at the trees on every side with furrowed brow. He was sure he'd forgotten matters known the night before. He shrugged.

'Fools,' he muttered softly, 'we're all fools.'

Then he rode down into the valley after Tschea with the fire still burning and the porridge still hot in the bowls left by the cave.

Soon afterward, Lonawi saw the three Darsans arrive.

15 : Darsans and Dark Shadows

While in Schroun Clarai had sent three Darsans after the red-haired madman with orders to catch and kill him. Now everyone had forgotten their mission except for them. They were two men and a woman – Vels, Inilo, and Yelinne. Vels was tall and dark and clean-shaven; Inilo was a squat

man with a perpetually brooding expression; Yelinne was
wiry and narrow-framed, her flat brown face was framed
by short black hair, and her eyes burned with dedication.
All three were experienced professionals.

They'd started west on the first day, asking questions
everywhere. They'd begun by scouring the area around
about Tsarsa, where they'd unearthed a decrepit scarecrow
of a man whom they'd killed because he'd cursed them as
he shook. But they'd heard nothing of a red-haired madman
with a strange noise-machine. Inilo soon grew irritable and
disinclined to press the futile pursuit, and he was soon close
to falling out with the other two.

On the second day, they covered the area north and west
of the Boribet. At the end of that day they heard that Nikosner had fallen on the caravan. They rode all night, Inilo
complaining fiercely. They reached the grasslands before
dawn. The caravan was gone. All they found were the shattered remains of the munitions wagon, many unburied
bodies, scavenging birds and dogs, and a wounded, dying
Darsan who raised a feeble hand at their approach.

'Kill me, brother,' she implored Vels. 'For pity's sake.'

Vels had been about to do this when Yelinne held back
his arm.

'Have you seen a red-haired madman?'

Yelinne's voice was crisp and without any pity at all.

With her clouded eyes fixed hopefully on Vels's drawn
sword, the Darsan gasped out how she'd seen a red-haired
man ride away to the north at the end of the storm, ride
away with a woman from the caravan.

'He was ... one of them,' she whispered, features
stretched with agony. 'From here I could feel his vibrations.
Even through Nikosner's madness. Now I'm infected and
dying. All night I lay here, enduring the demons of death
while still alive. Kill me now, set me free ... please....'

'What direction?' Yelinne demanded, making absolutely
sure, so that even Vels was disgusted by her hardness.

The dying Darsan had again pointed to the north.

Then, while Inilo waited with cynical fretfulness to the
rear, Vels put an end to the life of their comrade.

The three of them rode north, up onto the deserted moors

as the sun rose. They picked up a trail. With Inilo lagging
to the rear, Vels and Yelinne pressed on as fast as their
horses would carry them. Yelinne in particular was in a
desperate fever to catch and kill the madman. Her mind was
blooming too hot and ugly for her own comfort, and she
felt sure that the madman's execution would in some way
exorcise the demons nibbling at her own soul. Thirty years
old she was, and never such doubts as the ones which flooded her now. Vels ... her sometime lover ... could she trust
him? As for Inilo ... he was sure to run out on them – he
might even betray them. What if they should suddenly
chance on their quarry? Inilo might well shout out perversely and warn the lunatic, just to spite them. She could believe
anything of Inilo, for he had no dedication. As they rode
down through the pastures, past the long-horned cattle, she
didn't look back at him in case she gave him wind of her
suspicions.

Then they found the cave, with the fire still burning.

Vels dismounted warily, dipped a finger in the porridge,
tasted.

'Warm. They can't be far away. Maybe they heard us
coming.'

'What does it matter?' grumbled Inilo, coming up behind
them. (*Slouched like a slug in his saddle*, thought Yelinne
with distaste.) 'Clarai's captured, everything's changed, our
allegiances are dead. We should be sensible and look out for
ourselves.'

'All madmen must be killed!' Yelinne glared with wintry
face.

'Who's to say who's mad?' Inilo's eyes were filled with
suspicion. 'We're all going mad. Both of you look so strange.
I can feel how you hate me. You don't even trust each
other. Why should I trust you?'

Yelinne's face flooded with unhealthy color; she looked
to Vels, who was close to the breaking point.

'You talk too much!' growled Vels, heavy body shifting
uneasily.

'Will you betray our mission?' Yelinne hissed.

'What mission? I remember no mission. This is a daydream!'

Inilo's contempt triggered Vels, pushed him over the edge.

'See if you find your death a daydream!' he bawled, drawing his sword and rushing at the mounted man. Inilo dug in spurs, but his horse, instead of carrying him off to safety, stood up on its hind legs and spilled him. And while Yelinne watched, unmoving and emotionless, Vels used his sword for the second time that morning.

'He was a treacherous fool. He deserved it,' Yelinne remarked sharply as Vels, panting, wiped the weapon clean on emerald grass before sheathing it.

'I didn't mean it!' Vels was rigid, his eyes fixed on Inilo's body. 'He did not deserve it. He spoke his mind. My temper snapped, and now his blood is on my hands.' He kicked at the fire, scattering burning embers, he could not look Yelinne in the face. 'Two days ago he was my friend – and your friend too. Have you forgotten that already?'

'We'll eulogize him later!'

Yelinne, trembling, was looking to the woods ahead.

'We won't leave without burying him and paying our respects!'

'We don't have the time!' snapped Yelinne. 'We must catch and kill this madman before he infects more decent folk. Hold yourself! Remember your duty!' Her voice was scolding.

Vels glared at her with sudden hate. 'My duty's toward Inilo whom I've murdered!' Before she could answer he'd grabbed a spade from his horse and was digging into the soft earth with paroxysmal fury. Not knowing what to do, Yelinne watched him through a haze of angry impatience.

'If you want to save time,' he shouted, 'you'll help me dig.'

She felt damned if she would. And she couldn't afford to wait. Yet somehow she was doubtful, so she couldn't go on without him. The dilemma only increased her anger, so that she sat on her horse and gave him no help. He ignored her. After the first rapid onslaught he worked more slowly, grimly, so that she began to think he was deliberately wasting time to spite her.

By the time Inilo was buried and Vels, sweating and tired, had replaced the last clods of turf, they were cold on the pursuit and their trust in each other was dead. Each was held to the other by a brooding rivalry centered on their prey. Now Liam was their mutually exclusive purpose as they rode down into the valley, attended by a horde of biting insects. They watched each other angrily while trying to suppress the delirious shaking fits which more and more frequently caught at them.

She talks to me of duty, thought Vels, *I'll show her duty....*

If we lose them now, thought Yelinne, *it's my duty to execute him.*

And a crow was strutting on Inilo's grave.

Scratched, maddened by the snatching briars, Tschea had fled headlong down into the valley until she lost control and crashed into a thick rhododendron. She lay exhausted in the dappled half-light, without will or strength to get up again. Her head was churning as foully as her stomach; nature's ceaseless motion nauseated her. Why couldn't it keep still? The trees mocked her with their whispering, and the birds with their insolently happy singing; she was sickened by the overwhelming richness of her perception, terrified by her own state of mind. She couldn't get the vision of Ussian burning out of her head. Fresh waves of giddiness surged, and she couldn't hold her food.

She didn't look up when she heard the red-haired lunatic approaching. She couldn't care, she didn't care that she couldn't. What did it matter? He was standing behind her, probably laughing at her despair and about to tell her how sublime ecstasy lay beyond this madness. He probably enjoyed seeing her degraded like this; he came from Phadraig, he ...

Then her bitterness was giving way to a pleasant calm which filled her, spread through her, eased and relaxed her.

When she lay utterly still he stopped playing and reslung the sirena.

He'd hardly dared, for memory of Tatung was still strong. But something of the forgotten experience of the night before must have come through; the music he'd played for her had been soft, hardly audible at all, very gentle.

He helped her to her feet. She could hardly stand without assistance. Dazed, she saw him now without hate. A sharp face. A mess of ruddy hair and beard, twinkling eyes.

'Are we friends?' asked Liam. 'Can we help each other?'

'What did you do?' she whispered drowsily. 'Was that your music? So peculiar. I heard nothing. I felt ...'

Then she started to fall. He caught her, set her on the horse, and swung up behind. It was a single movement which flowed so well that she smiled briefly before yawning and taking him for a pillow.

'Sleep if you want,' he said. 'We'll go west now.'

His arm around her was comforting; he smelled of earth, of grass. Distantly she thought how good it would be to have a bath. But she was asleep before they reached the sunlit glades and groves at the floor of the valley. Insects danced, maples flamed up the hillside. Liam was humming almost contentedly as they came to an overgrown drovers' trail which took them west, out of the valley, into the open land beyond. The valley was rich with wild life: rabbits hopped, birds sang, it was a fulsomely sunny morning between summer and autumn. From time to time, Liam looked back, but never saw any signs of pursuit. Tschea's face was peaceful and his mood was good, for he felt that they were going in the right direction ... whatever that was. ...

Though by the time they'd left the valley behind he couldn't deny an increasing sense of foreboding. The landscape ahead was vague and inchoate. Now it was early afternoon, the sun was bright above, the sky was clear – yet the horizons were invisible. And the shapes and colors about them seemed all wrong. Dirty yellow fields were blackened by harshly premonitive squadrons of low-beating crows; the sky ahead looked unhealthy, and much lower than it had been.

Then he saw the crossroads ahead, and the ominous building which straddled it. It was a hostelry and coaching post, but it emanated no hospitality. Liam realized it was the focus of his unease, had been subtly affecting him for many minutes. He thought of Nikosner. Something bad had happened here. He was tempted to take to the fields and avoid it. But ... the fields ... were no longer there. Of a sudden everything was hazed over, and nothing was clear but this packed-earth track leading sharp and straight to the crossroads, to the wooden building stilted up over the crossing like a black and dreary drunken spider.

Liam spurred on the reluctant horse. He refused to look away from the crossroads: he accepted it as a test. It was then that Tschea was driven from her long sleep. She surfaced, fleeing the accusing faces of her deserted children – she surfaced into nightmarish wakefulness.

Dread seized her when she saw the ominous building so close ahead, when she saw her captor's eyes gleaming so cold. She struggled.

'Let me off, madman! It's hell. You'll kill us!'

'No other way!' he hissed. 'We must go through here!'

'For pity's sake ... let us go back and find another road....'

'No other way,' he repeated.

Now the dark wooden building was almost on top of them, and to her it glowed, cold and hungry. She went rigid and couldn't move, felt death all about. The road brought them under a wooden arch, under the building, through to the open central space where the roads met. The air here was leadenly pulsating and the sun could not get through; ponderous waves ebbed from the building on every side, from the ground beneath the crossroads, so that Liam's neck creaked with the effort of turning his head. The horse drooped, seemed about to drop. It was difficult to move. Difficult to think. Blank windows stared, and painted gargoyles grimaced above each of the four arches. Nothing moved. Nothing sounded. Then something caught the edge of Tschea's eye, and she snatched at Liam's hand.

'What was that? Did you see that?' Her whisper echoed around.

'See what? See what?'

'A deer leaping ... changing into a – oh, no! A child laughs! Oh, we must ride on, the shadows here are ...'

But Liam's attention was caught. He stared, his neck-cords standing out, to a point some fifteen feet away in the northwest corner of the enclosed crossroads.

He started to dismount as he whispered, 'See – the woman there – by the open door. She rocks a dead child – it's dead of a broken neck, but she sings a lullaby. She does not see us – and the door is open. . . .'

Tschea saw the open door. It was a black hole. She couldn't see the woman or her dead child very clearly at all – they were wraiths. Liam approached the door as if his legs were dragging him to it. 'Wait,' he jerked back over his shoulder. 'I must go in. I must see what's happened. Remember: you're Tschea. I'm Liam. Stay there.'

She didn't call him back. She was leadenly glued to the trembling horse. Pausing by the door, he looked down at his lullabying ghost. He couldn't pause for long. The black space drew him in, sirena unslung.

Tschea was left with a chant running through her head: . . . *Tschea . . . Liam . . . Tschea . . . Liam . . . Tschea . . . Liam. . . .*

It was meaningless. She was alone. The high-charged place was shivering through her, and shadows began coiling in her, pressing other names and allegiances into her. The world of sun and song was lost as she dismounted heavily, clumsily, her eyes gleaming.

Liam slipped into darkness. Into a thick, turgid atmosphere. It was like standing at the bottom of a stagnant pond, breathing thickness which slowed him, drew him farther in. The place was a trap. *Turn around and leave now*, he thought with difficulty. *Take another step and I may never come out. What am I doing? Why enter at all?*

The step was taken even as he wondered.

A child's triumphant laughter pealed all around him.

He spun. He whirled. He fell into the ungainly dance of the lost folk stranded in this unraveled place, into a dance of forgetfulness where nobody knew anyone else, the laughter malicious in his head. But nowhere in the broth-thick darkness did he sense a child. Instead, he found himself plunging uncontrollably through the tenuous forms of faded people, all of whom were performing grotesque dance-rituals of private compulsion from the solid world they'd ceased to occupy. Many had lost all substance – their ghosts mouthed, acted, pranced before mirrors in the walls. Without sense of dimension Liam went careering through this dark mirror-dimensioned dancehall of ghosts; with them he whirled on the mad pealing laughter, spinning through the shadows of jugglers, merchants, soldiers, beggars, stranded travelers who'd been drawn inside this place. Then he came to a bright door which beckoned, and a wild-eyed man stared at him from it. He was about to go through when something warned him that it wasn't a door at all, but a mirror, and that if he went through it he'd be lost forever. It squeezed his mind; it pulled at him, ordering him to go through, give up self and sirena. Shutting his eyes he forced himself away from it – and walked straight into a solid wall.

He collapsed, stunned. When he opened his eyes he saw beside him the bare feet of a boy who was painting the stone wall with dripping eyes – red, yellow, purple, orange eyes; eyes which glared, lazy eyes, smiling eyes, a multitude of eyes.

The boy looked down without stopping his painting.

He was curly-haired, with yellow-flecked gray eyes.

They appraised each other. Then the boy smiled sadly; he brought down his brush and stepped aside. Liam saw that he'd been concealing a door with his thin body, which meant that the door must be very small. This didn't seem to matter. Liam found himself walking through quite easily, quite calmly, with plenty of room to spare, sirena slung.

He entered a flagstoned room. The white stone walls were lined by wooden shelves cluttered with jars, bowls, implements. Large iron bins by the door contained flour; they were getting low. There was a man kneading dough at a table in the middle of the room. He was surrounded by dough. It rose in lumpy white mountains around his massive, sweating body. His back was to Liam and he didn't turn; with thick but dexterous hands he continued to pound, knead, roll. Liam didn't want to interrupt. The man worked as if his life depended on it. He was huge, a giant silhouette through the flour-cloudy light of the oil lamp on the table before him. Liam waited by the bins, silently.

'Stop standing like an idiot, boy, ferry me flour!' barked the doughmaker without turning around. 'This useless painting besots you.'

Liam cleared his throat, stepped forward, and faint laughter echoed.

'I'm not your assistant,' he said. 'I was traveling through—'

The doughmaker turned, suspicious and hostile. His face was red and lumpy, bristling with golden hairs, and his eyes were fanatical, expressing an all-too-human hunger. Liam stood his ground. The doughmaker glared.

'Be you devil or man!' he shouted in incantatory tone. 'I command you: take this bowl. Bring me flour! Bring me water!'

'Willingly,' Liam agreed, 'if you'll tell me what happened here.'

The doughmaker made a sign of self-protection, and his eyes narrowed. 'No bargains with the Mutant's minions. I see you. You are one like the one who came here. All the others who heard him laughing have faded. There's only me and the boy; work alone can keep us real. Don't tempt me. The Mutant laughs all about!' His voice was increasingly ragged, and he was creeping closer, brandishing a rolling pin. 'The Hou'ons take their revenge through One-Eye – this is their conquest!' Agony twisted his face. 'Ah, no, no, don't think about it – work, work, work! I must work! You ... you're a one-eyed devil like the rest. I see through you. Be gone, or work!'

Liam looked weary. He laid his head on one side, gesturing agreeably. 'To you I'm a monster, to me I'm a man,' he said. 'I was traveling past with a friend and I let myself be enticed inside. Here I am. I'll work – if you tell me what happened, and how to get out. . . .'

'The only way out is through work.' The doughmaker thrust a bowl at Liam. 'Get me flour.'

'What when the flour runs out?' Liam scraped the bottom of the bin.

'Bake!' snapped the doughmaker, turning back to his kneading.

'What when the bread's baked?' Liam brought him the flour.

'Break!'

'Then what?'

'Eat!'

'Then...?'

A shrug of massive shoulders. Resignation, and anger. 'Sleep.' Then he threatened. 'No more questions. Work!'

Liam folded his arms, raised his brows. 'Work to die? That's no escape. You'll have to leave this room. And I think I can help you.' He touched his sirena.

'Ridiculous! There's no door. The Mutant laughs all around!' Now the doughmaker's desperation was apparent even to himself.

There was something he couldn't touch ... something drowned by the glare of this one-eyed monster tormenting him. He heard the monster's tormenting words. He thought of how all his fellow-travelers had become shadows since that madman came to the hostelry with his laughter. He trembled on the edge of attempting a decapitating blow with the heavy rolling pin.

'One-Eye's what you make of him,' mouthed the one-eyed monster. 'It's this senseless production of dough you have to escape, not One-Eye. He has you already – you know it, I know it. You don't even fool yourself with all this pounding and kneading. Not any longer....'

The rolling pin cleaved down. Liam jumped clear.

The doughmaker's head was filled with the sound of children laughing. The monster tormented him. 'Get thee hence!' he howled.

'There's a remedy,' the monster protested, 'a music which ...'

'You'd spell me! Degenerate devil, get out!'

So Liam left the doughmaker to it. The boy was gone. Now the lower eyes were blinded by dribbling tears – red, yellow, purple, orange.

Liam stopped. *Perhaps I should play for him whether he likes it or not.* He thought a while, then shook his head, and plunged back among the jerky dancing shadows. Once more the laughter pealed through him. He found himself swim-

ming against a tide of shadows which was dragging him
back and down.

He could hardly believe it when at last he found himself
framed by the outer door again, facing a world of fairly
solid appearances. The light was blinding. Slowly, he saw.

The horse was there, nervous on the crossroads.

But Tschea wasn't to be seen. Nor the woman with the
dead child.

He looked up. The gelid haze persisted. He looked all
around. Blank windows stared like negative mirrors from
every side of the crossing. Cautiously, he stepped out. The
dense air was flickering, coiling, and half-glimpsed forms
like electric worms pulled his eyes here, there. The horse
whinnied in fear, kicked up dust and grit, bolted abruptly
through the western archway. Liam stopped. Had he heard
laughter? Was he out of the house at all? What ... another
horse where the first had stood? He licked his lips, felt for
the sirena, and his pulse raced.

For the black ghost-horse was turning on him.

Its shadowy rider had drawn a sword which, raised
threateningly, seemed to be drawing energy in from the
haze, so that the phantom was growing steadily more substantial.

Black beard. Black leathers. Burning eyes.

Even as the silent phantom came gliding at him, he remembered another time, and he sensed a more substantial
threat immediately behind him. The ghost-rider was a
decoy. Forgetting it, he spun. Saw Tschea. Coming at him
with a knife. Her face pallid, agonized, her eyes so wide that
the whites were visible all the way around. He caught her
wrist even as a ghost-hoof came plunging through his shoulder. It had enough substance to leave a numbing tingle. He
lost her wrist as her fierce momentum spun both of them
through the dissipating shreds of her ghost. They hit the
ground hard, Liam on the bottom. He was stunned.

'I looked in a mirror,' Tschea hissed in an abnormal
voice, 'and the mirror said that you have to die!'

She was terrified. Her voice pronouncing sentence, her
arm about to strike in execution, she couldn't stop it. He
lay there momentarily helpless. She fought against the com-

mand to strike, and turned her eyes away from him. And she saw—

'Namahon,' she whispered, 'you look at me as if I'm a monster....'

Liam opened his eyes. Through a blur, beyond her he saw, standing in the doorway, the boy with the yellow-gray eyes.

For a moment the boy smiled at them – uncertainly, sadly, hopefully.

Then he seemed to half-turn. And he was gone.

Tschea cried out. She dropped the knife. Shivering, she scrambled away from Liam to the door. She could get no farther. She strained against the blackness, arms stiff, fingers spread flat, as if pushing against a solid barrier. Then she collapsed where the woman with the dead child had been, lay stiff in her torn yellow dress, staring fixedly into the darkness which had swallowed her son yet refused her a second entry. Liam was gone from her mind.

He picked himself up with slow concentration. First of all he examined the sirena, fingered it almost ritualistically. He wasn't so much checking it for damage as trying to draw the power of its own ancient indestructibility to cure the damage to himself. Realizing this he drew himself together, picked up the abandoned knife, stuck it in his belt, and went to Tschea. He squatted beside her with the utmost wariness and a kind of embarrassment. She continued to stare longingly into the darkness. His heart softened. She looked so lost, so ill; beneath her tan the pallor of her face was unnaturally luminous.

Why should I feel pity? he thought incredulously. *It could be suicidal.* Nevertheless, he took her gently by the shoulders, turned her around to face him. Her skin was hot, dry, bramble-welted. For a moment she stared at him with a mute intensity, still seeking to see someone else. Then she touched at her tattoo, bit her lower lip, and turned back to the blackness of the door.

She began muttering fiercely, almost incoherently: 'How can I help it? How can I help it? Just as you said – mind whirls away, nothing can stop.... Don't know who I am, who I was, where I come from ... It spins!' She clutched her head. 'You led me here,' she accused in a pitiful voice, 'into the mirrors ... dancing, dancing, all dancing, ghosts, full of hate for the living, kill, kill, kill! The present's horrible! You're in the present! I hate you ... I have to ... but the music you ... ah! No!' Her face fled through a chaos of expressions. 'I should never have ... Namahon, please ... the mirror ... I can see how ... I must go inside again....'

'You can't go in a second time!' Liam hadn't released her shoulders. He was fervent, scared. 'It's not possible. I don't know what this place is – I sense it's taken over by the same force that's behind Nikosner. Some kind of culling station ... I don't know. But no more talk of mirrors. It's all right now; they failed, because of the boy. He wasn't a ghost; I saw him too, inside, and he was solid!' She was hardly listening. He had a flash of difficult recognition. 'Your ghost-rider isn't Algon – it has too much of Nikosner in it. Your memory's weaker. Algon's at the delta. I'm sure. And the boy was sent or came to ...' Wondering what he meant even as he said it, he lost it.

But it was effective. Stung, she gave him her attention. 'What do you ...' Then she bit her lip, cast her eyes down, obviously perplexed.

'Is Namahon your son? Is he Algon's son as well?'

Her head snapped up, her eyes were moist. 'How can you know where Algon is when I haven't seen or heard of him in thirteen years?' Her voice was dark, jealous. But before he could answer, her eyes switched to a point behind him, and her mouth fell open. 'Darsans! Two of them. Looking at us, whispering ...'

Liam felt, heard the presence behind. His hackles rose. But he didn't look around; he wasn't going to be fooled again.

'I hear,' he said, very carefully. 'I'll keep my eyes on you.'

'They think we're ghosts! They're not sure, but one's dismounting. She's coming toward us – her eyes are full of hate. They were sent to kill you!' Her eyes widened. 'Now I remember – in Schroun, Clarai sent them! Fool, do something; they're really real!'

Liam didn't move. He heard a horse snicker nervously, heard the sound of feet scuffing closer. Now in Tschea's eyes he saw the Darsan reflected – a grim, stocky woman in uniform; and a second one, a man, following the first. Tschea seemed to be paralyzed. Still, Liam didn't move. He heard labored breathing. The Darsans were right behind him. They were close to the door – it was pulling them in. He felt the waves of their helpless fear; in Tschea's eyes he could see their stiffly futile resistance. He thought he heard a distant echo of childish laughter, and he wondered why he couldn't move.

He stopped breathing as blackness pulled the Darsans in.

Yelinne first – furiously tantalized by the untouchable ghosts.

Then Vels – grimacing, guilt-ridden, resigned to madness and death.

Tschea let out her breath in a long, shivering sigh.

Liam clapped his hands, jumped to his feet, barked with laughter.

'They couldn't touch us!' he shouted jubilantly. 'They were at the other side of the house! Going-in and coming-out are different places!'

Then he shuddered fiercely at the echoing of his voice. The house was still on top of them, still influencing them. He saw Tschea's distress. She was trying to get up, but her legs were like jelly, and her eyes beseeched him. So he raised her up. They felt a sudden need for each other. Taken aback by it, they clung together on the spellbound crossroads, reassuring each other that they really existed, hugging with a glad amazement ... which quickly died as the melancholy of the house reasserted itself. Liam broke away, taking her arm. 'Come on,' he insisted, eyes bright. 'We'll take those two horses in exchange for our one which bolted.' Then he stopped. 'Which road is best ... for the delta?'

Tschea wavered, made a gesture of self-abnegation. 'South. West. Either. You choose. I don't care.'

'What lies south? Ussian?'

She nodded, her face flushed as she remembered her children.

'What about the west?'

'The hot spring resort at Gurdiangar. And beyond that ... the Cyclone College at Dulankir. The only one they have in

Miir.' She was whispering. 'I sent Namahon to the Cyclones. I think they made me do it. . . .'

'Cyclones?' Liam's brow crinkled. 'Who are they?'

'A very secretive brotherhood.' She was bitter, clipped.

'Do you think Algon could be a Cyclone?'

'Don't be ridiculous!' she flared. 'I never met anyone less like a Cyclone. They're pedants and manipulators. I think they're using me; probably they made me take you from Schroun. Tschea is just a puppet!' Bitter, she stared at the door which had swallowed the Darsans. 'The Cyclones want you alive; those in the mirrors want you dead. You must be very important. Both use me as an instrument. How can you trust me? Or do you find me attractive because I tried to kill you?'

Liam shrugged. He was anxious to be away.

'I come to Miir, I find myself in a mystery, and you're at the heart of it. ' His voice was brisk. 'I think – the west. If the power here is the same as the one that Nikosner's brought to Ussian, then I prefer not to visit Ussian – yet. It may be I have to. But if these Cyclones are protecting us, or watching us, then we should go to them.' He tapped the sirena. 'Perhaps they wait because they have a use for me, perhaps they want to see if we can make our own progress. Let's go!'

Tschea hesitated. She knew she could leave him here. Her face showed it. 'Ussian,' she muttered, struggling with her conscience. 'My children. I should . . .'

'Do what you will.' Liam released her arm. 'But think: this place is confusing, and Ussian will be infernal. First we should know what we're doing and find out why these forces struggle over us. It may well be that your children have escaped; perhaps the Cyclones helped them.'

'You don't know the Cyclones.' She was uncertain.

'Do you? Don't you want to learn what all this is about?'

'I couldn't care less,' she muttered. 'They use me. They have always used me, kept things from me. Now they use me further in this mad confusion. . . .' She waved an arm in sudden defeat. 'Yes! Yes! Very well! We'll seek Cyclones, and curse everything else!'

They started out toward Gurdiangar without altogether realizing how much the crossroads had influenced them. The
flat road speared past nondescript fields and groves into the
saffron haze which concealed the distant hill above Gurdiangar. The road was unfenced but seemed separate from the
land on either side; trees loomed like tenuous two-dimensional ghosts, fields were vague and colorless, and only the
straight and unpaved ribbon which they followed had any
reality.

They started off riding side-by-side, and for a time they
met nobody. Liam had lost his earlier clarity and the atmospheric haze echoed his state of mind. Though he felt the
energies latent in the land about, he was tense and heavy.
He rode with a frown, beating ponderous rhythms on his
thighs. Beside him Tschea rode without present difficulty. It
was such a relief to have left the crossroads that for a while
she was almost relaxed. After several minutes she grew
curious about him. For he and his scarlet machine affected
her so strangely. In particular, his noise-machine seemed
almost ... familiar....

'What exactly *is* your noise-machine?' she asked after a
while.

'It is not a noise-machine!' Liam was affronted. 'It is a
sirena!'

'Very well!' She heard herself laugh. 'But what is it?'

'A very ancient instrument.' He scanned her with brooding hauteur. 'Sirena is the name that came to me when I
found it on a sorceror's isle, fifteen years ago. I'm sure it was
made by the race which lived before the Great Forgetting. It
has a soul of its own, and it translates the world-currents
into sound. It doesn't like being called a *noise-machine!*'

She giggled, she was beginning to feel giddy again, and the
machine pulsed at her even though it was inactive on his
back.

'I beg its pardon,' she whispered, slightly frightened. 'Its soul – its soul is the soul of the delta, I feel that. . . .'

'Please tell me about the delta,' Liam interrupted. His expression was odd and he was taken aback. So she told him A'Yaya's Tale. She told him how Analee had fired Miir with premature enthusiasm, and how Formalism had attacked the ancient beliefs. But soon her voice faltered, mad pictures were flickering in her head, and it was all she could do to stay on top of the gray Darsan horse. She forgot him as the windy afternoon grew intermittent, its hazy reality cut with distressing internal visions. Mirrors . . . the crossroads weren't completely left behind. She was being crushed by giant forces flickering on the edge of visibility.

Meanwhile Liam had started to sing in a powerful baritone; he sang and chanted at the sky and at the surrounding landscape as if protecting them both from all evil. For the afternoon grew even stranger as they began passing other travelers. People were filtering onto the highway from the countryside, drawn by incomprehensible compulsions, some starting east and others going west. Several times Liam stopped singing to shout questions at the passersby, but all of them hurried past the red-haired maniac and his shivering lady, their eyes averted. For his singing made them giddy. He had no idea what he sang, and he remembered very few of the strange people who passed.

There was a man hobbling east inside a cage of hooped iron which was studded with spikes inside and out; he squinted violently as if he hoped to grow one-eyed and wise through pain. The powerful emanation of his self-indulgent agony was sickening. Tschea saw him through the grotesque distortion of her imagination, and she felt ill. Then, with the sun getting low, they passed an old man dead by the roadside. Crows had taken his eyes. Tschea fell dizzy through the empty sockets. So she gazed at the watching sky instead, but it was even more menacing.

Liam grew to feel just as oppressed. He stopped singing and held grimly to the directional pulse which throbbed around and through him. Soon, Tschea found it impossible to remain silent, and where he'd been singing now she babbled out everything on her mind, suddenly bringing out stories of the Tarasse and of her past as evidence of the fact that she had no identity of her own and didn't know what she was doing. Liam listened, saying little, willing to listen all the way into Gurdiangar if she wanted. For she was talking about a way of life completely strange to him, one he'd never known – Miir before the Change. So different from Phadraig. Different ideas, different gods had dominated their lives. Yet ...

He interrupted her passionate description of Cuinneale's iniquity.

'What sign were you born under?' he asked.

'I have no idea,' she answered angrily. 'I never even knew my birthday ... I was given one, but – this is what I'm trying to tell you! My earliest memories are of Schroun, of the Communal Hearth. Yet in my earliest memories I know that was not my home; they were not my people! They treated me well, all progressed so smoothly toward the Tarasse that ...' She checked herself. 'I'm sure the Cyclones know who I am. But they never told me. I have no identity. I'm an easy one for the mirrormen to take over. I have no loyalties, no certainties, no ...'

She was interrupted by the approach of a great crowd.

It was growing cooler. Mists were forming, adding to the haze, laying themselves down across the road. From the mists came the sound of bells ringing, horns blowing, cattle bellowing, wheels creaking, drums beating, voices raised in ragged song. It sounded like an entire community on the move. Soon they saw that the whole road was blocked. They reined in by the road and waited for the multitude to pass, stone-faced and reserved, side-by-side.

Most of these people came from the mists on foot, carrying banners which proclaimed they were the Holy Humans from Kharsee on pilgrimage to Zagrin. They were of all ages and descriptions, from very young to very old, dragging carts and driving animals, with bundles on their backs and barking dogs behind them; they came in such a pandemonium of din and dust and energetic sense of direction that Liam and Tschea forgot themselves and stared agape.

Ragged, excited children came running ahead of the main

body, laughing as if they were on holiday. They stopped
short and stared curiously, unafraid.

'See his eyes – he's from the battle.'

'Ask him if he's seen One-Eye – go on!'

'No! You ask him!'

A pug-faced boy stepped forward, called up.

'You have seen the Savior – and the mumen?'

'I have seen the Mutant.' Liam was grim.

'Then why do you go west? We go to Zagrin to pay
homage. We ...'

But the main body was starting past, and the children
were called or snatched away. Liam and Tschea were all but
swallowed up and swept along on the tide of the huge
company, on its enthusiasm and sense of purpose. Tschea
felt their happiness, their certainty; she was so tempted.
Liam watched with an ambiguous smile, for many voices
called out to them to join, to come to Zagrin; bells were
rung in their faces so that their horses stirred nervously, and
dancers capered, cattle lumbered.... Half the immense procession was past, and Tschea was looking uncertainly at
Liam, sorely tempted to fall in with people who *knew*, when
a tall man on horseback reined in crisply beside them. He
was dapper, immaculately cloaked in blue, carried gold rings
on every finger of the one hand he had, and his face was
strong, deeply lined.

'Welcome,' he said matter-of-factly. 'We are the Holy
Humans from Kharsee and we go to Zagrin to pay homage
to the Mutant.' He nodded formally to each of them. To
Liam he said: 'Forgive my bluntness, but I sense that you
were at the battle.... Why is it you travel in the wrong
direction? Join us. All are welcome to praise the Light of
Transformation.' His eyes gleamed. 'The Mutant will make
Holy Humans of us all. Nothing will be allowed to divert
us.'

'I thank you,' said Liam soberly, glancing at Tschea as he
did, 'but the Mutant has done enough for me already. And
I've done enough for the Mutant. One-Eye took all he needed
at the battle. With the dance of the mumen he lit us up
with our energies: humans are holy already – humans are
mutants themselves!'

'Certainly. But One-Eye is the *Divine* Mutant. Praise him!'

Liam was impatient. 'He doesn't need our praise, he has his dream!'

The leader of the Holy Humans spread arms wide in sublime simplicity. 'The End, the Beginning ... all is the same in One-Eye's dream....'

'I'm not a philosopher to agree or disagree,' Liam answered hotly. 'All I know is that this Change takes place in every individual head, in the whole race! And that other forces fight for our souls in the confusion. We should use the Mutant light, not just worship it!'

'First you must forget yourself,' said the Holy Human softly.

'I've done enough forgetting to last me a lifetime!' Liam stared at the Holy Human. 'Thank you, but we will not join you!'

The man grew frosty as Tschea stared from him to Liam and back.

'Then, where are you bound?' he asked Tschea.

She said nothing. Tight-lipped, she looked away.

'To the delta,' said Liam, keeping the sirena hidden under his cloak.

The Holy Human barked with laughter. 'Ah, the delta! The Cyclone project! Many go there, hoping for the Fifth Element to spring out of the mudbanks – even the whales, or so I've heard!' And he laughed harder, leaning back, until suddenly reaching forward, serious, beckoning confidentially to the pair of them.

'You're fools to have hopes of the delta,' he whispered, as if fearing the sky might hear him. 'Take my advice – turn around. Many are going to the delta. It's a powerful place. But those of the mirrors prevent its activation and mean to destroy it if they can – which they will do when Nikosner has succeeded in persuading the people of Ussian to burn and curse their city ... and he is succeeding! What can stop him? The Cyclones? They sit besieged in their Colleges, fluttering their hands. Miir is doomed. Take good advice – come with us!'

The crowd was almost past. Liam twitched his reins, west.

'Continue to the east,' he said in farewell, 'and you'll

come to a crossroads wrapped in reflections. Thanks for your advice.'

The Holy Human laughed again as he wheeled away. 'We have come through many crossroads; we have our direction. You – continue to the west, you'll come to Gurdiangar!'

Then he was gone, and the rest with him. Tschea stared after them.

'What – did – he – mean?' Her hands were tightly clenched.

Liam was restless, already forgetting what had been said, thinking only of Gurdiangar, of the rhythms of the Change. 'We'll find out when we get there.'

'No – I mean about Ussian ... being burned and cursed ... by its own people....' Her head was bowed. She could not look at the sky in case her face reflected in it. 'Why is that necessary to destroy the delta?'

'Perhaps they need a physical base nearby....' Liam's voice was faraway. He was examining the strange landscape ahead, all bumped and broken and knobby in the last of the sun, crowned by a hill which for all the world was like a baldheaded man, complete with ears. '... Perhaps Ussian must be made alien before aliens can be solid there; perhaps the mirrormen can't take a place until they're invited....' He shrugged, turned to her. Her eyes were fixed on the road. She looked unwell, weak, lacking in energy. 'Ah,' he said, 'come on. We'll crack those mirrors with music. I can feel it! Tonight, at Gurdiangar, come what may, the sirena will sing!' And he leaned over, took her by the shoulders, shook her with energetic encouragement. 'Come on!' he exhorted. 'Come on!' He shook her until she looked up angrily and threw his arms off, calling him a cold-hearted barbarian.

'Wake up! Don't dream of Ussian. Be here and now!'

'Don't shake me like that, ever again!'

'That's better. But don't stare at the road like that, you'll ...'

'Don't tell me what to do!'

The air quivered with her shout. Liam shrugged; then, raising hands in supplication, he turned and rode off, arguing furiously with himself, wondering what he'd done wrong, why he felt so affronted. After a hundred feet or so he stopped, turned, looked back. She hadn't moved. They faced each other across the space, each waiting for the other to make a move. Then Liam laughed suddenly, slapped his thigh, and cantered back. She met his eyes with a brittle dignity.

'Mad I may be, but you could show more tenderness.' She was sharp. 'You shook me as if I'm a thing to be coaxed along. I don't think we could ever understand each other at all.'

Liam shrugged expansively. He felt restless, troubled by her.

'I'm a boor,' he admitted gruffly. 'No doubt about it. But you definitely needed a shake. Now, will you come along?'

'You're a strange man,' she said, more easily, seeing the lines around his eyes, reading them for the first time. 'I don't think you were ever happy.... Why did you take me from the caravan?'

'One good turn deserves another.' Liam was abrupt, and he looked away, anxious to reach Gurdiangar. The sun was very low, and the air was getting colder.

Tschea realized how tired, hungry, and saddlesore she was. The rocky, knobbled landscape ahead ... it seemed alive. It was difficult to cling to sense, to hold herself down in her shivering body. Her teeth were starting to chatter. 'Very well,' she said, 'Gurdiangar.'

'You're cold.' He was gruff, as if embarrassed that he hadn't thought of it before. 'Here.' Folded in the saddlebag of his uncomplaining horse, the one Yelinne had ridden, was a woolen Darsan cloak.

With it wrapped around her she was much warmer. But still she knew that the sky was watching as they started through the broken land, through sharp irregularities of slanting sun and deep shadow. 'Tell me about Phadraig,' she insisted. 'Keep me here and now. Tell me what made you, and how you saw the world from the city of Norm Purity.'

'Oh, yes!' Liam's laugh echoed about, and his eyes cast ahead. 'Norm Purity!' He told her how the ancient hill-city had strangled itself with inflexible tradition in fear of Witch-goddess Earth and of change. He told her how the population had declined, how increasing numbers of deviations from the Norm had led to laxity in the execution or expulsion of Uncleans. 'It was practical necessity. Or nobody would have been left to praise Norm Purity. Even so, it didn't change that much.' He shook his head emphatically. The air was beginning to smell of sulfur. 'Phadraig wasn't a place where people could freely live and love. Love was a mythologized duty, Norm Purity was self-hate, Norm Purity was Gobhan, the First Servant!' Now he was fixing her with a rigid gaze, his eyes burning. 'Some of us were free for a time, but we were fools, we returned to aid the city against Kalnakill. Then Gobhan broke us with treachery. And he murdered Rix – I know he did. He killed Rix because we mocked him publicly. He killed Rix, and Liam stopped laughing.'

He fell silent. They were climbing now, up a corridor of bare rock. The skull of the hill ahead had the last of the sun to itself, and was hazed by the vapors. Tschea's eyes were watering. Her head was beginning to float again. She rode beside Liam, feeling sad.

'Who was Rix?'

'He was a friend ... a gentle maniac.' Liam scratched his head.

'Did you have affairs with women?'

Liam looked at her askance. 'There's a time for everything,' he said. 'Presently, it's time to save breath.' And he nodded ahead.

They'd rounded a rocky corner.

The hot springs of Gurdiangar lay before them.

It was a weird world at the foot of the bald hill. Vaguely, Tschea remembered being here before. The town itself was built in a timbered fold of the hill, away from the fumes. The road ahead was sulfur-scarred and steamy; she knew it climbed around and up above the springs. Liam looked at her. She saw through tears how he was tapping out fingertip rhythms on the saddle, how energetically nervous he was. She felt no easier. The horses were nervous. The air reeked, coiled with oppressing forms – watching eyes, ominous reflections, accusing faces. . . .

They advanced cautiously past outlying springs and bar-

ren rocks which were bleached and streaked with vivid
colors. Protecting their heads in their cloaks, they trusted to
the sure feet of the horses. The animals struggled around and
up above the half-bowl, above a withering hell. It was
peeled, blistered, splashed with raw colors; sulfur springs
jumped feet from fuming alum vents; iron springs shriveled
the air with heat; vapor rose in jerky puffs; the air was filled
with a cacophony of squeaks, groans, hisses – natural lamentations which sounded to Tschea like devils chattering at
her.

Fool, hissed the geysers, *what are you doing here?* And
the pools of scalding mud : *Traitor*, they bubbled, *coward*,
child-deserter! When she realized that her horse was treading only feet from the crumbling rim, she did nothing to
draw it away, for her guilt was extreme. Liam didn't
approach her, sensing she'd react as an enemy; besides, already they were passing the first of the resort buildings,
leaving the bowl and turning past small-windowed single-
story stone buildings : bath-houses and departure points for
treks down to the bowl.

Then they were over the ridge, able to breathe again,
looking down on an extensive jumble of bright-roofed
buildings all crammed on top of each other in the fold of the
hill. The narrow streets were filled with people. Liam's eyes
gleamed. The pulse from the southwest was throbbing
through him – the time was come. The gates of Gurdiangar
were wide open. He spurred eagerly forward. Tschea followed blindly, abandoned inside as they rode into Gurdiangar, with Darsans forgotten, mirrors forgotten, Cyclones
forgotten.

A Cyclone of the Outer Vortex saw them come through
the gates.

His name was Harne. He was a slight, dark man.

Like Lonawi, he came from Baethnan.

Save for a short closed season each year the stocky local people of Gurdiangar were always outnumbered by the tourists and sick pilgrims who brought wealth to the place. Now the resort was filled with stranded travelers and others inclined to stay put until it became clear what was happening in the world outside. Nikosner seemed a much more potent threat than the vague delirium about mutant conquerors and changes in reality. No glaring madman had infected Gurdiangar, so far. But many upset and upsetting travelers had passed through during the last twenty-four hours. The Holy Humans in particular had left confusion and dreadful tales in their wake, and quite a few people had gone with them. So far, there had been little violence. The people who came to Gurdiangar were hardly warlike. They'd been sweating out the hours in the bath-houses, or drinking in the bars, or watching the strange people passing through, growing increasingly uneasy at the breakdown in carriage services.

In midafternoon their unease became outrage when the local people withdrew all services and retired to their homes, hoping that the tourists would decide to go somewhere else once they found the bath-houses locked, the bars closed, the beds unmade, and all entertainments canceled.

By sunset it was clear to Harne that a riot was in the making.

He'd been in Gurdiangar since the morning: watching, listening, taking part in the arguments ... waiting....

By sunset he'd received the message that Tschea and the songmaker were approaching. They weren't to be contacted unless Baethnan's Master gave the word. And the Master, at the delta, depended on Dulankir to receive and transmit message and reply. Atmospheric confusion had grown too great for direct sending. Time was short and Dulankir was undergoing a strange form of attack. Frowning, Harne started toward the eastern gates from a garden behind the Green-spring Hotel, the resort's social center. Angry crowds were thickening in front of the hotel, overflowing from the Parade of Grateful Pilgrims into the narrow streets beyond. Patrons thrown out of the hotel were screaming abuse at its shut windows as Harne angled past arguing cliques, families, and national groups. The ornamental dwarf-trees planted along the sloping parade were being torn apart for clubs by incongruously holiday-costumed men. The visitors were filled with resentment and a strange new nervousness.

'... Even the bars. If I don't get a drink soon, I'll—'

'Nikosner's making Ussian's people tear their city apart....'

'Be glad he's not here! Where's your damned brother? I'll scream!'

'... Listen, sparrow-man of Kor, don't teach *me* man-ners!'

'Purplefield savage! You repulsive orphan-eater, you dis-gust me!'

'... Dulankir? Under attack by ... *ghosts?* That's ridicu-lous....'

A blustering fear was spreading generally. Many of the tourists desperately needed someone to blame for their dis-quiet. Harne left them and climbed the winding street to the eastern gates. He'd seen no local people about; he met few on the street. Their doors were locked, their windows were shuttered, and many had already left for the country-side.

He reached the gates before sunset and waited in shadow. When Liam and Tschea came through the gates he didn't show himself. They rode their weary Darsan horses down into the town without pausing, but Harne didn't follow even when the crowd-noise faded away into startled silence.

After three more travelers had reeled through the gates with streaming eyes, he came forward to meet Lonawi. Without ado he swung up behind his brother Cyclone. Lona-wi was grim, dusty, tired, pessimistic.

But, as they rode down, they heard and felt the music be-ginning....

* * *

Liam plunged down the twisting street to a bad-tempered crowd. He had no idea why. It was time for the sirena to sing, and that was all.

Tschea was horrified to find herself riding after him past locked-up houses with narrow shuttered windows, after him down around a final corner to rein in desperately only feet from the milling people.

If he's not a magician, I'm dead, she thought.

For Liam was picking a path into the crowd, an energetic scarecrow attracting immediate suspicion. He turned and called her on. For a moment she paused, confronted by twilight eyes on the edge of the Change. Then she laughed with dizzy contempt. *Why am I scared by a crowd of prosperous hypochondriacs? This is only Gurdiangar!* And she followed on.

But it didn't feel like a holiday resort as they rode into the silent press. The crowd opened in front of Liam and closed immediately behind Tschea. Nobody was willing to lay hands on the ... madman ... nor on the woman with her eyes so wide and blank.

They were almost at the Parade when they were challenged. A youth in a startling shirt of black-and-white zig-zags leaned out of the last first-floor window in the street, and his voice was loud and trembling.

'You! And the lady! Who are you? You burn, you must be ... mad!'

'How can someone wearing a shirt like that call me mad?' Liam roared back as Tschea felt the fear and doubt of the people around her. 'Your shirt's disturbing! And what's this? You say we burn?'

'Yes! You're crowned with auras! You shake with chaos!'

'Auras?' Amid mounting babble Liam felt the air above his head in mime of search for an aura. 'Yes, we shake with the Change, true! As for the auras you see ... to see them you must also be changing. Everyone has always had an aura. Vegetables have auras! Everything's energy!'

'You're obviously insane!' came a shout from the crowd. There was a roar of agreement. Confusion was developing: some of those closest were trying to get away while others more distant were trying to get closer. A hand grabbed Tschea's ankle, but she kicked it away as Liam beside her swept his cloak aside and unslung the sirena. 'A weapon!' someone screamed. In the surge to get away many fell and were trampled. Tschea fought to hold her head and her horse.

'Listen!' shouted Liam, standing in the stirrups, holding the sirena high. 'We must celebrate the Change and not deny it. Let's see what lies where!' And he jumped so positively from his fretful horse to the cobbles that those creeping forward fell back again, for the madman and his strange machine seemed to glow. Liam paid them no attention. He walked around the horses and helped Tschea to dismount. His eyes were dancing. She was resigned to death at least, she was smiling faintly, somehow amused to be about to meet her end at the hands of a savage horde of elderly socialites and tourists.

Liam was ecstatic. And obviously deranged.

'Sit down,' he suggested. 'Why wear yourself out?'

He set himself comfortably down on the cobbles with many eyes staring, ignoring the clamor of demands from the Parade to know what was going on. Folding his legs beneath him, he laid the sirena across his lap and was immediately engrossed in the control board of the scarlet machine which glimmered in the twilight. Tschea, still standing, sensed that even those bent on violence were puzzled and increasingly mesmerized by the nimble magic of Liam's fingers which alighted here, there, doing a touch-dance over the instrument to establish connection with it. Swarthily top-knotted people from Phrenge and austere High-Hats from Spokane predominated immediately around him; in their doubt they were forming a bulwark against the hostility behind. Tschea sat down stiffly.

How long could this assumed inviolability last?

Then Liam sounded an opening note, a sharp punctuation that alerted the crowd. Quickly he followed it up with a barrage of cheeky pops, whines, and hisses. People along the Parade stared wildly up and about. They heard hot springs bursting in the air. Had he infected them with madness already? But fresh demands for his death were contested by

startling laughter from the neck of the street – the laughter
of those who'd seen the grotesque faces Liam pulled to illus-
trate each different sound. Not everyone had laughed.
Tschea saw how some trembled fearfully. And Liam's face
was dreamily distant now, completely . . . gone somewhere
else.

Gazing up at the purpling sky he started to play so softly,
beyond hearing, stirring her back to that night of the Harvest Festival when she'd wished for a new music. The evening was beginning to sparkle. Her doubts were falling away
as a slow wave of relaxation rippled through Gurdiangar.
The youth in the zigzag shirt who'd come down to the
street to kill the madman got as far as the doorstep. Shortly
he was sitting there with head on knees, drifting in the
sparkle which flowed from the well of songmaker and
sirena, in the current which crept through doors and drew
out the townspeople to share in the trance.

The broad calm river rippled through Gurdiangar and
beyond.

Liam had forgotten about watchers and invisible politi-
cians.

He was in the shaping of the pulse, one pulse of many in
the disordered lands, the signature-pulse of the garden he'd
visited the night before. It was the song which had carried
him over the night-land in the gulf, a song inside and a song
beyond, not so much a conscious choice as a fortunate hap-
penstance. The sirena breathed out a wave of light which
washed these people gently into their own uncharted terri-
tories, which eased them into themselves and into the
Change on the edge of which they'd been trembling. It grew
so that everyone was alone with his or her vision of the
current, alone and together, for at times they all reacted
identically – when as one they laughed, sighed, or groaned in
fearful awe. For as the pulse grew stronger it became familiar, something they'd known all their lives without recognizing. It was a great river within and without, and there
was no holding back the meetings with rocks and rapids and
dizzy whirlpools, for now the journey was begun.

And in time, a question was sung :

It's good. It's so good
To be flowing here with you
Do you think we could agree
To flow together to the sea?

And when he'd sung out the question, Liam stopped playing.

The current died away. Like a man awakening he opened his eyes, very slowly. It was dark. Far above, the stars were remarkable, sparkling like crystals. The hill above Gurdiangar was a smooth-domed blackness, silhouetted against the starry night like a two-dimensional cutout. There was a coldness in him. He sensed danger.

Gurdiangar breathed soft all around, its lamps unlit.

Somewhere, someone muttered, otherwise the silence was complete, save for a slight stir of breeze – save for the sound of shod hooves on cobbles, coming rapidly closer from the eastern gates.

Tschea moved. Her face was a dim whiteness.

'We forgot about the Darsans,' she whispered.

Far below, the hot springs gleamed luridly in the night as the two mirror-bound Darsans climbed on horseback toward the gates. Vels and Yelinne had forgotten their lives before the crossroads. They'd emerged from the house enmeshed in murderous reflections which amplified the importance of their duty : to kill the madman. They'd started out on the Gurdiangar Road without hesitation, at first on foot, but before long on a horse taken from a traveler whom they'd left dead in a ditch. Soon after, they'd claimed a second mount in similar fashion. They'd ridden furiously west, past the Holy Humans, cursing the delta, cursing the devil madman, Darsans no more. And when they neared the hot springs and felt the atmospheric flood of Liam's music, it affected each of them differently.

The music told Vels that he was deranged; it reminded him of what had happened before the crossroads. The reflections had caught him, the house had taken him, done something to him, to Yelinne ... she was crazy too. Something had happened ... he couldn't quite remember ... and

she was determined to be the executioner. They forced their
way to the gates. The flood's full force struck them. Immediately, Vels felt relaxed, the killing compulsion slackened.
But Yelinne stiffened and fought. 'Give me strength!' she
muttered. 'Let me destroy the devil!' But the flood was too
strong. Shuddering with agonized pleasure she groaned at
the stars, unable to go forward. She saw Vels slumped in his
saddle, grinning idiotically. 'Traitor,' she moaned, 'fight it!'

Then she heard Liam's invitation to flow to the sea and
she cried for help again. But Vels thought of A'Yaya's Tale
and found himself in tune with an anciently familiar tide
that drowned his wish to kill.

The flood died suddenly. The two Darsans stared down
into a dark pit of silence. Yelinne's face twisted, and she
goaded her horse forward through the gates. Shouting with
anger, Vels pursued her down into Gurdiangar as she spurred her horse viciously down the twisting street and around
a sharp corner. Then she was dragging hard on the reins.
Her horse bucked only feet from the somnolent crowd, dim
in the darkness; she was righteously shocked. Their minds
had been stolen. Where was the thief? She felt him very
close, and she notched a bolt in her crossbow.

'You've heard the music. Will you come to the delta?'

The voice was quiet, close. An iron fist gripped her heart
as she made him out. He stood not fifteen feet away, watching her, unmoving, impaling her with his gaze as the crowd
began to stir. She raised and aimed her crossbow stiffly as
Vels caught up with her. 'No!' he shouted, snatching at her
arm as she fired. 'It's sacrilege!' And the bolt flew high and
wide over a rooftop. Howling, Yelinne smashed the crossbow into Vels's face; she drew a short sword and charged
without care for those her terrified horse trampled. They
were lost already! She had eyes only for the archfiend. He
stared as she neared him. One-eyed, hypnotizing her!

With people screaming and cursing, she faltered in her
charge.

The man in the zigzag shirt vaulted onto Liam's horse and
sprang at her, swept her to the cobbles, knocking her unconscious. Liam grabbed the reins of her panicking horse
and soothed it. And the man in the zigzag shirt stood

shakily as commotion spread. Vels, knocked dazed from his horse, was hauled to his feet, threatened. A woman whose man had been trampled was screaming. The peace of communion was gone. 'Throw them in the hot springs!' somebody roared, and there were cries of argument. Tschea caught at Liam's arms. The happiness was over. Doubts were breeding again, confusing her, so that she was already bad-tempered.

'Why didn't you defend yourself? Why did you do nothing?'

He shrugged. Taking the sirena, he winged out a sharp note.

The silence was immediate, broken only by sobbing, breathing.

'Be still!' he called out. 'Confusion's over.' He breathed deeply. 'Let's have some light!' he demanded. 'Let's see where we are!'

The Darsans were defeated. But not the force behind them. Yelinne's eyes had almost frozen him – they'd been like reflecting mirrors. Now she lay, crumpled, unconscious. Someone brought a lamp. Liam scratched his head, and thanked the man in the zigzag shirt.

'I'm Liam.' He extended his right hand. 'And you?'

'My name's Tairo.' The young blue-tattoo's voice shook. He took the proffered hand cautiously. Liam met open eyes shining from a strong brown face, eyes shining with respectful ardor. 'My father is Jaos the Guide. Sir, are you all right?'

'Am *I* all right?' Liam was taken aback.

Then he realized how possessively the enormous crowd was surrounding him, taking him in, awaiting more music to soothe its nerves. . . .

Tschea bent to his ear, her eyes glinting mischievously, sadly. 'Ah,' she whispered for him alone, 'now you've done it. You're their god. Do you think they'll let you leave them without music?' And she started laughing as his disciples surrounded him.

It was ludicrous. Liam went to the conscious Darsan with Tairo like an acolyte at his shoulder. The wounded were pulled from his path, and anxious hands reached out to touch him, his cloak, the sirena; torches were held up to light his way, some heads bowed as he passed, and many pairs of eyes were filled with awe. The Darsan was thrown roughly at his feet to croak for forgiveness.

Vels looked up in fearful awe and hailed the red-haired being as a manifestation of the Zuni Bird, sent to lead people through confusion. Uproar broke out, as if the identification was likely enough to be disputed. Liam found himself at the center of arguments, denials, agreements, fantastic counter-theories to explain his nature, his origin, his miraculous music, his strange machine, his apparent disregard for death. Several times he tried to interrupt, but nobody paid him any attention. Not even Tairo. They were too busy deciding what kind of god he was. They wanted a visible, tangible, reassuring god. He was reaping a whirlwind which he should have foreseen, and they would hardly let him go. What were the watchers doing? Had this been foreseen?

Surrounded by excitement Liam stared up at the sky, briefly excited himself. Was he to lead thousands to an as-yet-unknown apotheosis at the delta? Perhaps this explained the battle above his head, perhaps this explained Tschea's intervention. His elation was wry, short-lived. It was ridiculous to think of personal triumph, he was only a deluded songmaker, probably still in One-Eye's dreaming grasp, no more than another puppet agent employed in some incomprehensibly vast scheme of human engineering.

'Will you play again when you've judged these assassins?'

Tairo was hopeful, respectful. The tumult was slackening. Liam saw a blur of shadowed faces, close-pressing. They were waiting for him, these unknown people starting on the

Change. None but Tairo and the Darsan stood out as individuals. It was oppressive. What could he do but accept their
collective idea? – for the time being.

He squatted beside the trembling Darsan, said softly,
'What you say – could the mirrors have told you to say it?'

Vels shook his head violently. 'No! They told me to kill
you. Your music made me remember!'

'Then, since you see me so well, how do you see yourself?'

The Darsan met his eyes. Vels was terrified, determined to
admit the truth. 'This morning,' he hissed rapidly through
his teeth, 'I murdered a friend in rage at the truth he told
me. He said we were all mad, and living in a daydream. I
killed him.'

'And tonight you save my life,' replied Liam, as rapidly.
'Go free to the delta – wash your spirit clean.'

Amid an approving murmur he was escorted to Yelinne.
She was conscious again. Her left arm was broken, but not
her fervid hate. She spat at him. 'One-eyed devil! Delta-
spawn! Kill us both!' Her eyes glittered, and she had to be
held back. 'You'll fail nevertheless.'

Torchlight flickered, and the shifting crowd muttered
angrily.

'You're not very generous.' Liam's eyes were droll, interested. He pondered for a moment. 'I have only two eyes.
And your punishment is: a doctor will set your arm, then
you're free to do what you want.'

She screamed at his severity. And though there were
mutters of surprise, nobody questioned the decision. Depressed, tired, Liam turned away, looking for Tschea where
she'd been by the horses. He couldn't see her anywhere. He
couldn't feel the night. A dozen people were trying to
attract his attention. Others were already crying for more
music. He felt smothered. They'd crush him with their
hunger. He had to get off the street. He turned on Tairo as
Yelinne was led away, started to explain his human needs.
Tairo listened, but his face grew sulky: he wanted more
music like the rest of them.

'The spirit can't be forced!' Liam shouted, barely audible
above the uproar of increasing demands. 'I must wash, eat,

rest, be with my lady, and have time to contemplate the
beauty of creation. I....'

A girl came out of the door which Tairo had used; she
wriggled through the crowd, and said something in Tairo's
ear with her eyes fixed on Liam. Her beguiling face was
framed in rich chestnut hair; her small, neat figure was provocative, wrapped in green and white linen spirals from
shoulders to ankles. Liam was in no mood to consider a god's
prerogatives. Tairo turned to him. 'My sister Aleen tells me,'
he explained, teeth gleaming, 'that your lady's already rest-
ing in my father's house.'

Liam sniffed games. He didn't care. It was enough to get
off the street.

Tairo shouted explanations and assurances as he slammed
the door in the face of people trying to push through. 'He
won't be long! He has human needs! Wait patiently.'

The mounting bellow of protest was reduced almost to a
murmur by the thickness of the door.

Tschea was upstairs, collapsed on a bed in a lamplit room.
There was a mirror in the room – a large one, in a plain oval
frame, hung on one of the low walls. It had caught her
attention immediately. Hardly daring to breathe, she had
looked. Had seen a haunted, dirty face ... her own face.

It had been quite a relief. She hadn't looked a second time.

She'd refused food, a bath, insisting that all she wanted to
do was lie down. Aleen had come upon her in the street,
eagerly calling her by name and Tarasse rank. 'My father
took us to Ussian five years ago,' she'd explained, 'to show
us the room in the Tarasse where he was born Unique. I saw
you there!' She'd practically dragged Tschea into the house,
into a room where a dazed old man was sitting, apparently
overwhelmed by the chance to succor a Red Feather. Tschea
didn't believe it. The girl had Liam on her mind. How
sensible! She could have him.

'A bed,' she'd said, 'a room alone, please, that's all.'

When the door slammed below she was stretched out,
still in the Darsan cloak, staring at a violently colored painting on the wall beside the bed. It depicted an intrepid
Guide (no doubt Jaos) leading masked and goggled tourists

through the inferno of the springs. She continued staring, wide awake, abysmally depressed. Only sleep would solve this misery. But sleep was impossible. There was racket outside, downstairs, and in her head. Had Liam foreseen this? Did he want it? What did it matter? The peace and certainty of the music was gone, and her head jangled with accusations again. Namahon ... and Cassa, Flath, Larene – they might be dead already. Or changed into something terrible.... She glanced fearfully at the mirror, but all it reflected was the heavily shuttered window. Nikosner had Ussian. In any case, she couldn't reach them. What was worse, she didn't care. She sat up, violently.

'I have to care!' she shouted at the sloping ceiling. She fell back. 'But I can't.' Her voice was faint. *All my life*, she thought, *nothing but transient loyalties*. She saw the image of Algon. But it was old, and mixed up with newer confusions and horrors ... mixed up with Nikosner and the mirrors, with this madness which Liam called Change. His music. Why wasn't his personality as sparkling and clear as the music? Was it Phadraig, or his nature too? She groaned, she was aching; he had to play again. He *must* play again! No, she could live without ... No, she couldn't.... She sat up again, rigid. 'I'm as stupid as those fools shouting outside,' she muttered. 'It's meaningless – and there's *nothing* at the delta, nothing but mud and water and birds and idiots!'

Besides, she thought, more calmly, *how can we get to the delta now?*

When Liam came in, she was shaking with her face to the wall.

No peace he'd had. The moment he'd got inside, what seemed like generations of Tairo's excited relatives had appeared from various parts of the house. They took him over while Tairo held the sirena as if the touch of it would make him whole. A bath had been already run, and Liam accepted it gladly before discovering that a god couldn't be expected to scrub and shave himself. His fragile patience dissolved when they tried to discard his trousers and cat's-eye tunic in favor of a garment patterned with flaming rainbows; he roared at them. Next they sat him down amid cushions, brought him food and drink. He picked while they hovered and tried to choose what he'd like. Outside the crowd was getting louder ... it was all too much. Beckoning to Tairo, he stalked out.

'Where's Tschea?' His voice was curt, and he snatched his sirena.

Shaking, Tairo pointed up the stairs to a green door.

'You'll play again soon?'

Liam didn't reply, but took the stairs three at a time. When he entered the room, he saw the mirror before he saw Tschea.

'Have you looked in it?' he demanded.

She didn't reply or look around. Compressing his lips angrily, he approached the mirror, not realizing how much his peace of mind had been upset since the coming of the Darsans. 'Ridiculous,' he muttered, glaring at his own wild face. 'Hear them howling outside. It's a trap, they won't let me go, they'll suck me dry; if I tried leading them to the delta I'd drop dead long before we got there. Cyclones! Hah!'

Tschea continued staring at the tasteless mural, temper no better.

'Don't make me angry,' he said, very quietly, approaching the bed. 'You can at least acknowledge my existence. You can....'

Tairo burst in at that moment, without knocking, very nervous.

'They'll break in and tear us apart if you don't come out now!'

Tairo was appalled by the uncontrollable shivering, by the acceleration of the seizures. He feared he was falling apart.

'God, madman, whatever you are – you must play peace again!'

Liam didn't reply; he was regarding Tschea's obstinately turned back with simmering eyes. Tairo couldn't stand it; greater fear overcame lesser, and he grabbed Liam brusquely by the shoulder, spun the songmaker around to face him. Liam's eyes narrowed. Tairo was breaking out in a sweat, and he removed his hand. 'Curse this shaking!' he hissed. 'You *must* play now, before we all go mad!'

'Yes!' Tschea stirred around, her expression sad and ironic. 'Play again,' she whispered. 'Perhaps the Cyclones will hear this time.'

'You were sent to lead us to the delta.' Tairo didn't seem to have heard her; his eyes gleamed with conviction. 'Even the foreigners.'

Not knowing what he felt, Liam nodded hopeless assent. He sensed conflicting currents which would surely tear him apart. He sensed that something was lost, something was forgotten. But Tairo's eyes had leaped from midnight to midday. He let Tairo carry the sirena downstairs. Tschea wouldn't follow. They gazed at each other uncompromisingly before he turned and went with reluctant eagerness.

Wildness shivered in him. What did the watchers matter? Perhaps they were delusions. The outer door was opened. Tairo handed over the sirena with reverence. Taking it, grinning like a wolf, Liam walked into the crowd. He was chaired shoulder-high to the steps of the Greenspring Hotel. The roaring and stamping died away. The currents of the night were surging through him again. Raising his head to the stars, he set his feet firmly apart and started to grow an enormous gonglike drone which reverberated through the town.

It took Tschea off the bed, and she stood with gritted teeth. 'No!' she groaned. 'He goes his way, I'll go mine!'

The room was oppressive as the drone faded; she had to look at the mirror. The reflection of wall and shuttered window was hazy. Something was interfering with the light. Now she half-understood. Liam had lost confidence with the coming of the Darsans. She sensed danger. She ran out of the empty house, past the two horses still standing unstabled and nervous. She began pushing through the crowd toward the Parade as she felt the heartbeat growing from the sirena....

Everyone felt it. Vels in the crowd felt it. Yelinne at the edge of the drop to the hot springs felt it, and she paused. It grew like the beat of the earth itself – it pounded through everyone. A mercurial rhythm snaked over it, demanding a shaking-loose. Then hundreds began to dance as the music grew stronger, stranger; as high fragments of melody came fleeting over the heartbeat, diving and soaring through the rhythm, touching every mind with bright ecstatic wraiths.

Liam was an open channel. Miir was exploding through him with a mounting irregularity of signals and pulses which the sirena transformed into music more powerful than anything he'd ever played. The instrument seemed to be singing of its own accord; he wasn't aware of it when his feet were taken on the urge to climb to the summit of the hill. At some point, though, with the crowds spreading out and discarding unnecessary clothing, he left the steps. With rhythm looser but earthbeat solid, he burned a path through the dancing crowd and took an alley leading to a path which zigzagged up the side of the hill.

Tschea was among the hundreds who followed like children, their tensions and dignities dissolved. Yet ... part of her wondered what was happening. Why up the hill? Liam was halfway up the path's first diagonal as she started up. At first he was torchlit and visible to the followers – swaying and stamping up with the sirena molded to him, moving faster, doglegging up among the first of the fir trees. As he climbed further and further ahead the night seemed to grow colder, and people began to lose the beat. For the music changed. It became ominous; it echoed through the firs like an icy wind and broke the dancers out of ecstasy. Tschea stopped moving. She shivered in malevolent darkness, for the sound reminded her of the crossroads....

Then the dark music faded and failed. There was a moment of stupefied silence. Here and there on the hillside, torches flickered. Then clamor erupted above her, and she heard Liam roaring angrily.

'I'll not play that! I'll not destroy you with my madness!'

Then the slopes were a confusion of cursing, floundering people.

With an icy heart Tschea started scrambling straight up the side of the hill, tripping over roots and running into low-hanging branches. She intersected the path again, thrust terrified people aside in the dark, and continued climbing despite her sudden exhaustion. She was sure he'd make for the summit, and she had to get there in time....

*   *   *

The first part of his ascent was a beautiful delirium.

It was when he reached the trees that the music became utterly ugly. Sinister images descended into him as he climbed higher. They were images of personal triumph, haughty and chill, and they paved him with ice. They flickered and reflected and drew his lips back from his teeth so that he snarled as he played; his body climbed and his mind descended through blood-red clouds of living vapor. The clouds coalesced into glaring eyes, and ...

And it was then that he stopped in his tracks and remembered.

Numb, cursing himself, he stopped playing. There was an instant of silence. Then clamor broke out behind him and he shouted out his self-disgust. He ran. Tormented, he ran around the side of the hill until a branch clouted him across the forehead. When he came to, he heard voices calling out in terror and he had no idea where he was. With the sirena clutched in one hand he continued up the hill in an automatic daze. His thoughts were fugitive; he was scarcely puzzled by his inability to remember who or where he was. When the trees thinned out he found himself gazing toward the summit of the hill, less than two minutes' walk away. But the night sky was pressing down, the stars were spinning like whirlpools, spinning closer so that he ducked, afraid that they'd press down too far and his throbbing head would burst through into whatever lay beyond. He didn't want to climb another step, but the summit was a compelling fascination. So he stumbled on up over the bare rock, vainly trying to remember what was wrong and what land he was in. The sky was exploding about him: the charged atmosphere flickered and sparkled and crawled with electric worms which urged him on toward the flat marble table that marked the summit.

He saw a man seated on this table with folded arms, a man who waited for him in the center of the electric storm.

Liam approached with the utmost reluctance.

For the man's aquiline profile was familiar, and now he was turning to greet the songmaker like a friend. Liam stopped dead. Something was very wrong.

Yet – it was Rix who awaited him, there was no doubt.

It was the voice of his friend he heard in his head, he was certain.

Come on, Liam, rejoin the Company. We're united again. Step up on the table with me, it's a door, and the way is open. . . .

Rix the Sculptor stood on the table, beckoning. Liam's mind was as thick and obscured as molasses. He took an uncertain step forward.

'How did you know where I was?' he called out suspiciously.

We heard your music. Could we fail to recognize your talent? And you sensed us, for you played at the frequency which admits us. Come on!

Liam took another forward step, unable to decide what was wrong.

As he did, he heard through the storm's bright crackling a little snatch of melody that stopped him in his tracks.

It was a simple tune, played on a flute. For a moment he found himself somewhere else. Instead of standing on this hilltop, he seemed to be standing in a beautiful garden amid the warm glow of unknown blooms which filled him with energy. He shook his head. The garden vanished. He saw Rix again. But Rix held no flute. Besides, the sound seemed to have come from farther down the hill. He looked about suspiciously.

Ignore the phantoms which hold you back! Your friends are waiting – Patrick, Scalaman, all of us. Don't hold back! There's no time!

The voice in his head was severe, slightly cold, and Liam frowned. Then the flute piped again. There was a bright explosion in his mind. And Liam remembered. 'You're dead!' he shouted with sad disgust. 'Gobhan murdered you a year ago. You're a trick, a reflection, a trap!'

Liam turned and stumbled away as Rix shredded into nothing, as the enshrouding electric storm rotated away into some other space, leaving the songmaker alone at the top of the hill, beneath high stars.

For a little while he lay like a bag of bones near the summit, shivering at the narrowness of his escape. His first coherent thought was to wonder who'd played the flute.

Who had saved him? And the garden ... slowly he recalled what had happened during the day, and for the first time since leaving the crossroads he realized that his mind had been darkened, his commitment to the delta had been insecure. The garden ... he'd seen it the night before, he'd walked there, and intermittently throughout the day he'd half-remembered the experience. He'd been there upon arriving at Gurdiangar; he'd played the delta-pulse. But his hold of it had been tenuous, and the Darsan had snapped him into the killing current....

Liam stood. He heard distressed people crashing about in the woods on the lower slopes. Now he could clearly distinguish between the opposing currents which streamed through Miir tonight. *Both* of them came from the southwest – one from the delta ... and one from Ussian. Now he stood above Gurdiangar and felt them plainly, and he began to understand their different characteristics. They were not so much opposed as aspecting. The current from the delta he sensed as a broad calm avenue of light rippling in all directions, its colors inside him were pure and sparkling, its essence was compassionate love, it brought integration with the natural world. The current from Ussian was choppy, agitated, and frantic; those caught in it could be concerned with nothing more than survival, lust, and power. Its colors were muddy with the dark and de-energized red of stale blood predominating; its tendency was to separate and confuse. The conflict was a matter of whether Miir was to be a garden – or a charnel house. It was no choice at all.

'... Yet I was almost confused into choosing confusion,' he whispered to himself through chattering teeth. 'It's not just the conflict of Miir, it's the basis of history. We must hate ourselves very much to have let this psychic gravity drag us down for so many thousands of ...'

'Liam! Where are you? Are you all right?'

It was Tschea! He'd forgotten all about her. Bellowing out her name, he started through the darkness toward her.

She had seen how nearly he was trapped and destroyed. She'd heard the melody of the flute, twice, coming from a different place each time. She hadn't caught any glimpse of the player. Now she moved urgently toward Liam, ignoring her bruising and confusion. She was filled with yearning and with a hope that the yearning might be fulfilled, and she wanted to help him, knowing now that it was the same thing as helping herself. Not far behind were furious people with torches – they'd tear him apart if they reached him first. She called again. He answered, very close. Then he loomed out of the darkness. They caught and clung together; their mutual relief was tangible and embraced them both.

'I hurt many people again,' said Liam rapidly. 'I played the wrong current, invoked the wrong power. I was almost tricked with a dead reflection, just like you were. Are you all right? Did you hear the flute? Can you feel how the night beats now?'

'Yes! Yes!' She stroked his gaunt and stubbly cheeks. 'People are coming – you must play the delta-current again and repair the damage!'

And for a moment both remembered the high-energy circumstances of their first meeting in Schroun, and they kissed, but only briefly, for Tairo was approaching. In the light of the torch he carried his face was an ugly devil-mask, filled with hate. There were others behind him.

'Madman!' shouted Tairo. 'You're no god!'

Ducking aside as Tairo rammed the torch at his face, Liam laughed.

'We're all gods, Tairo. Prisoner gods.' And, taking Tschea by the hand, he slipped away from the torchlight before Tairo could lunge at him again. Everything was suddenly clear. Smiling, he reset the sirena and let himself go into the pure flow from the delta with a full consciousness.

Tairo stumbled furiously after Liam and Tschea, but by the time he reached them, he was dancing instead.

Soon many were climbing the hill again and there were dancers at the skirling summit of the hill above Gurdiangar. The ripple of the threatened delta-pulse was boosted again. All over the land were new sensitives who felt the vibrations and began remembering a universal cellular knowledge which took them from their troubles into the desire to dance southwest to the delta. It was received by some who were locked and lost in Ussian's confusion. It was felt at the delta.

Yelinne – who'd been hovering between the hill and the bowl – saw how the stars were starting to slither into a vortex at the zenith of the sky. It was as if their light were being sucked into an invisible tunnel which led down to the top of the hill. The hill itself was beginning to glow with a violet radiance which hurt and distressed her. For she wanted to go to it, but could not. She turned back toward the edge of the drop down into the steaming, bubbling hot springs.

The mirror-power had failed here tonight. But Yelinne knew that it was doing very well in Ussian as she threw herself to her death.

Many dancers were converting their oppressing phantoms in spontaneously rhythmic movement when Liam noticed the disturbance at the zenith. Singing through the sirena he felt the great spiral coiling of energy above and about the hill. Then, moving lightly around the summit through the dancers with Tschea dancing close by, he saw the violet glow which appeared over the marble table. It was a will-o'-the-wisp, gently hanging, at first no more than an insinuation of energy.

Then it attracted attention as it began a rapid growth, burning an intense violet hole in the fabric of the night.

The stars seemed to plunge.

Liam stopped playing.

The dancers stopped dancing.

Then a general withdrawal, a concerted gasp of astonishment.

The violet had gobbled out, up, and ... there it was. . . .

The Gateway was open above the table, shimmering and rectangular, a film of energy which looked the same from any and every side.

Everyone stood still, their faces glowing like velvet.

Then in the door for an instant there appeared a middle-aged man, tall, craggy-faced, sharp-eyed, striking in Liam a chord of dreamlike memory. Then Liam saw how Tschea reacted to this man, who smiled briefly at them both, and at two more behind.

She was trembling like an autumn leaf as the man faded out.

'Algon,' she whispered, shaking her head in agony, 'no ... no....'

Then Harne and Lonawi came to the pair of them. Before the dancers realized that the songmaker was leaving them, the four went to the Gateway with Tschea too stunned to protest ... though there was a part of her which wasn't surprised. Liam went first – he almost ran into the shimmering violet film, his heart hammering. Then Harne. Then Tschea, with Lonawi's hand on her arm to guide her.

Lonawi tucked away his flute as he went through, the last of the four.

After all, he hadn't intervened ... all he'd done was play a little tune, a favorite melody....

They vanished from the hilltop before anyone else had moved. The Gateway began to lose its luster almost immediately. Suddenly Tairo cried out; he ran forward and threw himself headfirst through the violet screen, and he felt the wrench which the others had felt.

Then he was gone – so was the Gateway; the night was dark again.

So fifty people or more were left shivering atop a bare hill in an alien land: alien even to those who'd been born in it. For now the nature of the conflict was plain to them, made clear by the music, by the growing Mutant light inside them. Vels was among the first to set his eyes to the southwest. He was shaking, but he was determined not to fall foul of the mirror-power again.

'We must make our way to the delta,' he told others. 'We must go now, singing, holding ourselves to the music we've heard, or else we'll be distracted. It may be that every extra person who comes to the delta will make a difference in this ... struggle, this ...'

He couldn't express what he sensed, not in words. But he was among those who left Gurdiangar before dawn, setting out on the road which led past the Cyclone College at Dulankir.

The white College resembled a man sprawled flat on his back over the top of a low hill about a mile from the road. It was surrounded by a dark and flickering haze, a dreary influence which persisted even in the sunrise. The pilgrims avoided it, turning south through the Zaidam Marshes toward the delta.

Vels got there. Many others didn't.

Many found themselves in Ussian instead.

Part IV : At the Delta

About the time that Liam and Tschea had reached the
cave the night before, Chimalus na Yaahnem had been
among the first of Ussian's crazed wild-eyes to look upon
Nikosner, to fall under the spell which Nikosner projected.

Chimalus had lost all sense of self – he'd forgotten his
name and his consular past. Half-naked, armed with a
bloody scythe, he'd become the natural leader of one of the
violent mobs which had been rampaging uncontrollably for
the previous forty-eight hours. He was to the fore of those
who flooded to the back of the Tarasse when the caravan returned to Ussian.

Many team-masters lost control of their teams when the
caravan first dipped into Ussian's deranged field of consciousness. The passengers were plunged into a sudden chaos
in which it was difficult if not impossible to know what
was real. Their natural terror was tempered by confirmation
in Nikosner's vision; many of them were howling with
fierce delight as carriages picked up speed and careered
wildly down behind panic-stricken teams. There were
crashes, collisions, uncontrollable flights down dark avenues
packed with angry, savage, bright-eyed, seemingly … luminous beings. Human beings. Citizens of Ussian who didn't
recognize the caravan from the Tarasse at all; a gathering
mob taken by the blind cellular desire to consume these invading foreign bodies.

Several wagons and carriages had been engulfed.

But half the caravan and all but two of Nikosner's horsemen reached the back gates of the Tarasse. The gates were
closed. They remained closed. The clamor had died with a
startling suddenness. Chimalus was at the front of the vari-
ously armed wild-eyes who converged on the crumpled,
apparently defenseless remains of the caravan. For the
threats of the mounted brigands had no more influence on

them than did the white faces peering from the carriages.
The mob crept closer with a slow stealth, a reluctance to
leave the shadows and enter the field of the still-lit gatehouse
lamp. Chimalus was part of a single creature united in the
stalk, in the shivering anticipation of the final rush, his
gleaming scythe raised up on high, a growl rising in his
throat, in every throat.

The wild-eyes were about to rush when one of the carriages spat out a wailing creature which struck their minds
with numbing force.

All in black, the creature fell to the dirty flagstones: it
writhed, it shrieked, it shuddered bonelessly, its vibrations
rippled through them so that strange scenes immediately
began to form in their minds, it so hypnotized them with
its power that they'd stopped dead in their instinct tracks –
fearful, awed, impressed.

Nikosner's burning vision was already growing in them
as his men scaled the walls to the gatehouse, which they
found to be empty. Few people were left in the Tarasse, as
was soon discovered. The gates were opened, but by then
it hardly mattered. For the spell was growing as Clarai and
many others tumbled out of the carriages and off the
wagons to join the vision-spun wild-eyes; to shake in sympathy with their lord Nikosner, to grow his vision – One-
Eye's vision, their vision – much higher. They shrieked and
rolled about and danced with him, they had no fear of the
wild-eyes, and this confused the wild-eyes further. For
during the previous days and nights the one constant factor
had been the omnipotence of their terror-rule.

More denizens of the lost city came, attracted by the scent
of something weird. Tah Ti the Boaster was among them. He
was prepared for this, he had remained behind for it, and his
balance was steady, though he aped the general derangement as a disguise, for self-protection. He was cloaked,
hooded, and his cat Reb was not with him.

What he saw and felt was the same as everyone else. . . .

The beautiful green emerald was growing clearly from
the black night above, was growing in his mind. Its influence
couldn't be denied. It was a brilliant gem, a multifaceted
viridescence which took every mind with it as it transform-

ed from green to red, into a giddy flame of sacrifice. It took hundreds of people into a state of frozen hypnosis and only a very few of them, Tah Ti included, sensed that in this flame rested a watching intelligence.

Chimalus na Yaahnem was among many who trembled and crawled on the flagstones, his mouth open, tears streaming from his eyes; he was spiraling up through this flame, through images which translated inside him as a thundering voice:

We must tear down Ussian! We must curse every brick, every stone, every inch of land. We must curse the Cyclones, and those who are red-haired, and those who wait at the delta. We must curse the fantasy of the Zuni Bird. We must burn Ussian in sacrifice to the one-eyed lord, the Divine Mutant inside us all, the Master who has changed us in this new time. We must reject and destroy ourselves in order to be saved, we must take our place in the Mutant dream, we must obey the commands of the Mutant's emissary, Nikosner. Now we must begin our work.

Nikosner shivered and raved on foot all night through every quarter of the darkly haunted city, attracting from their holes many who'd not made a movement in days, followed by an enormous train of exultant wild-eyes who marveled at his flaming aura, at his godsent vision, at his transcendent purpose. He brought them certainty, perspective, understanding, and an opportunity to atone for their sins which undoubtedly had led to this catastrophe.

From shadows Tah Ti watched how they killed and destroyed with epileptic enthusiasm equaling Nikosner's. He saw how first they attacked those walls painted with the sign of the Zuni Bird. All night he padded the dangerous streets, softly, cautiously, certain that Ussian wasn't being sacrificed to the Mutant, but to that same hidden power which for years had obstructed the delta project. When dawn was near he went to an empty stable behind the Maple Park – the same place where Lonawi had met Namahon – and here the Boaster met a fellow adept of the Inner Vortex in order to make his report and to receive further instructions.

Chimalus was prominent among those who ran amok all

night, scything viciously at those who seemed less than ecstatic about the holy burning-to-be, at those who looked as
if they might be Cyclones in disguise, and especially at
those who looked or crept toward the delta. The delta was
very evil – those who loved it were enemies. Chimalus was
deeply convinced of this, so much so that he didn't even
have to think about it. Every time he found himself close
to shivering Nikosner, he became more certain. The holy
necessity of curse and destroy as epitomized by the flaming
flower had seized him almost completely. If some part of his
personality remained free to protest at this terrible savagery,
then presently it protested uselessly. For it was essential
that Ussian should quickly become the precise reflection of
the burning vision which had seized him. If it did not – then
he would be damned forever.

All night he ran about, without any real self-awareness of
where he was or what he was doing. On the wharves of the
Naenshe in gray predawn he killed a red-haired man who
looked too much like some demonic enemy whom he feared
deeply. The victim was already exhausted by having fought
off many such attacks already, and he died without understanding why he'd suddenly provoked such mass hatred.

When day came, Chimalus abandoned his scythe for a
sledgehammer. With enormous energy he joined thousands
of others – converted or otherwise persuaded – in the tearing-down of schools, libraries, museums, and consecrated
places. The night had been bloody, the day was shrouded in
dust. In his vision Nikosner had communicated a precise
plan of attack; it was a perversely well-ordered destruction.
The foundations of the attack had been laid during the night.
The road to the delta had been horribly blocked. The bodies
of men, women, and children who'd been killed trying to
escape had been arranged in the shape of a single giant eye.
By dawn the city was encircled by wild-eyed guards who
killed whoever they found trying to escape, guards who
admitted whoever wished to enter Ussian. Exhausted, Nikosner retired to the Tarasse. He had to be helped by his lieutenants – he was utterly drained of energy and could hardly
stand upright. But the vision was communicated, the work
was begun, his holy revenge was under way. Ussian's re-

maining population was working with a will – his will, One-Eye's will . . . in his exhaustion, he was no longer sure whose will.

Today, the tearing-down.

Tomorrow, the burning. Tomorrow night the Tarasse would flame, the cursing would reach its climax, and the site of the destroyed city would by then be completely alienated. His triumph would be over.

Nikosner's men had been disappointed by the Tarasse. They'd hoped for a milk-and-honey paradise of flowing wine and beautiful women. Instead, they found a place ransacked of all its valuables, a place with the atmosphere of a morgue. Those who'd stayed behind were locked in their rooms, or hiding in secret places deep within the mazelike complex. They were more terrified of themselves than they were of Nikosner. Some didn't even know that he'd come. Existence had become nightmarish, time had broken down days before his arrival, and life had become surreal, nonsequential, utterly cruel. Many lay still and silent on unmade beds, weak with unrecognized hunger, waiting, enduring the phantoms which crept through the walls of their rooms, of their skulls. They no longer cared what happened. Few of those who'd returned in the caravan with Nikosner reentered the Tarasse.

Throughout the day, they were too busy helping to pull their city to pieces, caught in the deranged communal ecstasy.

Hilgo descended into Ussian in midafternoon, many hours after Nikosner had disappeared inside the Tarasse, so far not to reemerge.

Tschea's ex-Contractual came riding a horse which he'd found along the way. He was fueled by unforgotten wrongs, by a sense of universal injustice. The world had betrayed him. The chaotic atmosphere had him shaking with fearful fascination by the time he'd rounded the Tarasse and come to the Inila Way. For a time his private grievances were strong enough to deny the entry into him of the methodically destructive lunacy which he saw on every side.

The afternoon sun was hazed by the dust. He came to the Inila Way where he saw hundreds of people tearing up the avenue, stone by stone, chanting curses on every one. Nobody so much as looked at him. His face was filthy, choleric. Their work was a pretense! They were conspiring against him, every one of them knew how Tschea had betrayed him, secretly they were laughing at him!

'Dogs!' he roared, riding in roughly among them over piles of rubble. 'Don't play games with me! Where is she? Where is she? I'm going to kill her!' But he couldn't even hear himself over the steady chanting of curses. He saw a man he knew. Kryle, Tschan's Contractual. Kryle was stripped to the waist, covered in dust all over, and his eyes were burning. Hilgo shouted questions at him, but Kryle didn't even look up – he was wielding a pick-ax like an automaton. Hilgo rode on, closer to the open main gates of the Tarasse, knocking down several of the single-minded diggers and smashers as he did. Not one of them paid him the slightest attention. They simply picked themselves up and returned to their work.

Before he reached the gates, Hilgo had forgotten why he'd returned to Ussian. Soon he was smashing and cursing with the rest of them.

It was after sunset.

Nikosner was still inside the Tarasse when Chimalus awoke to realize that he was one among thousands of lunatics who were completing the destruction of the Inila Way.

His awakening was sudden, quite unexpected.

One moment he was fragmenting stone with his sledgehammer as steadily as he'd been doing all day, the next ... he wondered what he was doing....

Something caught at him ... some influence, from far away; something stopped him, snapped the spell. He shivered convulsively, started violently. Stopped working, set down the sledgehammer, saw his hands. They were bloody, but the blood was not his. Shaking his head with incomprehension and fear, he looked about. Saw and heard the fanatic thousands who surrounded him. They hammered and chanted like a single beast, a frenzied beast with hot-glowing eyes, dilated nostrils, and mouths which vented a mad clamor. He saw Clarai not far away. She was one of a gang carrying broken rubble from the avenue to the piles at the side – she was recognizable only on account of her tattoos. In the twilight haze he saw others he'd known. All of them lunatic. He sniffed at the dust-choked atmosphere, stared up at the grim comb-topped heights of the Tarasse. Such an ... alien quality pervaded Ussian – it shook him to realize his separation from this power. He felt naked, exposed, somehow ... watched. He sensed powerful currents all about. Not all of them were currents of cursing and destruction....

There was another influence in the air, one which utterly denied this destruction of Ussian. It reminded him of the delta....

He gazed at his bloody hands with dawning disgust.

'What am I doing?' he muttered, horrified. Then he dropped the sledgehammer as people about turned, regarded him with suspicion and mounting hate, somehow sensing that he was no longer united with them in this great endeavor. He fled for his life. A thrown knife narrowly missed him, and he leaped across the rubble, thrusting people out of his way. He ran down a narrow street toward the wharves, past a crowd which was throwing cursed books into a fire blazing at the waterfront, fled across a bridge pursued by a gang of shrieking children. When he lost them, he found temporary refuge in an empty and looted house on the south side of the Naenshe.

Here he collapsed on dusty floorboards and listened to the sounds of a dying city. For the first time in days he recalled his former life as Jerezid Consul in Ussian, and he realized he had no idea of what had happened to his wife, to the lands ... to reality....

'I'm stranded in a death-trap,' he muttered, eyes wide as he remembered the madness of the night before, how he'd slaughtered without any compunctions.

Behind him, someone coughed.

Heart beating wildly, Chimalus spun around. 'Tah Ti,' he whispered, 'the Boaster....'

Tah Ti stepped forward, grimly, cautiously; he squatted

in front of Chimalus and eyed him sternly. Chimalus stared, speechless.

'I followed you from the Inila Way,' said Tah Ti in a low voice. 'I watched you starting out of Nikosner's spell.'

'What's going on?' Chimalus was dazed, hungry, exhausted. 'I ... woke up, I ... felt something, something which ...' Words failed him.

'You felt what Nikosner and the power behind him wish to destroy,' said Tah Ti crisply. 'You felt the influence of the delta, boosted by those at the delta; you also felt it being boosted from Gurdiangar to the north. Ussian doesn't die for One-Eye, but on behalf of another power which has fought us subtly for many years, a power which intends to take over Ussian and destroy the Zuni Bird. Ussian is dying, but it need not die accursed – the conquest isn't certain.' The Boaster spoke with quiet vehemence, and Chimalus didn't know what to think. 'If sufficient people awaken by tomorrow night, then we have the chance to regain our freedom, our dignity – we will be the People of the Zuni Bird again, as once we were, many centuries ago....'

'But I'm not of Miir,' objected Chimalus, 'my land is ...'

'Here you are. Like it or not, you are of Miir.' Tah Ti gestured sharply. 'What's your preference? To destroy yourself? Or to live as a free being?'

'To be free, of course ... but ... what is this power ... the enemy...?'

'It is dangerous to name it. Accept my word.' Tah Ti rose. 'Now we must leave this house. It's dangerous. Nikosner must come out of the Tarasse to reconfirm the people and combat the delta-influence before too many awaken. Fate has granted us a gift, an unexpected gift; it may suffice to change the course of Ussian's fate from destruction to celebration. Now – quick – follow me – if you want to live.'

So Chimalus na Yaahnem followed the Boaster as darkness grew, as Nikosner emerged from the Tarasse for the first time since dawn.

Nikosner had passed the day mostly alone in the Eagle Chamber atop the Tower of Naka'es, the highest room in the Tarasse. He had slept until the middle of the afternoon. He'd awoken in a dispirited state. Until the sunset he paced restlessly from one oval window to another, garbed in black silk, drinking from a bottle of wine, feeling strangely uninspired by everything he'd brought about. The view from the Eagle Chamber was superb, but not even the sight of the city dying according to his vision gave him any pleasure. Perhaps his triumph had been assimilated too many times in prevision, so that its actuality was empty. He felt like a husk, like an empty being – there was nobody he wanted to see, nothing he wanted to do, and he had no wish to go outside again. The mania of the night before had resulted in complete exhaustion. The thought that it might be necessary to repeat it was somehow appalling. Hadn't he done enough to ensure his triumph? Far below, thousands chanted with manic enthusiasm as they tore up the Inila Way – why this suspicion that it was going to be necessary to recharge them with fresh enthusiasm?

Ussian was his. Why did he feel so empty?

His triumph was halfway to completion.

But still there was no vision in him of what would happen after the burning of the Tarasse. That was certain – however, it was followed by vagueness, blankness. As the sun sank lower over the Bay of Whales in the southwest he was filled with fears and half-understandings which ate at his self-confidence, at his certainty.

There was a high-powered telescope in the Eagle Chamber, and he spent some time at it, scanning the city, but questions of a kind he'd never asked himself before kept distracting him.

His triumph.

But was it?

What of the delta? What of the Cyclones, of the red-hair? What was happening, what threatened his triumph, and why? There was nothing at the delta but mud – that and many deluded fanatics ... surely....

Doubts. Questions. Why such a flood of doubt, of human weakness?

His incomprehensible fear was growing as the sun set and he sensed a change of atmosphere in the city, sensed that something inimical to his triumph was radiating from a point north of Ussian ... and from the delta. He realized that he was going to have to go out and repeat the previous night's performance.

He also realized that he did not want to ... that he was afraid....

He left the windows. He came to the mirror set in the carpeted floor of the round, exotic Eagle Chamber. His reflection stared back at him. It entered him.

Then he forgot his doubts, he forgot himself as the depths of the mirror drew him down on hands and knees.

Soon afterward, there was a sharp knocking at the door to the Eagle Chamber. The door was at the bottom of the stairwell sunk in the north side of the Chamber.

When Nikosner opened the door, he was shivering with energy again. But his eyes were not so sure as they had been the night before.

Descending to the streets, he was trying to remember what had just happened ... and what had happened during the last few months....

Clarai was working close to the main gates when Nikosner emerged, when the thousands shouted their greeting. She did not immediately join in the welcome. She'd been on the verge of realizing her exhaustion, her madness. Once or twice before Nikosner came out she'd half-stopped in her ferrying of rubble, and a puzzled expression had crossed her face, as if she suspected herself of being on the edge of remembering something she'd never consciously known.

But she – and all the others beginning to feel impulses which might deny Nikosner's triumph, which might prevent the sacrifice of Ussian – quickly forgot her vague doubts when Nikosner shivered and raved again.

Though there were some like Chimalus who'd escaped the mania, when dawn came around again, the burning of selected outlying areas had already begun. People chanted the strange curses learned from the burning flower in their minds while joyfully firing their own homes. The western breeze was mild, the city well spread out; so it was difficult for the flames to leap from one quarter to the next. But the burning progressed with the day. Nikosner had been carried back into the Tarasse, utterly exhausted. If many were puzzled and increasingly dubious about his fire-raising and cursing, the majority were well confirmed in the necessity of destruction.

By midday, the city's western districts on both sides of the Naenshe were well ablaze. The pall of smoke which drifted up, black and lazy, was clearly visible from the delta.

It was at midday that several hundred people, specially selected, set out from the delta toward the doomed city. It was an army of liberation spearheaded by twenty Cyclones and led by the Master of Baethnan; its chief weapons were the red-haired Fire-dancers of Danaimon ... and the red-haired songmaker with the sirena....

20 : Algon's Tale

Plunging from Gurdiangar to the delta through the Gateway was like being turned inside out and back again, instantaneously. It was some seconds before Tairo realized that he was sprawling atop a small grassy hillock in the darkness, overlooking the huge encampment by the delta. The other four who'd preceded him were gone already. Tairo picked himself up slowly, his head was spinning and he felt nauseous, but there was an idiotic grin on his face. He'd come through! Hundreds of camp fires flickered through the mist before him.

The atmosphere was throbbing, and the delta pulsed through him with a massively steady calm, reminding him of the heartbeat which the songmaker had conjured at Gurdiangar. The difference was that this pulse was directional, and there was no doubting the direction from which it came. He started down toward it, wading through the damp long grass toward the outlying encampments.

'I'm at the delta,' he told himself, not quite believing it. 'I'm at the delta, the Zuni Bird is going to sing, I feel it!'

*   *   *

It hadn't been Algon who'd met Liam, Tschea, Lonawi, and Harne as they'd reeled from Gurdiangar onto the hillock, but another Cyclone, awaiting them with four horses, shadows in the darkness.

Liam had helped Tschea up onto her mount.

She was dazed, too dazed to think properly.

They rode down behind the three Cyclones with the atmosphere pulsing around and through them. The pressure of the night air varied with the pulsing – at one moment they felt expanded, at the next, compressed, then expanded, then compressed again ... it was a most peculiar feeling. Liam's heart was hammering as they rode into the huge camp, along newly created alleyways of makeshift tents and driftwood shelters, past staring faces which flickered in the light of hundreds of torches which flamed from the tops of poles stuck in the uneven ground. They passed a great open space surrounded by shelters: here communal meals were being cooked over extensive beds of fir alight in trenches; hundreds were waiting in orderly queues; children were running about; there was a sense of great communal purpose, of restrained expectations – restrained, for Ussian wasn't so far away.

Tschea knew that she was about to meet Algon. It was difficult to believe, more difficult than the fact of the Gateway which had transported them here. Her feelings were so mixed. She was desolate, excited, furious, exhilarated by the atmosphere; simultaneously she felt she was a single cell in some vast natural organism and she felt alone, weak, and apart from everything happening about her.

They were led across scrubby dunes to a row of large white tents. Cyclones and others were commuting between these tents with the delta muttering not far away; they were moving with purpose, some at a half-run. But none of them were so busy that they couldn't stop to gaze interestedly at the newcomers, at Tschea so white and nervous, at the thin and ragged red-haired man.

Outside the last tent in the row Harne and Lonawi dismounted with the silent Cyclone who'd led them here. Lonawi turned, indicated for Tschea and Liam to dismount and follow him. A flap of the large single-poled tent was folded back, and yellow lamplight gleamed forth.

'The Master of Baethnan will see you,' Lonawi said. 'Come.'

Tschea tried to speak. Her voice was little more than a croak. 'Is he . . . is he . . . Algon. . . ?'

Lonawi nodded slowly, his smile a trifle grim.

Liam gave her support as they entered the tent.

He felt in some need of support himself.

Algon and Namahon waited inside, alone.

That morning they'd been rowed around the outer periphery of the delta, accompanied by schools of dolphins who'd leaped and dived around them while Namahon, eyes screwed tight shut in concentration, had concentrated on locating the precise place amid the mist-shrouded mud-banks from which the pulse thudded most strongly. The pulse had been growing stronger every hour, as if the growth of the waiting multitudes stimulated it into ever more intense emanation.

Eventually, with eyes still closed, he'd pointed with a trembling finger. 'There!' he whispered. 'It's strongest there!'

The area at which he'd pointed was occupied by a long and curving bank of slick mud which disappeared into the mists that tendriled the delta – it was an area where the birds were especially thick.

Now they waited inside the tent. An oil lamp stood on one table; the lamp was surrounded by maps and geometrical diagrams, and wooden chairs were drawn up around this table. On another was food and a pitcher of water; there was a cot behind it. The battle for the delta was being coordinated from here. Several times today Algon had led the crowds in communal meditative ceremony which strengthened their unity. The people had also been divided into companies. Each was a hundred strong, each was under the tutelage of an adept of the Inner Vortex. Each had been assigned a particular task – one collected wood and kept the cooking fires alight, another cooked the communal meals, a third acted as a messenger corps, and so forth. All new arrivals were assigned to whatever group best accorded with their particular talents.

Ten companies were busy constructing a wooden road which already extended two hundred yards out into the delta. It was flexible and segmented, and the work continued around the clock.

The adepts were training the people in the one-pointed directing of their combined life-force powers. The people were learning quickly, influenced as they were by the delta, by the Mutant Change, and particularly by their own wills.

Now Algon felt the approach of the songmaker and of the woman he hadn't seen for thirteen years. He regretted the necessities which had been imposed upon them all. He and Namahon were seated facing the entrance. The Master wore an unadorned maroon robe; his craggy and beardless face was calm, and his blue eyes were deep and expectant. When Lonawi led Tschea and Liam into the tent, he stood easily. Namahon also stood, biting his lower lip and wondering how Tschea would react.

Tschea hung back uncertainly at the entrance.

She saw Algon. He saw her. Neither moved.

He wasn't as she remembered him at all.

She saw a man much graver than her memory-image, she saw the Master of Baethnan. And Namahon ... her son looked well. But she didn't move forward to greet him and nor did he. Nothing was said. Liam stood watchfully, trying to ascertain what Algon was thinking.

When the Master spoke, it was to Lonawi. 'Your flute, please,' he said with a slight smile.

Liam was surprised, amused, and grateful to the Cyclone of the Outer Vortex who handed over the instrument with a faintly comical expression.

'Leave us,' said Algon as he laid the flute precisely on a table. 'I'll speak with both of you later.'

The two Cyclones backed out of their Master's presence.

'He knows everything,' Lonawi commented ruefully to Harne.

'Did he do wrong?' asked Liam sharply. 'He saved my life.'

'He disobeyed an order.' But Algon's smile was gentle and embraced Tschea's wooden face as well. 'Sit down,' he invited.

Liam sat. But Tschea didn't move. Namahon saw how the color was burning high in her cheeks. Recognizing her anger, he took his mother's arm with an anxious expression and tugged her to a chair. She collapsed into it, staring at Algon as if unable to believe he had the gall to speak to her in such a friendly fashion after thirteen years.

'I hope you can explain everything.' Her whisper was dangerously soft, and she started to rub at the tattoo on her forehead.

'You are at the explanation,' Algon replied as softly. He sat at the other side of the table on which the lamp stood, and he eyed Liam. 'You. Songmaker. Are you also angry with the Cyclones?'

'I'll hear you before deciding what I feel.' Liam shrugged and selected a peach from a bowl on the table beside him. 'I suspect that being here is sufficient. I have no judgments to make.' He took a huge bite and chewed with obvious enjoyment.

Tschea said nothing more, for Namahon at her feet was gazing up at her and his expression pleaded with her to listen. At the far side of the lamp, Algon's face was a mask of light and shade. She realized that it was difficult to maintain her anger in this atmosphere. *But I will not beg!* she thought. *Let him explain!*

And this was what Algon did.

'Toward the end of the time we call the Great Forgetting, when there were only three hundred and sixty-five days in the year,' Algon began, 'the world groaned beneath the weight of a densely material Age of Iron. The ruins of cities of that period demonstrate that the people considered drainage systems more important than places of worship. They cobwebbed the planet with systems and structures and roads which bore no relation to anything but their own supposed desires. It was a dark time in which humankind's natural relationships and functions were all but forgotten, an era of wars between nations, of confusion in every soul. The world was full of projects which involved the release of huge amounts of half-understood energies. We know little about them. The era is a violent disturbance which we cannot enter. Moreover, the majority of their works were destroyed in a cataclysm which set the planet on a new axis, which altered the shape and climate of the lands and extended the length of the year. Some believe that there was a great war; others believe that the planet was brushed by the tail of a comet....'

Algon paused. Tschea's expression was sphinx-like.

The songmaker was fascinated.

'I've heard tales,' Liam whispered. 'In *these* lands ...'

'... In these lands.' Algon smiled briefly. 'Yes. Before the cataclysm these lands belonged to a group of islands which, in an even older time, had been thought of as a region of the spirit. Yes. Before the cataclysm many people came to these lands to work together, intending to engineer their own evolution according to ancient doctrines of shape and number which had been reconfirmed as sets of scientific probabilities. They worked in awareness of the coming cataclysm, possibly hoping either to avert or to transcend it. Their prime task was the building of instruments to act as intermediaries between God and Man, to draw down and distribute the cosmic life-force, to praise and glorify the holy world anew ... to awaken the Fifth Element within themselves....

'Many such instruments were built, on greater and lesser scales. Phadraig was such an instrument. But the most potent of all was in this land ... *was* this land.' Now Algon spoke with an absolute clarity. 'The whole of the region of which Mantrim and Miir now constitute a part was designed as an extra-dimensional face of a structure which they built – a structure the influence of which you are feeling at this moment ... the pyramid which lies buried beneath the delta....'

Liam's mouth fell open. He leaned forward.

Tschea gripped Namahon's shoulder hard – she was electric.

And the waters of the delta muttered in the near distance.

'... I'll come to the pyramid itself in a minute or two,' Algon continued as Liam poured a cup of water and passed it to Tschea, who needed it. 'First, I'll complete the history.

For the cataclysm came. And, by and large, these lands survived. The climate was warmer once the dust had cleared; there were mountains, volcanoes, seas, rifts, and deserts which hadn't existed before. The Abeltine Lakes were formed. Mantrim was virtually divorced from the mainland. The rivers Naenshe and Lansalle were born to flow into a bay where there had been land ... where there had been a pyramid. For the structure was buried during the convulsions. Its existence was forgotten in the chaos of the Middle Kingdom. The lands were darkened, there was sterility, mutation, and the Mutant was formed. The nature of the Mutant during its first incarnation resulted from the psychic aspect of the cataclysm. It was born of energies no longer bound in any specific physical form – it was idea of itself. In a sense it was the deranged Fifth Element – deranged, because it lacked stability, coherence, or compassion....'

He could see that they were only partly following him.

'At any rate.' He shrugged. 'When in time the Middle Kingdom faded into a new cycle, the people of this land could no longer see the giant work of the landscape. All they recalled of the pyramid came to be expressed in the legend of the Zuni Bird : a legend which explained why it was that Miir seemed so much sweeter and more gentle than the other lands about. For though the pyramid was buried, its influence remained at work. The reality behind the myth remained totally obscured until the time of An. It's said that he was sitting near the delta when he began to wonder why the sea-beings persisted in coming so close to the mudbanks that they were frequently stranded. He wondered why they and the birds found the delta so attractive. He began to feel how the delta pulsed strongly at certain times. At night he saw violet lights flickering above the outermost mudbanks. At length, he ventured out and disappeared. Three days and nights he was gone. When he appeared again he was changed, he emerged with a prophetic gift, with a vision of Miir's future and a partial recall of the past. This gift of prophecy was symbolized in myth as the white feather of A'Yaya's Tale; An himself was immortalized as A'Yaya. A'Yaya may have had actual existence in an earlier time, but with the passing of the years An and A'Yaya have become inextricably confused.

'It was An's inspiration which led to the creation of the
Cyclone brotherhood, to the foundation of the Tarasse College of eugenics, to the building of Ussian. He retained his
own name only in the writing of the book of prophecies
which is kept at Baethnan. In the Old Tongue, "Baethnan"
means "the wisdom of An." It was he who began the project which had resulted in our rediscovery of the pyramid
and its purpose. He foretold what would happen in this
time. He foretold a war with an invisible enemy. He
foretold the Mutant's return in a new form. He foresaw
the reawakening of the Zuni Bird, he prophesied about Analee....'

Then Tschea interrupted for the first time. 'Analee ...'
Her voice was strained. 'His name – *Ana*lee ... who was
he? Was he a Cyclone from Baethnan?'

Algon regarded her very seriously. Then he said, 'He
wasn't a Cyclone. He was trained at Baethnan.' After a
pause, the Master added, almost casually, 'He was your
father.'

Tschea went white. Liam tensed. Namahon showed no
surprise.

'I don't understand,' Tschea whispered hoarsely, feeling
chill. 'If so, why wasn't I told? What am I? And who are
you?'

'Had you been told,' replied Algon levelly from the flickering shadows, 'it's probable you wouldn't be alive to hear
about it now.'

'What do you mean by that?' she demanded angrily.
'How can you justify the fact that I've been kept in ignorance all my life?'

'The decision was made when you were only a few weeks
old,' said Algon calmly, 'when it was first realized that we'd
begun a war with an invisible enemy. An enemy who wishes
to prevent the reactivation of the delta, the enemy which
occupies Ussian now....'

'Oh!' she snapped. 'You blame the Unmen and their mirrors?'

'We *suspect* that the Hou'ons are involved. But they cannot be our enemies unless we are our enemies too.' Algon

was emphatic, and Liam was listening with a different kind of fascination now. 'To blame the Unmen categorically may be no more than another way of saying that we attack ourselves, then seek to find an enemy in whatever is conveniently alien, external, and incomprehensible. How can anything be hostile to intelligence but intelligence itself? We had hoped to have the pyramid activated in time for the Mutant's return. But for thirty-five years we've been prey to mistakes, confusions, and false trails in our researches. Indeed, there's negative evidence to suggest that the Hou'ons have interfered with the project. But we lack the slightest idea of their natures or their motives. To call them "Unmen" is parochial separatism. Should we succeed in activating the Fifth Element, then we will understand much more clearly in the banishing of our *own* negativity. Had you known that Analee was your father, your own frustrated yearnings would have probably driven you to suicide.' He paused unhappily. 'That, or you would have been murdered. It was thought better that....'

'Oh, an easy way out!' snapped Tschea, cheeks burning. She was shivering with intense passion. 'None of this is explanation! Yes, I feel the pulse – I admit I'm tempted to believe much of your incredible tale – I've always felt the power of the delta. Now that you tell me that my father was the Herald, some of my feeling for the delta makes sense to me. But you can't seem to explain why I was kept in ignorance. I want to know much more before I forgive you! I want to know about me, about you, about Namahon ... about Liam here. Why was I abandoned outside Schroun as a foundling? Why have I wasted so much time in the Tarasse, uselessly resisting Formalism? I suppose Cuinneale was a puppet of the mirrormen too! Why did I send Namahon specifically to Baethnan when I didn't know that *you* were at Baethnan? Will you claim coincidence, or unconscious knowledge on my part? What of the dream I had on the night of the Harvest Festival? Did you influence me to save Liam from Schroun so that you can make use of his talent and his sirena now? And while we're about it, Namahon's here, but what about Cassa, Flath, and Larene? They're my children, I'm their mother, I can't simply forget them because reality's turned upside down! Where are they now?'

Her voice was violent – she was straining forward, quivering.

Algon shifted into a more comfortable position at the other side of the table. He eyed Namahon, whose face was sorrowful, and Liam, who seemed quizzical but remote, as if the songmaker were unwilling to interrupt a family squabble.

'Nothing you've done these last few days has not been done of your own accord, of your own instinct,' Algon replied emphatically, meeting her eyes. 'I admit I was never happy about the way you were treated, about my part in your life. But I was as bound as you. You were not "abandoned" – you were placed with a Communal Hearth which succored you and brought you up with every advantage. Would you have preferred to be locked up in a Cyclone College all your life? Your own ambitions led you to the Tarasse – recognize them! Certainly, once you were there we began to hope that you might become White Feather, that you might influence the Guild – and thus Miir's people – back in the direction which Analee had heralded. And I – I came to Ussian from Baethnan....' Algon was briefly silent.

Tschea's fists were clenched. Liam sensed the pulse getting stronger, as it rippled through him like a giant tide. From the direction of the delta came the sound of flutes and drums, the sound of many people chanting in mass counterpointed response to a single tenor voice which made him shiver with its purity. Liam understood that Tschea felt she *should* be furious, bitter, resentful; he wondered when she'd admit to herself that she felt none of these things, not here, but only the ghosts of them, ghosts of the past....

'... I came to Ussian from Baethnan,' Algon repeated thoughtfully. 'I was in the Outer Vortex then. The Master – my predecessor – chose me. He gave me ... orders ... to meet you. It was hoped that ...'

'Orders?' she hissed. 'You had *orders*?'

'Yes!' Algon, though clearly unhappy, was under tight control, while Namahon was gazing at the floor in embar-

rassment. 'Just as now I have orders from the Grand
Master....'

'And did you take me over with some Cyclone spell?'

'There was no coercion!' Algon's eyes burned. 'My orders
were these: *Go to Ussian, seek out the Green Feather
Tschea, return after three days whatever happens.* That was
all. And it was your will which chose me, as much as mine
chose you! I did not want to leave so soon ... but I have
taken the vows of obedience to the brotherhood.'

'You see?' Tschea swung on Liam. 'Just as I told you! I
was used, cold-bloodedly used!'

Liam's gesture was vague, and he looked away.

Tschea had expected his support. She was taken aback.
Even Namahon wouldn't meet her eyes. She was so dizzy!
The pulse – it boomed through her, crying to her to accept
the situation. But she had to have explanations! She had to
know!

'Not so,' Algon replied candidly. 'Or if so, then I was
used equally. I'm glad to have been of use; I only hope that
now we'll succeed.'

'You rebuke me!' Her voice was flat. 'You think I should
humbly accept the inexplicable. What of my questions?
Where are my children? Do you ...'

'Cassa, Flath, and Larene are in Mantrim,' said Algon patiently. 'A Leaper friend of yours brought them to one of
our Colleges. He said that you asked him to do this before
you left on the caravan.'

Again, Tschea was taken aback. 'I ... never ... did....'

'It's true, Mother.' Namahon looked up. 'I met the Leaper.
He said that you told him to do this. I think you must have
forgotten.'

Tschea averted her eyes in confusion, stared at the tent wall.

'Furthermore,' said Algon, eyeing Liam, whose head was
cocked toward the delta, 'this dream you talk of – it's your
private property, I know nothing of it. You knew about
Liam before we did. You reached him before we could ...
before we were sure that we wished to contact him....'

Liam looked around, and snorted with feeling. 'I'd have
been dead by now if she hadn't!'

'Exactly.' Algon was a trifle grim. 'We've been much ob-

structed these past days ... these past years. Our reputation
has grown evil; many bad happenings have been blamed on
us by Cuinneale, by many others.'

'Perhaps all of them looked in mirrors!' Half mocking,
half serious, there was spirit in Tschea's voice.

'Maybe.' Algon smiled slightly. 'Mirrors are universal.'

'Cuinneale was known to look in mirrors,' Tschea whispered, her hand tousling Namahon's hair. 'If he was their
agent, and if it was he who drove Nikosner mad fifteen
years ago, then ...' She looked up. 'I've looked in many mirrors too. But still you haven't explained why I sent Namahon
to you!'

'You're a daughter of the delta.' Algon was ambiguous.
'How could we have forced you to do anything against your
inner wishes?'

Namahon said: 'Mother, you told me you thought I'd be
safe at Baethnan, that the Cyclones would train me, but
... but I sensed you had some other reason which you yourself didn't ...'

At that moment Liam started laughing. He couldn't help
it. Algon and Namahon gazed at him, but Tschea glared.
'Oh, please,' he asked, pulling a self-deprecating face, 'I
don't want to interrupt, but ... here we are! Why deal in
explanations of words with the pyramid pulsing and the
sirena ready to sing much higher than any words can
reach?' He indicated the delta with urgent good humor
which was so infectious that Tschea relaxed and even
smiled slightly. To Algon he said: 'You were going to tell
us about this pyramid. Can we not walk down by the delta,
can you not tell us about it there? For whatever differences
arise from the past, here we are. We chose to come here. I
know I have ... I know that Tschea has, whatever she says.
If she hadn't, I'd be dead!'

So the four of them went walking by the delta in the
strangely lucid brilliance of the night, beyond the tents and
fires through the saltily luminous mists which curled where
the waters lapped in reedy inlets.

They came to a spit of sand and shingle which curved out
past more energetic currents. The flexible wooden road was

being built outward from this spit. On it a large number of people were gathered around the Fire-Dancers from Danaimon. They were whirling in dance while several Cyclones led the people in rhythmic chanting which ebbed and flowed to the delta's rippling pulse. The tenor who led the celebration was a graceful albino androgyne.

Tschea was thrilled through by the purity of the androgyne's voice and movements, and of a sudden she knew that she was home at last. She began to flow in dance with a faraway expression, her eyes fixed toward the hidden outer limits of the delta, and the night wasn't dark at all. She could see quite clearly: the mists were layers of golden veils and the night was permeated with an immanent glow which haloed all the people around her. For the first time in years she felt that she was part of a family : she danced.

Liam was glad to feel her happiness. Exhilarated, he walked with Algon and Namahon out into the delta as far as the road presently extended. Sufficiently wide to accommodate five people walking side-by-side, it was anchored to mudbanks and the sections in between rose and fell gently on the waters. A triple guard-rope on either side was slung along between wooden uprights stationed every twenty feet or so. When they came to the mudbank which was as far as the road had been extended, they stood silently for a while, watching the rhythmic coordination of the work-gangs who bound and placed the timbers down, bathing in the pulse.

After a while, Algon turned to Liam. 'The road is being aimed directly at the apex of the pyramid,' he said softly. 'The apex lies only a few feet beneath a mudbank in the outer margins; my son located the point yesterday morning. Stand there and you'll be sharpened in the direct focus of the pyramid, and the sirena will sing out the transmuted energy as it was made to do. Tell me : where did you find the instrument? We didn't know that any still existed.'

So Liam told him about the sorceror's isle.

'Well,' said Algon, his voice resonant. 'I think that soon you'll play the song of the Zuni Bird ... if you're willing, and if first we can transmute the cursing of Ussian into celebration. The negative pressure of a total cursing would prevent us from attaining the necessary communal

clarity of spirit. And the Unmen – whether inside us
or separate from us – would win.'

'I'm willing,' Liam replied, 'and we'll prevent the cursing.'
He had no doubts. The atmosphere made doubt impossible. They stood aside on the mudbank as several men
came jogging past, carrying lengths of timber between
them and chanting softly in the pulse. Somewhere farther
out, a white wave frothed out from the Naenshe. Liam felt
light and outside time – it was another man who'd come
demented into Miir a little over a hundred hours previously.

As they stood Tschea came out to join them. She was
animated and radiant, and she threw one arm around Liam
and the other around Namahon.

'I feel I'll never need to sleep again!' she declared.

Algon laughed. 'I'll remind you of that sometime,' he said.

'Has he told you all about the pyramid?' she asked Liam.

'No ... we've just been standing here ... feeling it.' The
songmaker turned to the Master of Baethnan. 'Will you tell
us about it?'

So Algon told them what was known of the pyramid from
the readings of Cyclone sensitives while the gangs worked to
extend the road, while the mists drifted across the waters
and breathed suggestive shapes in the air about them.

'It has four sides – one for each of the elements which
define our earth. Perhaps you can feel how subtly the Fifth
Element is generated from the alchemical fusion of these
four. Its power is derived from the geometry of its shape
and number-relationships. It draws down cosmic energy,
which it transmutes and generates at variable rates and amp-
litudes of vibration according to the positions and relationships of the heavenly bodies. The essence of this cosmic
energy is that antigravity which is consciousness which is
the universe which is light which is the life-force.' Algon's
voice was hushed, he spoke as if praying. 'This energy has
the power to awaken the Fifth Element in all who worship
here. The state of the Fifth Element involves the full realization that we ourselves are our own evolution, evolution
being the transformation of energy from solid slow-vibra-
tion forms up into the ethereal forms of light. Light is life is
energy in harmony – to Fifth Elemental vision the universe

is an ever-glowing and ever-dancing field in which every unit is interchangeable and part of the whole, in which all's the same and all's as it ought to be because it can be no other way. The Song of the Fifth Element is the Song of the Zuni Bird is the Music of the Spheres as revealed in our transforming plane between earth and sky. And this is the time which is set for our awakening from time.'

As he spoke the mists were clearing, the late night sky was opened up above the delta, and he pointed.

'See up there – the ringed planet and the planet ruling wisdom, they seem to lie so close together.' Then Algon reversed the direction of his pointing to the grayly glimmering mud beneath their feet. 'And could we see through the earth and through the brightness of the sun, we'd find the spheres of love and war and intellect similarly disposed in a close conjunction. We're the third, and though the other six cannot be seen with the naked eye, perhaps you can feel how they too share in this conjunction. It's why the pyramid pulses more strongly with every passing hour. The ancients predicted a holocaust of fire and flood when such a conjunction should occur.' The strangely pellucid being tapped his forehead. 'We are embarked upon it again. Now we realize ourselves or fail – again. Such changes are as old and as new as time – there are always such changes: those who built the pyramid underwent such a mental conflagration at the termination of their Age of Iron. The world is always ending to be born anew. The Mutant has returned to dream again, but this time the aspects are different. Dreaming us, the Mutant is the stuff of our dreams. Locate the Mutant inside ourselves and we'll know and name its essence....'

Then Algon sharply clapped his hands. 'Dawn approaches,' he said briskly. 'There's much to do. Let us return to the shore now.'

When the eastern sky was red and gold the Master of Baethnan conducted a silent service by the delta. The thousands sat in a vast semicircle, their hands linked, their wills meshing in the pulse which beat stronger, stronger.

'The time has come.' This was all that Algon said.

The thousands sat for two hours without moving.

*   *   *

Later in the morning, with black smoke shrouding the eastern sky and with preparations for the march on Ussian under way, Liam and Tschea strolled through the bright sunlight until they came to the placid main stream of the Lansalle. Finding a grassy hollow, they stretched out and gazed at the early autumn woods on the farther Mantrim bank. The woods were beautiful and infinitely varied in tones and hues; leaves of gold and russet and lemon were spiraling lazily down on the breeze. They lay silently for a while and their mood was bittersweet for, though now they felt very close, they still weren't in agreement. Tschea had insisted that she was coming to Ussian and remained adamant despite Liam's attempts to dissuade her. Now she lay close beside him with hands cradling her head; her eyes were clear and there was warm color in her cheeks. She seemed calm now, and she was no longer shivering. But her uncertainties weren't yet banished. She clung to them despite the night's events, partly in stubborn self-definition and partly because room for doubts still existed.

Liam knew it. He had asked Algon about his vision of the garden from the night of the cave. Algon had denied all knowledge of it, but Liam hadn't been able to help his suspicion … mild suspicion, but suspicion nevertheless. It was a negative feeling which detracted from his pleasurable sense of wholeness. Watching Tschea restlessly, he plucked blades of grass and flung them into the breeze. The day was so beautiful, the pulse so strong, and his doubt so small … but it existed, all the same. . . .

'. . . When I was very young,' murmured Tschea after a while, 'I thought that the whole world was a sparkling diamond, and that every being was a facet of the diamond. I believed that it was the pleasure and obligation of every being to shine more brightly, to praise and glorify the diamond in every possible way. . . .' Gazing up at the high white clouds, she sighed. 'I thought I'd outgrown such romantic silliness … but perhaps I was wiser then. . . .' Her expression was dubious. 'What do you think?'

'A beautiful belief. We'll know its truth – when Ussian's saved.'

'Do you think we'll succeed?' Her eyes were searching.

'Of course we will!' But his certainty was too abrupt.

'You're worried about me – you think I should stay here with Namahon.' Her voice was perceptively humorous. 'The men go to war and the women stay with the children – is that right?'

'Not at all!' He wasn't smiling. 'Why must you come?'

'I don't know,' she admitted. 'Perhaps Analee's daughter is tired of feeling ... *pushed* all the time. Why don't you want me to come?'

'Because I'm afraid that something terrible will happen to both of us – and unnecessarily so.' He was both angry and tender.

'Are you scared to die?' She rolled over onto her stomach.

'No. But it would be stupid to die worthlessly. And something in your intention seems fatal. Do you do it to spite Algon?'

'Algon?' She laughed, then shook her head decisively. 'No. No.'

'Are you sure?' His eyes narrowed. 'You hated him last night.'

'How can I hate a false memory?' Her voice was soft as she took his hand. 'I don't know this new Algon at all. I think you're jealous....'

'Perhaps, a little.' Liam's smile was reluctant and surprised.

'You have no need to be jealous. None at all.'

'I know.' He stared away. 'It surprises me more than anything else.'

'Well,' she whispered, drawing closer to him, 'then let's give ourselves a big surprise before we change too much to be surprised by anything anymore.' Her eyes glowed. 'You said, there's a time for everything....'

She kissed him tenderly and he found himself responding with equal passion. So they made love in the soft grass with the sun beating down and the pulse of the delta heightening their pleasure. Liam was amazed to learn he wanted her much more than he'd known.

When eventually they picked themselves up and returned toward the camp, Liam asked her once again not to come to the delta.

'It's no good,' she said, softly implacable. 'My mind's made up.'

He knew then that nothing would make her change her mind. They returned to Algon's tent, where those going to Ussian were being briefed. His prayers were silent. For nothing was certain yet. Nothing would ever be certain so long as human beings were involved.

21 : The Dance of Fire and Flood

Darkness and flame.

The people from the delta approached the terrible delirium of Ussian through smoke and swirling hot ash. They pushed forward into infiltrating reflections which had already roasted many minds.

Algon accompanied the main group that penetrated the city by the road blocked by the horrible eye. All the lunatic guards had withdrawn into the ecstatic holocaust. Through the dense smoke the sky was livid purple and bloody red, and the Fire-Dancers whirled grimly past the eye. The possibility of celebration here seemed most unlikely.

Meanwhile Liam and Tschea and Harne and Lonawi picked a different route down the north side of the valley. They were thickly cloaked and hooded against the heat and groaning lamentations of the atmosphere. Below them was Ussian's lap – through the ruddy and choking smoke it was beaconed by a dozen major blazes. Confusion assaulted them more strongly with every downward step they took past ransacked villas, across torn-up avenues, through withered parks where lost people gasped for breath.

The two Cyclones led, then came Tschea, and Liam last of all. He felt already fragmented by the complex syncopation of the dying city. Rising from the glaring pit came the overloaded and manic broadcast of beings caught in mass delusion and alienation from themselves ... and the howling updraft was surely filled with hordes of invisible watchers

who'd not reveal themselves until the moment of final cursing ... if that should come to pass. He could feel them
crouching on top of his spine – their presence grew more
implicitly necessary with each step he took into their lair.
He gave Tschea a hand as they slipped down a steep grass
bank behind the two seemingly imperturbable Cyclones.
Her eyes were bright with fear and a strange delight; she
was muttering at the visions which jumped and jerked
before and behind her eyes. She had forgotten about the
delta and looked at Liam through the smoke and glare as if
she hardly knew him. The cacophony made conversation
impossible. Liam was fearful, for the weight of forgetfulness here was enormous.

The garden ... he could feel it flowering inside him
still....

Hold on to the garden and all will be well, he told himself.

Then the smoke cleared momentarily and caught them
halfway across a razed area above the scorched Maple Park.
Ussian was revealed. They saw tidal waves of the possessed
streaming through the flickering streets, past skulls of fire
and bleached bone ruins and dark as-yet-undamaged blocks.
They saw ant-sized maniacs flirting with the flames which
licked greedily along the terracings of the Chuunlan Oval;
they saw the demented capering across fused green glass
fragments in the blazing Kuwa Quarter; they saw the thousands converging on the cursed remains of the Inila Way
in front of the Tarasse and heard the great chant which
rose up through the roar of crashing buildings and the
hissing of the flames.

'Nikosner! Lord! Nikosner! Curse! Nikosner! Master!'

The Tarasse was utterly dark. Not a single chink of light
shone from the enormous complex. Its curtain-walls hung
mournful and backlit by the ruddy glare of the confront-
ing inferno.

It's waiting to die! thought Tschea. A shudder of fascination coursed up her spine.

Even as they watched a light came on high above the
roofs beside a shadowy cluster of combs ... a light shining
from an oval window....

'The Eagle Chamber!' Tschea hissed. 'I see ... a man....'

'It's Nikosner!' Liam grinned wolfishly. 'He feels us here....'

'Come on!' urged Lonawi. 'We must meet Tah Ti. No time!'

So they moved deeper into delirium as the smoke returned. Soon they reached the stable behind Maple Park. Armed men led by Chimalus na Yaahnem slipped out behind Tah Ti and another Cyclone. Tschea was briefly forgotten as the Cyclones, the songmaker, and his bodyguard squad conferred. She hesitated. But she couldn't resist the lure of the Tarasse.

When Liam turned to encourage her, she was gone, and nobody had seen her slip away. His fears rushed back and he started spontaneously toward the Tarasse. Lonawi caught his arm. Lonawi felt as chill inside at her disappearance as Liam did.

'*Because of the help you gave them at Gurdiangar,*' Algon had told them earlier, '*neither are wholly confirmed. Tschea may try to lose herself. Watch her! And watch Liam too!*'

'Too late!' Lonawi shouted. 'You can't go chasing her now!'

'How can I forget her just like that?' Liam blazed.

'Abandon your task,' snapped Tah Ti bleakly, 'and we'll all die!'

'Gentlemen!' Chimalus felt powerful. 'We must not fight ourselves!'

Liam gestured with angry resignation. What could he do? 'Very well,' he muttered, 'lead me down. Let's get on with it!'

His anxiety for her slipped away as they descended into the heat and clamor. They came to a half-burned house at the bottom of Maple Park by the outer wall of the Tarasse. The atmospheric friction scraped his mind – it was difficult to think, to remember, and death was all about.

Here they were close to the insane crowds and the songmaker forgot about Tschea. He forgot everything but the necessity of retaining the delta-pulse in Ussian's blackened and demonized heart. How could such a feral death-song be transformed into celebration? At the delta it had seemed straightforward. Now he was being crushed by pandemonic

weight. But he had assistance. The Cyclones were irradi-
ating him with energy. He was surrounded by Chimalus and
another fifteen men were ready to die if it were necessary.
He fought to hold on to his connection with the delta as he
prepared the sirena. He pictured the immanent garden and
the memory of songborne flight above a cruel night-land,
visions awaiting realization, visions so personal that not
even this chaos could drive them out. With closed eyes he
sweated and trembled inside the baking ruin, breathing lung-
searing air which was filled with hate and discord. The Song
... the Garden ... the principles he had to hold in order to
stay afloat. Like a drowning man he prayed for strength as
he launched himself into the increasingly feeble beat of the
delta.

His first notes were ferocious and discordant as the Fire-
Dancers approached the Chuunlan Oval. They and their followers were finding equal difficulty in retaining the spirit
which they had to spread.

But negative assistance came from an unexpected quarter.
Nikosner heard the chanting of the crowds. He knew the
enemy had come; he sensed red-haired danger all about. He
knew that if he didn't quit the Eagle Chamber now his
triumph would end in anticlimax and in what amounted to
self-destruction. But he was light inside.

For the Tarasse was bound to burn, and he was bound to
burn with it.

He knew much now that he was calm. Calm and utterly
blank for the first time in fifteen years. He knew that the
madness resulting from Cuinneale's bungled experiment on
his brain wasn't the same as the Mutant effect. He knew it
because the Change was affecting him now. Though the
burning vision had first descended when he'd caused the
mumen vaults to be found, now he was sure that it wasn't
derived from One-Eye.

Nothing mattered anymore. Now he was a shell without
purpose or desire left to drive him. Hunched up on the floor
he sat, staring at the empty mirror. Outside they waited for
him to fire and curse the Tarasse, to complete the destruction and alienation of Ussian. Why? He had no wish left to

do it. His agony was gone. His energy was gone. His fits were gone. There was nothing in the mirror but his own haggard reflection, the image of a being burned up for no good reason of his own. The second night had drained him completely. Again he'd slept into the afternoon, to awake with the strange knowledge that the motivations for all he'd done recently had come from ... mirror-indoctrination? It was as if the clarity of mind in which he could hold such a realization had crept up on him as a result of total exhaustion. Now demented people were chanting for him as though he were a great leader. But now he knew himself to be no more than a bewildered human being.

'I charged them to burn and curse their city,' he mumbled in his isolation, 'but what charged me? It was right to kill Cuinneale. But why should I want to burn Ussian? That means plunder....' He thought further, staring at the furrowed brows of his reflection. 'Why did I plunder in the first place?'

As he stared the mirror began to glow. Now his reflection was enveloped in a cloudy haze. But he looked away with stubborn determination. He came to his feet, staring at his own two hands rather than at the treacherous reflection.

'Of course. I plundered because Ussian rejected me. But Ussian rejected me because I was a dangerous lunatic, because I killed my wife. It was my own stupidity. I let Cuinneale experiment because I wanted an easy enlightenment – I thought there was such a thing as a shortcut....'

Something stirred in the mirror independent of himself. Strangely fearful, he saw a red-haired man, one-eyed, with a scarlet machine.

'I see you,' he whispered. 'Do what you will. Prevent the cursing if you can. I won't burn the Tarasse – I won't take my commands from mirrors again!'

The image blurred, faded, changed into a somehow unhuman being which was as bald as an egg and had two hypnotically lustrous green eyes. In his mind's-eye Nikosner saw himself cursing the Tarasse. His mouth fell open, and he jerked. Then he laughed harshly and seized a chair, and he brought it down with all his strength and smashed the mirror into shards.

'Now I see you for what you are!' he shouted in sudden jubilation. 'You've failed! Perhaps you've used me up too quickly, perhaps you underestimated the effect of the Mutant upon us, perhaps you don't really understand how we humans are!'

At that moment began a frantic knocking at the locked door. He ignored it and went to a window, shivering to a newly sensed beat. As he looked out over the blazing city once again he realized that this beat was at least in part responsible for what he'd just done.

'It's the pulse of the delta, of Miir,' he told himself with a painful smile. 'The Zuni Bird may sing, but it's too late for me.'

For he was on the edge of the time beyond his vision. Already the first torches were being applied to the ready-tindered Tarasse by people running through the dark maze far beneath his feet.

The knocking continued for at least two minutes.

When it stopped he knew that his men had abandoned him. Still smiling, he went and opened the door: there was nobody outside it.

Then, gazing at the fragments of the mirror, he took a knife.

Outside, the rhythms of human distress were gigantic. But many people were no longer moving to the destruction beat. The city was shrivelling them, and still Nikosner had not appeared to set the climactic seal on the cursing. With every passing second more and more of them were snapping out of the incendiary thrall and falling out of tune with the spirit of the sacrifice.

They awoke to find the Green Emerald devastated and burning around them, to find their bloody feet trampling the ash-strewn rubble of the Inila Way, to find their fists waving in the air ... to realize what they were doing. Clarai was among them. Clarai from the streets, now back in the streets and suddenly more free than she'd been in twenty years. She awoke to find herself ragged in the inferno and locked in struggle among a mob of savage people who bore no resemblance at all to the gentle people of Miir. She awoke in realization.

'It's not the Mutant who moves us to curse our city and worship an unhinged brigand!' she screamed, fighting to keep her feet in the surging crush. 'It's something else, which lies and cheats! Wake up! Wake up!'

Her strident voice cut through the pandemonium of questions, terrified curses, astonished exclamations. Tschan heard Clarai's call, but the Purple Feather was dying. She had miscarried, and now she lay crushed beneath fallen masonry near the Inila Way with the flames creeping closer. She wept to remember how sweet life had been only a few days before. Only a few days ... an absolute gulf separated her from the past and the future.

Hilgo too heard Clarai's call. He was among those who struggled near the open gates of the Tarasse. Here the confusion was greatest. Some were fighting to enter the doomed complex, others were struggling to get away, while most had lost all sense of direction and were striking out in indiscriminate panic. Hilgo stopped fighting when he heard Clarai. Wake up? What was going on? Suddenly he was wretched in memory of his own home and family lost so many hundreds of miles to the north. His no longer plump face sagged in horror. Was Ghillechly also in flames? For a moment he couldn't believe what he saw, heard, sensed, and smelled all about ... it had to be a dream ... surely they were being dreamed ... none of this could be real ... could it...?

'Yes, it's real!' he bellowed furiously. 'Ussian burns. I'm here, I'm Hilgo, I'm in Ussian, I'm ...' Then he recalled why he'd returned to Ussian.

'Tschea!' he howled, adding to the babble. 'Wherever you are, I forgive you. Don't let them kill you. You're right! The games are dead – they don't matter!'

He was one among many awakening and threatened by panic, for it seemed impossible to escape the madness they'd accepted so unconsciously. They awoke into a crackling and lurid bedlam with peculiar sounds filtering into them from the direction of the Chuunlan Oval; they were surrounded by still-spelled lunatics who were hurling their torches up and over the walls of the Tarasse and clamoring for Ussian's death like demented animals. The heat was intolerable, flames were leaping closer through the market this side of the blazing Kuwa Quarter, and the Tarasse itself was beginning to burn.

Hilgo was one of many now struggling to escape, wide-eyed and horrified, seemingly awakened just in time to experience his death. Strange sounds boomed and muttered through the flames and crumbling buildings. Behind and beyond the pulse of these mind-twisting sounds, he began to feel the cleansing subliminal current which had helped him to awake, and he realized that other people were feeling it too. As his awareness of it inside him grew stronger – so calm, clear, and steady it was – he looked about with dawning hope and met other eyes reflecting the same hope ... reflecting it but also transmitting it themselves, at first uncertainly, but soon enthusiastically. For it showed him how to escape, it told him to dance and to join in a general celebration of life, it told him to deny the wishes of the invisible watchers which now he sensed for the first time. They throbbed in the scorched and disordered atmosphere ... and he laughed at them. By the time he saw the songmaker and the Fire-Dancers whirling closer – by the time he realized that this *music* came from outside him as well as from inside – he was already moving to it and seeing with it.

The flaming city possessed an unforgettably eldritch beauty. All about Hilgo were heavy buildings transformed into bright flowers of flame, and he cursed no more, for he felt the desire to dance instead, to run and laugh and caper like a child set free inside a magic garden.

The first moments of Liam's playing had been crucial. He'd all but lost the delta-pulse. He'd left the half-burned house with hood down and the sirena sounding out dubiously. Many lunatics had seen his red hair and their immediate instinct had been to kill him, but his guard had been strenuously active in his defense. The attackers were held off, not just by his guard, but soon by the increasing numbers of people awakened in the music. Every step that Liam

succeeded in taking toward the main gates strengthened his
grip on the pulse which had almost been lost. With the
Cyclones around him he held to what he knew inside.

It became irresistible – the music soared higher with every
forward step he took into the seething crowds, so that soon
he wasn't aware of being in Ussian at all ... he was flying
high above the cursed night-land and it was transforming
into a sparkling garden. As hundreds gladly took their cue
from the music the Fire-Dancers came dancing past the
Chuunlan Oval with their own uncertainties diminished by
the rising flight of the music. Algon followed them with the
singing, clapping, leaping army of liberation from the delta.

At first many still-deranged people rushed to attack these
red-haired enemies, and some were caught and dragged
aside. But soon the Fire-Dancers and their followers were
moving much too nimbly to be caught by the clumsy
charges of increasingly confused antagonists; they slipped
past and through their attackers, and as they did, they transformed their enemies into fellow-celebrants. The patterns
they spun in the music's wake became mesmerizingly
beautiful, and they whirled like dancing flames, creating
shapes which touched the minds of those they'd come to
convert...which touched, turned, and transformed them....
Soon, without there having been a precise moment when
one could say that negative cursing was decisively transformed to positive celebration, the remains of the Inila Way
were being vibrated by the movements of thousands awakened into synchronization with the shape and sound of the
delta-pulse. The Fire-Dancers separated, each one flowing
out in a different direction, each taking people along to
imitate, then merge with the dance.

There began a general exodus from the Inila Way to
cooler and more open ground about the burning Chuunlan
Oval. Now Algon knew that the battle was won. In the
atmosphere hung the pressure of a hideous frustration,
which was divorced from the people who danced. The
watchers were excluded from the celebration – and just in
time, for the Tarasse was burning in several places.

The battle for Ussian was won.

But a victory for the Zuni Bird wasn't yet certain.

Liam was near the gates now. As he rode higher on the music pumping through him, he remembered all that had happened until he'd started to play. He remembered Tschea. Abruptly, he stopped playing. The Tarasse! Flames were licking at the walls.

'No!' he shouted. 'I'll not abandon you!' He slung the sirena on his back and ran through the gates.

Lonawi prevented Tah Ti from running after the song-maker. Lonawi was filled with fear and joy. 'Let him go! We've won!'

'If he dies we won't awaken the Zuni Bird!'

'It's his choice. How can we coerce him? If he dies for her, then the fault is mine! Besides ... listen, look about....'

Tah Ti paused. Liam had stopped playing, but thousands still danced with the pulse of the delta inside them. The Cyclone of the Inner Vortex bowed to Lonawi of the Outer as Algon joined them. Lonawi told him what had happened. Algon didn't seem surprised. He'd suspected that something of the sort might happen. Lonawi had played the flute at Gurdiangar, and the two had been brought to the delta not quite totally confirmed of their own accord. He saw that Lonawi blamed himself.

'We'll wait,' he said tightly. 'This is necessary. Be patient.' The Tower of Naka'es wasn't yet alight, but it would become a flaming torch in another minute or so.

Tschea had entered the Tarasse by a side gate, sure that her heart was about to explode, with no idea what drove her. For a time she met nobody in the gloomy maze. Her feet took her high and low, as she roamed like a distraught ghost. Here and there at unexpected intersections she heard the echoes of distant voices. They echoed and pulled her like the Tarasse itself. The Tarasse! A hollow and outdated creature. Let it burn. Increasingly vehement, she roamed until she came near the Tower of Naka'es. Here were people running through the doomed building's arteries and teasing it with torches. And here she remembered Nikosner....

Nikosner. Mirrors. Nikosner. Mirrors ... shivering mirrors....

Even as she felt the music beginning she started to climb up the spiral staircase of the Tower of Naka'es, her face a sad mask of determination. Now she knew she'd returned to die. She was a failure. All these years she'd been used, she'd been a pawn. Algon's explanations did not make sense ... she couldn't believe them ... she couldn't believe the fantastic tale of the pyramid beneath the delta. Algon had betrayed her, Namahon had turned away from her ... even Liam hadn't tried to make her stay at the delta when she'd told him she was coming to Ussian. None of them cared. Now she hated herself for the enthusiasm she'd felt earlier in the day, for the sense of homecoming. It had been an illusion. She hated herself for giving in to it. Mirrors. One thing she could do right in this universe of illusion: she could die. Mirrors. Like Nikosner, she'd been used. She had more in common with Nikosner than with any of the others who were supposedly her friends.

And what did it matter if the Zuni Bird sang?

It was all illusion, flickering around her, through her....

If nothing else, her death would be her own.

So she climbed, as Nikosner's lieutenants came tumbling down past her. They'd abandoned their insane master, for he wouldn't come. They felt the music, they wanted to dance, and they didn't want to die. They ignored the lady who climbed up past them. Tears were streaming down her cheeks as a timber-roofed hall adjacent to the Tower of Naka'es began to burn. She wasn't aware of being watched.

Liam had never known such a warren as the Tarasse. He ran blindly, following his instinct, agonized by the thought that she might be dead already. With smoke in his nostrils he pelted along plush corridors, up wide stairs, sniffing where she'd passed. He ran through a hall that was already ablaze, into luxuriant gardens around the base of a high tower. The Tower of Naka'es. It glowed, backlit by flames....

He started up the spiral staircase, climbing with teeth gritted and breath hissing through them, with pain stabbing fiercely behind his ribs ... with acrid smoke in slow chase behind him.

And he came to the Eagle Chamber.

The carved wooden door was ajar.

No sounds came from the chamber.

He entered cautiously, his breathing rapid with fear.

He saw Tschea sitting on the carpeted floor. She was gazing at a shattered mirror. He saw a black-garbed body hunched up motionless on the floor at the other side of the mirror. He recognized Nikosner. Nikosner's eyes were closed. A knife was clenched in one of his hands.

His black clothing was stained with his own blood.

Liam stood frozen as Tschea looked up slowly.

'Dead,' she said flatly. 'He's killed himself.'

'Do you want to die too? Let's get out of here!'

Tendrils of smoke coiled in the flickering air.

'Why should I?' She met his eyes but didn't stir at all.

'It's time to live!' He bent down beside her with his heart beating horribly. 'I want you to live. I love you.' But he was curt rather than tender, and her smile was cynical.

'I think you love nobody but yourself!'

'Not so! Have you forgotten this morning?'

He was shaking, and she considered his savage expression.

'That was desire! If you love me – then stay and love me *now!*'

He gaped. In a shard of mirror he saw his own unrecognizable reflection. 'We'll be burned to death!' he whispered. *'We must get out!'*

'If you truly love me you won't mind dying,' she said simply. She coughed as smoke caught at her lungs, then she smiled brightly.

Liam felt numb all through. He couldn't see her clearly at all. There appeared to be two of her, a double-image. Which was the real Tschea? He shook his head in disbelief as he sat down beside her. What was he doing? Slowly he drew his fingers down her arm and the air was sparkling coldly; his thoughts were growing vague, but he sensed that something very terrible was happening to both of them as she cupped his head in her hands.

'Come on,' she coaxed with gentle insanity, 'prove what you say. . . .' As he lay down with her Liam half-knew that he was abandoning himself and the delta. Heavy smoke swirled about them in their doom-laden embrace. Then they were distracted by a hideous bubbling sound.

They looked up to see Nikosner weakly humping himself up onto an elbow. Blood ran from his mouth, but there was humor in his clouding eyes. The bubbling sound was his blood-choked laughter.

'... Fifteen years I've been mad,' he wheezed. 'Tonight ... I am sane and choose ... to die. I opened the door expecting you ... didn't expect my conquerors to be as mad as me ... see the joke! Have ... compassion on your self-damned selves. Mirror's cracked ... their last attempt to ... kill you with your own stupidity.' Then he choked, his eyes closed, and his body jerked convulsively. When his eyes opened again they were still staring in amazement, for the pain in Nikosner's eyes wasn't the pain of death. He gestured with a feebly angry arm. 'Fools! Take your lives, get out, make love elsewhere. You confuse love with self-hate. Why destroy yourselves so ... pointlessly? Go ... to the delta. Make the Zuni Bird ... sing before it's – *Go now!*

He shivered violently, then he choked on his blood and died.

Consternated, Tschea and Liam met each other's eyes in the smoke.

Liam bowed his head and laughed in pain and astonishment. 'Ohhh ... he's right ... he's right ... this is not our fate.'

Tschea scrambled to her feet, staring at Nikosner's body. She sniffed the dangerous air like a frightened deer as Liam grabbed her hand.

'Algon was right as well!' he gasped. 'We're our own enemies. No more! Come on!' Then they went plunging together through the door and almost fell down the Tower of Naka'es in their sudden haste. With blackened faces and smoldering clothes they came staggering out of the main gates with the Tower of Naka'es blooming in flame behind them.

Algon met them with heartfelt relief on his face.

The city was flaming, but the dancing people were departing.

Ussian could be built again ... after the Zuni Bird had flown....

Conclusion : The Song of the Zuni Bird

Time to sing.

Thirty thousand people were together at the delta the following night when the Cyclone Grand Master arrived through a Gateway. It was generally whispered about as he was litter-borne to the delta's verge that he was more than a hundred and twenty years old and that he hadn't spoken since taking a vow of silence thirty-five years before.

His body was wizened, but his eyes were bright and clear.

Liam felt the old man's energy when he took two gnarled hands in his.

It was time and Liam knew it.

As the sky faded into night there was a great communal service of thanks and celebration. Thanks for the deliverance of Ussian, celebration of the incipient conjunction of planets and human minds. The Grand Master watched from his litter as Algon addressed the songmaker at the beginning of the road that led out to the apex of the buried pyramid.

Tschea stood beside Liam. She knew it was going to be a very beautiful night. The mildest of salt-laden southern breezes wafted over the mistless delta. The waters were quiet and the bird-colonies were silent. The craggy bluffs overhanging the Naenshe were sharply etched in the fading light. Tschea was dressed in white and so was Liam.

'Are you ready?' Algon's voice rang out.

'I'm ready,' the songmaker firmly replied.

'It is time!' called the Master of Baethnan.

'*It is time!*' echoed the multitude in one vast voice.

It was time. It was the thirteenth night after the battle which had signaled the beginning of the Change. It was shortly before the rising of the new moon.

Liam the Songmaker set out to complete one journey and to begin another. All doubts were gone. Phadraig, Ussian, the madness, his losses and gains – all were behind him now.

Now was now. It was time for the garden to grow in every mind. His face was radiant. Of his own accord he'd discarded his old clothes for a white robe. How could he give himself up between sea and sky in clothing impregnated with so much confusion? It would not be fit.

It was time, and he led the multitude out upon the delta toward the heart of the pulse as it grew dark. But the night was utterly clear and bright, and the atmosphere became so splendid that he heard himself crying out to the lustrously star-spangled sky with every step he took along the gently rocking raft-road toward the apex. It was all like a dream, a dream more real than the waking dream he'd been content once to call reality: with every step he felt less embodied, less confined, more and more an energetic spirit who happened to reside in an increasingly tenuous material envelope of flesh and blood and bone. His human body was an instrument purposefully evolved to bring essence through change to itself.

Onward he moved with his two eyes set to the sky in which the fifth and sixth planets would shortly rise so close together that it would be difficult to see them apart from this third planet. Eagerly he advanced across the mud-banks and rippling waters through the colonies of birds which took screaming to the air as the multitude came winding behind him. Hundreds and hundreds followed like children, singing and dancing and bathing in the deep heart of the pulse, following as gladly as some among them had done at Gurdiangar. But this time there was no chance of confusion. The pulse was all: it was a joyous energy that took them all as one.

When once he looked back the people seemed no longer separate and solidly flesh-bound but instead appeared as one incandescent stream of light flowing through the night, pulsing violet and single-minded. The great procession was immanently etheric in mass joy and all individuals were merging into one coherent body of pulsating energy. Like a serpent of violet fire this being drew closer to the origin of its life, grew more greatly united with itself and with those who wheeled in the air above and with those who waited in the sea, became more and more the single being of the third planet. And the aspect which was the songmaker's individual essence felt like a flower reaching for the light.

Every step was a step in time as well as one in space; every step was a growing-closer into an undifferentiated state in which Liam was Tschea was Algon was Namahon was Clarai was Hilgo was Chimalus was everyone at the delta who had ever been at the delta including the spirit of those who'd built the pyramid and the sirena. All became increasingly basic and only the universe was mirrored.

In time the songmaker reached the end of the wooden road at the beginning of the long mudbank which curved out toward the point Namahon had located. He was individually drunk on the wine of the pyramid's pulsation and it hardly seemed necessary to go any farther before starting to play the energies out across the land – surely all could feel them already?

But a practical aspect remained which said that he – the matrix of consciousness who was Liam from Phadraig – must continue, and must continue alone, for it was his personal destiny to be completely spent in the playing of the music. But those behind – transfigured in the music, they'd have their parts to play in the dream the Mutant had begun. And he – he would die, he would live : it was all the same. He would live in them and they in him : he must play the music. What was he but a channel through which the energies of the universe might stream – what greater ecstasy and joy could there be?

So he stopped and turned to Tschea, who was a foot or two behind him with Namahon and Algon at her heels.

The whole procession all the way back to dry land came to a halt.

Together the two stood ankle-deep in alluvial mud and saw each other as they'd first seen each other in the cell at Schroun. He saw Tschea, a lady he'd never known so well as now, a lady of intense individuality, which tonight at last found its best expression in the mounting communal ecstasy. They loved each other deeply. For a moment as their eyes met they wished they might have known each other under the former circumstances which had been called normality. But such wishing was pointless entrapment in irrelevance and they knew it very well. Nevertheless there was a hint of quickly passing sadness in them both as they embraced in good-bye and hello. They loved of their own accord and in the delta's concord; the energy which washed them tonight was such that only love was possible. Everyone here tonight was in love with each other and with the world from which they grew. The great river of human light was silent beneath the radiating stars and planets as the two embraced. No words were spoken, for their eyes transmitted all the necessary messages. Liam had to continue alone, but they knew there was no aloneness, for all shared in the same being, all were god and no longer prisoners in isolation; they'd meet again in the garden.

Tschea's eyes were dry as Liam turned and went on toward the apex of the pyramid. She could see and feel it now through the former impenetrability of mud and sand and rock and water – which, after all, were only denser forms of the binding energy that was universal. She stood above the northern flank of the pyramid. The waters were glowing a dull gold. When, after looking one last time at the already-distant dot of the songmaker, she turned back to Algon and Namahon and all the others, they were radiant beings. They were each a field of spectral energy and color merging with every other field about, descending from the violet radiance of their crowns to the green heart-fields to the root-red of their loins.

The river of light waited on the delta, beneath the stars.

The songmaker floated on to the heart of the pulse. The pulse had consumed his sense of self by the time he came above the apex and unslung the glowing sirena. He was merging with the currents – he was the music, he was an instrument now, a transformer, a hollow bamboo.

And so the Song of the Zuni Bird arose.

There were some on dry land who watched from a distance, for personal reasons unjoined in the communal trance. Some were local. They'd never known the delta so calm. No waves came crashing over the fragile and thickly populated wooden road that night, nor during any of the days and nights which succeeded it. But those at a distance lost all awareness of passing time, for they found themselves unable to resist the visions in music which came to lie on the waters of the delta, of their minds.

Like a tingling electric feather the Song came brushing through the many minds and transformed them into a collective in which every individual, though individual, was individual merely in relation to the whole.

The Song was an amalgamation of direct experience, of sight and sound and sense and taste and hearing and extrasensory perceptions.

The Song was the pyramid itself, the pyramid unburied and glowing magnificently with slow shifts of color. The Song was a garden of incandescent primal energy in which every being was a bloom. In this garden grew an enormous variety of flowers, every one united in common purpose, every one aiming to reach the light from which each was similarly descended. The garden was limitless and utterly familiar; in its shape and sound were included all possible forms of events which had happened and which were happening and which would happen. Everything of note in the disordered lands was occurring and known in the garden and was seen to have its potential order in a universal scheme of things. It was known how the Hou'ons turned their backs on their crossroads mirrors and floated silently back to their lake-villages. It was known how the Mutant dreamed of and in the garden in Zagrin while the mumen danced and rejoiced about him. It was seen how the confusions and misdirections of energy that characterized the human struggle from low to high might be recast into a common aiming at oneness. For the flowers of the garden knew that they were responsible for the success of their own flowering. Though many flowers had died and were dying, some were evolving, some were vibrating faster and higher, and some were rapt in the garden's glory.

In time the music faded and the People of the Garden found themselves back on and about the misty delta with the full moon high above the bay.

They awoke back to the physical world, but the music

was sure inside them, and each knew what she or he must do in the coming days.

Many thousands left immediately as the rain-clouds of autumn came sweeping in across Mantrim from the western sea; they took their separate directions without any words being spoken.

Those on the road returned to the shore, but the song-maker didn't return with them. Within an hour of the music ending, a violent storm broke out and the outer mud-banks were swamped completely, the wooden road was destroyed, the birds took wing for the south, and the sea-folk turned toward the open ocean.

Among the last to leave the delta were those three beings called Namahon and Tschea and Algon.

They took their separate paths into the garden of the Fifth Element, two-eyed and wide awake in the divinity of their mutation, calling themselves People of the Garden, People of the Zuni Bird ... human beings....

So the change which One-Eye had begun was continued and redirected by those with two eyes. Mission-bound they spread across the turbulent lands with the Song inside of them, and the singer of the Song rested in each and every one of them.